Bewitching You

Viola Estrella

BEWITCHING YOU

By Viola Estrella
Copyright 2012 Viola Estrella
Second Edition

ISBN: 0985619813
ISBN-13: 978-0-9856198-1-7

More information about Viola Estrella can be found at:
www.ViolaEstrella.com

Cover art by Estrella Cover Art www.estrellacoverart.com

Editor for second edition: Helen Hardt
www.romanceeditor.blogspot.com

Disclaimer: *Bewitching You* was originally published in 2009. This edition has been thoroughly revised and reedited.

Praise for Bewitching You

"Estrella's quirky and endearing characters ensure an enjoyable reading experience that should satisfy paranormal romance fans." Carol from Bitten By Books

"This was a fast paced story that keeps the readers attention from start to finish. Viola Estrella writes a wonderful tale of true love. This is a story full of spice and adventure with a bit if humor thrown in. The bond that Sofia and Grayson have is a wonderful thing. Showing us just how wonderful love can be if it is fought for and cherished. With well developed characters full of emotion this book should not be missed." Gabrielle from Got Romance Reviews

"Kudos to Viola Estrella for one Spicy Hot Romance read." Larkspur from Long and Short of It

DEDICATION

To my husband, antics and all. Love you, honey.
To my sons, who inspire me to be the best I can be.

ACKNOWLEDGEMENTS

A special thank you to Patrice, my friend and critique
partner, and Holly, my email buddy. You make me LOL
every day.

Lots of love to my talented, funny, supportive writer buddies
at Colorado Romance Writers.
I heart you guys!

Also, I can't forget all the strong women in my life who are
more beautiful/quirky/amazing than any character I could
ever create. You know who you are!

Chapter One

The rocking chair creaked as Sofia Good pushed off the ground with the balls of her bare feet. The chair rolled back a heart-stopping distance and fell forward again. Back and forward again. Even after spending twenty-four years on this earth, she still loved the slight thrill a simple wooden rocking chair could give her.

Back and forward again.

Okay, time to grow up, Sofe.

Sofia planted her feet on the hardwood floor and pulled the pencil from behind her ear. With the flick of her wrist, she flipped her sketchbook open to where she'd left off and continued to draw *him*. Across the room in another rocker, her grandmother knitted yet another hot pink sweater for the winter ahead and hummed a familiar tune, one Sofia had heard throughout her life, though she'd never once asked the name of the song. What was the point? A title wouldn't make the melody any more or less sweet.

In this family, with these women, sometimes knowing less was more. Certain things were better left unspoken.

Like the majority of Sofia's dreams.

When sleep brimmed with powerful visions—some horrid and gruesome—wasting conscious time rehashing was hardly ever a good idea. She dreamed of the future. Whether she wanted to or not. Bits and pieces were revealed to her through strong emotions like fear, love, grief, and lust. The "gift" of extra-sensory abilities had run in her family for as long as time existed. Nana had always said their gifts lay embedded in their DNA. Sofia never questioned it.

"He sure is a looker," Nana said, cutting into the silence.

The late morning sun shone through the front window, forming a veil of light between the two. But Sofia had no trouble seeing Nana's mischievous blue eyes peering over her knitting needles. Unfortunately, Sofia knew exactly who her grandmother spoke of. The star of her latest sequence of dreams, Grayson Phillips, slowly appeared on the sketchbook in front of her. She swirled her finger over his penetrating dark eyes, to the wisp of his hair hanging low on his forehead, and down to his full, inviting lips.

This was the only time since her discovery of precognition—sadly, during puberty—she was ever able to dream of her own future. This man—this sexy, kind, loving man—possessed it as far as she could see.

Too bad she hadn't even met him yet.

"Don't, Nana." Sofia closed her sketchbook, the drawing of Gray half-complete.

"Don't what?" A smile quirked the seventy-two-year-old woman's red-painted lips.

Her Nana, Penny Jones, had her own special ability, and she seemed to exercise it to the fullest today.

Sofia shifted in her seat and tried not to smile back. The woman was shameless. "The rules are you can't read my mind when I'm visiting. It's not polite."

"Honey," Nana said with a wink, "it's impossible to dodge thoughts when they're as vivid as the ones you've been having lately. Is he now or in the future?"

"Future." Sofia didn't bother arguing the matter further. She'd been dying to tell someone about *him*. He'd been filling her nights with visions of their imminent lives together.

Conversations, romance, mind-boggling passion.

And emotions Sofia couldn't put into words.

"It's looking up, then?" Nana beamed.

It was no secret Sofia's past and present needed a happily ever after. Boyfriends were hard to come by. After one date with a potential love interest she dreamed of his future with his cozy house, cute children, fun-filled family vacations...and a wife who wasn't Sofia.

What was the point in falling for a man when he wasn't her destiny?

But Gray—he was there. No doubt about that.

"Well..." Sofia thought it over. "It almost seems too good to be true. He's funny and kind and *gorgeous* and, um, funny." No way would she tell her grandmother about his superb talents in bed.

A month ago, when it all started, Sofia dreamed of losing her virginity to him. He'd been sweet and gentle, everything she hoped for. Since then, the visions had grown more sensual. Her cheeks burned from the mere memory.

Nana winked. "That good, huh?"

"So good," she gushed. "It's hard to believe I'll be that happy one day."

"I knew it was only a matter of time before you'd find a man worthy enough for you to let into your heart."

Sofia stood from the rocking chair and crossed the hardwood floor with her sketchbook in her hand. "I'm nervous." She opened the page to where she'd been drawing Gray and handed it to her grandmother. "I can't tell when I'll meet him." Usually her visions were clear and succinct. But not lately.

Another dream haunted her sleep as well, giving her

snippets of details of a small plane flying through the sky with passengers who appeared to be dead. This dream was as hazy as those of Gray, making her wonder if somehow her gift were fading. She didn't really want to lose her power. She wanted to be able to help these people.

Although a part of her did long to just be "normal." To not have the responsibility of preventing a murder or a rape or some other tragedy. Most of the time it only took a simple anonymous phone call to the police.

How she'd stop an entire airplane of people from going up in the air, she wasn't quite sure yet. Not much she could do about it now. Her visions typically showed her anywhere from one day to ten years into the future, but there was no way to tell.

Nana studied the sketch. Her red fingernails traced Gray's strong jaw line. "Yes, he's a fine man. You'll be very happy."

"But when? It's driving me crazy. I've been trying to read his alarm clock, find a calendar on the wall, something. But there's nothing. I don't even know where it all happens. All I know is that I don't look much different than I do now."

"Then it has to be soon." Nana greedily sifted through the rest of the pages crammed with drawings of him. Gray wearing a suit and tie, a bathing suit, wrapped in a towel. Gray stepping out of the shower—

"I'll take that, Nana." She gently closed the book and slid it out of her grandmother's hands.

Nana looked up at her with a wry grin. "Boy, I miss having a man around. As soon as you meet him, I want you to bring him here. So I can make sure his thoughts are pure."

Sofia shook a reprimanding finger, but couldn't help giggling at her grandmother's silliness. "Remember the rules."

When Sofia met this glorious man, she'd have far

more exciting plans for him. Besides, bringing a man to Nana's house would surely be relationship suicide.

"Rules schmules," Nana grumbled, and picked up her knitting needles from her lap.

Sofia gave up. For today, anyway. Although her grandmother had a kind heart, she was a bit, *er*, eccentric. It wasn't her fault. How could anyone with the ability to read minds ever lead a normal existence?

Still there were a few details of Nana's life that put her one step closer to what some people considered bonkers. For instance, Nana insisted on living amongst the Amish people in a small town in rural Indiana, far from any major city.

Away from the electricity and phone lines that she claimed gave her migraines.

Like many Amish, Nana lived on gas-powered appliances, lit her house with kerosene oil lamps, and heated it with a wood-burning stove.

Unlike the Amish, she had a fine collection of jewelry and lipstick, wore bright colors, and had indoor plumbing. Thank goodness for that. Sofia's weekly visits would dwindle down immensely if Nana insisted on using an outhouse.

Batteries powered other things such as the radio and the small black-and-white television.

Sofia's mother, Laura, had grown up like this. No wonder the woman took off to the city to raise Sofia surrounded by cars, lights, and noise.

A person could stand only so much quiet country life.

The view wasn't awful. Watching the sunset over the serene horizon had inspired more than a few paintings. She walked to the window covered by plain white curtains and looked out at what her grandmother considered heaven. Nothing but acres and acres of farmland.

And a man on a bike.

Sofia squinted, trying to get a better view of him. He was at the end of the stone and dirt road, too far out of her range to get a clear picture. But he had dark hair, she could tell.

Like Gray's.

Could it be? Is this where they were to meet?

"What is it, dear? Do you see him?" Nana asked, clearly having read Sofia's mind. She stood from her chair and walked to the window to stand beside her.

"I don't know. And stop it, or I'm leaving," Sofia threatened weakly. Denying Nana her gift was almost pointless.

"Go see. He's just standing there as if he's waiting for something to happen." Nana nudged Sofia. "Go make it happen."

"What if it's not him? Or what if it is?" Her mind ran circles around all the possibilities. "Can you read his thoughts from here?" *If you can't beat 'em, join 'em, right?*

"No, he's too far."

"Darn." Well, if he was the man in her visions, she could finally meet him. If he wasn't, she could just say she was being a friendly neighbor. Yes, that's what she'd do. She took a deep breath and marched out the door onto the porch.

~ * ~

Grayson Phillips's legs burned after peddling his bike down the bumpy country road. He'd been riding for hours. He was overdoing it this morning, but at least the torturous bike ride through the country was keeping him from thinking of *her*.

Jeezus. The woman wasn't even flesh and blood, yet still she manipulated his mind with sexual thoughts.

Thoughts that should be exclusive to his fiancée, Rachel.

And the dreams... The dreams were so sensual. So realistic.

To be so preoccupied with a woman who didn't exist

couldn't be normal or healthy.

Gray took a drink of his water, then squeezed the rest of it over his face, letting it drip down his neck and onto his bare chest as he stared into the endless rows of corn that blocked him from going any farther. Where the hell was he, anyway?

All this nonsense had to be chalked up to sexual frustration. He'd been with Rachel for almost a year, and she was one of the rare women who wanted to wait until her wedding night to give away her virginity.

As soon as they were married, the dreams would stop. They *had* to.

He slid his water bottle back into its holder and turned his bike around. He had a long day ahead of him, ending with dinner with Rachel. She'd been working hard on planning their wedding, and thus far, he'd been no help. Even though he wanted this wedding, this future with Rachel, he couldn't get excited about it.

Especially when another woman consumed his nights.

Today, he would change that. Today, he was going to forget about the damned woman with the vivid blue eyes and soft, sweet-scented skin who knew exactly where to touch him and when. The one who whispered fantasies into his ear and then played them out without the least of inhibitions...

Giving up fighting the dreams was tempting at times. They seduced him like nothing he'd ever experienced. But they weren't part of *the plan*.

Thanks to the death of his brother, Gray knew life couldn't be wasted on frivolous actions and foolish choices that left the people who loved you with a deep, punch-in-the-gut sadness.

Yep. Life had to have a plan, and *she* was not in it.

"Of course not," he muttered to himself. "She's just a fucking dream."

Now, how the hell was he going to get home?

He'd been riding mindlessly since he woke up early this morning. He hadn't showered or eaten. He'd barely dressed, throwing on a pair of basketball shorts and running shoes.

Get on the bike and go, he'd told himself. *Peddle until she's out of your head.*

Stupid idea.

How he'd arrived in the middle of Amish country, with no recognizable landmarks in sight, was beyond him. Rows of corn stalks were in front of him, a plain white house and a lake to the left, crops of soybeans to the right, and a country road with nothing but the same behind him. The house had two cars parked in front of it.

Huh. No horse or carriage in sight. Maybe these people weren't Amish.

A woman stepped out onto the porch and waved her arms. How odd. Gray shaded his hand over his eyes and focused on the stranger with long honey brown hair and petite body. She dropped her arms to her sides and gradually descended the stairs.

What did she want?

She wore a yellow knee-length sundress that flowed with her movement as she walked toward him. Slow, then fast, then slow again, as if she couldn't make up her mind.

Gray gripped the handlebars of his bike. She reminded him of...never mind. That was ridiculous. It couldn't be *her*.

She stopped halfway up the dirt drive.

"Gray?" she shouted.

At least, that was what he *thought* she said, but there was no way some woman living way out here in the freak-zone knew his name, especially a woman who looked disturbingly like the temptress from his dreams.

His pulse pounded. *What if? Just what if?*

No. "Get your head out of your ass, Gray," he muttered.

The woman started toward him again. With each step, she seemed more and more like the impossible.

"Gray?" She braced a hand on the curve of her hip and tilted her head. Familiar blue eyes, searching and unsure, seized hold of him from the short distance, paralyzing him.

It *was* her. Her hair, her lips, her voice—everything matched up. Everything.

She's the one. Go to her.

He sucked in a gulp of humid air overfilling his lungs.

Go to her? Where the hell had that thought come from? He swiped a hand across his sweat-soaked forehead. Shit. He was losing his goddamned mind. That, or the blazing sun was playing tricks on him.

"Sorry," he called out, but his shaky voice didn't carry far. "I can't." He cleared his throat and tried harder. "I have to go." *And stop talking to a fucking hallucination.*

Determined to save face with reality, he planted his feet on his pedals and launched forward. Aching legs be damned. He was getting the hell out of there and finding his way home.

Going insane was *not* part of the plan.

~ * ~

Sofia shut the door behind her and leaned against it, her legs wobbly and her throat tight.

"Was it really him, dear? You don't know for sure," Nana said from her chair.

"He looked just like him." Sofia sank down onto her bottom and pressed her forehead to her knees. Nana's cat, Sam, rubbed against her leg and purred. "But he didn't act like him. He seemed horrified of me. He sped away before I could even talk to him."

"You called his name." Nana stood and ambled toward Sofia. Her pink polyester pants scraped together as she crossed the floor. Nana was a plump woman. More for hugging, she always said. Sofia had agreed.

"I did call his name, didn't I?" Sofia moaned and slapped her palm to her forehead. "Just brilliant."

Nana sighed and carefully sat next to Sam on the hard floor. "You must remember that most people don't share our gifts. Or at least, they don't realize they do." She patted Sofia's leg and then ran her fingers down Sam's tawny fur coat.

"I know, Nana. I was so excited, though. I half-expected him to run to me and pull me into his arms."

"Ah, yes, but he doesn't know you like you know him."

"Do you think it's over? Did I ruin my chance at love?" Cold panic had her thinking dire thoughts. Not being the perfect weight herself, why would an attractive man like Gray stop to talk to her long enough to show him how compatible they were? She really needed to start that diet her mom had told her about.

"No, no, dear," Nana said in a comforting tone. "I hardly think that's possible. This simply wasn't the right time. Not yet."

Sofia groaned. Twenty-four years without the love or touch of a man was too long, and Gray Phillips was the only man she wanted. She may have scared him away this time, but *next* time he was going to fall in love with her. Just like in her dreams.

Fate had plans for them.

~ * ~

"This one's called white chocolate raspberry," Nora Spencer said as she held up the bite of cake to Rachel's mouth.

Rachel sighed louder than she'd intended. Planning a wedding with her mother wasn't as fun as she'd thought it would be.

"Grayson's allergic to chocolate products, Mom. I thought I told you that." *Several times.*

Nora rolled her eyes and dropped the fork onto her plate. "But it's white, and it's delicious. What could the harm be? The guests will love it."

"Yes, but my husband will break out in hives, stop breathing, and die on our wedding night." Okay, maybe she was exaggerating, but the horrified look on her mother's face was priceless.

"*Really?* He's that sensitive?"

Rachel frowned and shrugged. "I don't actually know what happens to him, but I don't want to find out on my wedding day, okay?"

Her mother flipped her auburn hair and turned to the baker. "Can we get rid of all the chocolate products, please? My daughter *thinks* her fiancé is allergic."

Rachel ignored her condescending tone. *So, I don't know all about my future husband's allergies.* So what? That was the least of her worries.

The truth was, there were times she wondered if she really wanted to marry Grayson. The thought was silly, she knew. Any woman could see he was the perfect man. He was handsome, he had a successful career at Linden's Advertising, and they'd been through a lot together, including the death of Hayes, Gray's twin brother.

Her chest constricted.

Rachel didn't want to think of Hayes. Not now. It was too painful. She shook the depressing memory out of her head and turned her thoughts back to Grayson.

The clincher had been when he'd met her parents. They'd immediately adored him. He had them under his spell...or it could have been because he was the first man she'd ever brought home who wasn't an unemployed artist of some sort. Rachel couldn't help it. She'd loved the passion that exuded from a man holding a paintbrush or a guitar or a camera...

Consequently, Gray was the first boyfriend her parents had liked, and it felt good to have their approval finally. So good, that when Grayson had proposed a couple months after Hayes's funeral, Rachel had accepted. Time to move on.

No looking back.

The bell above the bakery door rang and she crooked her head to see Grayson walk in.

"Hi," Rachel said, surprised. She wasn't expecting to see him until dinner.

He wore dark jeans, a snug t-shirt that stretched against his muscular chest, and a smile that melted her heart. He really was a handsome man.

And he looked so much like Hayes.

~ * ~

Gray pulled Rachel into his arms and squeezed her tight. The morning's events had left him frazzled, and he needed to be with his fiancée so he could forget about who he *thought* he'd seen.

"Wow," she whispered into his ear as he lifted her off her feet. "This is a...nice surprise."

He set her back down and met her bemused stare. He brushed a lock of her strawberry-blonde hair away from her porcelain cheek. She was beautiful. Everything he needed in a woman, he reminded himself, even as an empty feeling settled in his stomach. "I came to help."

"Really?"

"Yeah." He forced another smile.

"Grayson?" Nora came up behind Rachel, wearing the same confused expression on her face. "Whatever are you doing here?" She walked around and gave him an air kiss.

"I'm here to help with the wedding plans. It's long overdue, don't you think?" He grabbed Rachel's tightly fisted hand and maneuvered his fingers in between hers. She always seemed tense around her mother.

"Of course not. You're a busy man, and Rachel, well, Rachel's just a student. She and I can take care of all the details. Your job is to worry about showing up to the church on time."

Rachel bit into her lip, probably holding her tongue

like she did so well. Gray wondered what it would take for her to defend herself. He longed for the day it would happen. Maybe at dinner he'd give her a pep talk. What she needed was a confidence boost. Being raised by a woman like Nora couldn't have been easy.

"Isn't that right, Rachel?" Nora cocked her head in that condescending way that grinded Gray's nerves.

"Sure," Rachel said softly, as she lifted some chocolate frosting off a piece of cake. "We can handle it."

Chapter Two

A car was parked in the driveway of the home Sofia and her mother shared, so Sofia pulled along the tree-lined city street and cut her engine. The old blue sedan probably belonged to one of her mother's clients. It didn't look familiar.

Sofia's mom was one of many fortunetellers in Indianapolis, Indiana. She read palms and tarot cards with an accuracy that bewildered and sometimes frightened. Occasionally, when urged by an eager, generous client, she brought the crystal ball into play. To Laura, a ball of glass was just that—a ball of glass. Still, it was the one prop that delighted most of her patrons and had them coming back for more.

"Who am I to argue?" Sofia's mother had once said with a devious grin and a handful of cash. "They only want to hear good things about their future anyway."

Sofia couldn't blame her mother. The few times a client had gotten a preview of an ill-fated future, they'd become irate and left without paying. Even though some might consider Laura Good a charlatan, what other choice did she have? This was her career, her lone source of income.

Sofia walked up the path to her home and noticed her middle-aged neighbor, Herbert Lawrence, from the corner of her eye. His thin six-foot frame cut across their adjoining lawns, coming toward her at a rapid pace.

"Ms. Good," he shouted, before Sofia could run

inside and hide. "Ms. Good," he said again, as she turned to acknowledge him. He had moved into the neighboring house five years ago, yet she was pretty sure he didn't know her first name or her mother's. They'd both been branded *Ms. Good*, and of course, always in an exasperated tone.

"Yes, what can I do for you?" Sofia asked with an innocent smile. *What has Mom done to piss him off this time?*

He jerked to a halt four feet in front of her with the standard grimace on his face. "You have to make her stop."

As usual, Sofia didn't have a clue what he was talking about, but no doubt her mother was guilty. The woman was like Dennis the Menace, and Herbert Lawrence was the unlikable, high-strung Mr. Wilson. Sometimes it was fun to watch their antics, but mostly Sofia wished her mother would grow up and leave the poor guy alone.

She inhaled a small breath and asked, "What should I ask her to stop doing?"

He shook his finger toward the side of the house. "Purple," he said, his voice hitting a new high. "Out my kitchen window, all I see is purple with little tiny flowers. Why would she do that to me?"

"She planted purple lilacs again?" Was her mother running out of ideas? She'd planted lilacs last summer after she'd discovered he was extremely allergic to them, *and* that he hated the color purple.

Herbert's elderly mother visited him every other weekend, and Sofia's mother used the kind, somewhat senile woman to get all kinds of information.

"No, she painted the side of your house purple," he gritted his teeth and continued, "with little tiny white lilacs. So every time I look outside my kitchen window, that's what I see."

Sofia bit her lips shut to keep from laughing. Her mother *really* needed a hobby. "I apologize, Herbert...or

21

Mr. Lawrence. I'll talk to her about it. I'm sure it was just a misunderstanding."

"See that you do." His silvery eyes matched the grey streaks running along each side of his head.

Had he been grey when he'd moved in five years ago? Sofia couldn't remember. She nodded and turned, making long strides up the porch and into the house. Thankfully, Herbert let her leave without another word.

The door to her mother's den was closed. The sign on the dark walnut-stained door read, "Reading in progress. Do not disturb."

Her mother's murmuring voice reverberated out into the sunlit hallway. The sound was familiar and comforting. One she connected with her childhood.

Sofia used to sit against the wall and listen in on her mother's sessions, falling asleep at times. Of course that always angered her father, she remembered. He'd scoop her up into his arms and tell her to read a book or go outside and play. He hadn't believed in the powers of the mind or any type of "nonsense that couldn't be explained by science."

Oh, the arguments her parents had battled through. He'd yell and her mother would yell louder. In the end, he decided to leave and never come back. His leaving was for the best, Sofia realized now. How would he have handled knowing his own daughter was *full of nonsense* as well? Ever since puberty had set in.

Yep, it was better this way.

Her sandals tapped as she took the curved hardwood stairs up to her room. It had already been a long day, and all she wanted to do was work on her latest painting.

She'd dreamed of a beach, late at night. Gray Phillips, of course, was there, not too far ahead of her. His pant legs were rolled up, as if he'd walked through the water along the shore. His shirt was unbuttoned, revealing his broad, muscled chest. He held a camp lantern. That, along with the light of the moon, allowed her to see him waiting for her. His smile was white compared to his dark features—brown hair, dark eyes, and olive skin. He seemed happy, or was he amused by her? Who knew? At any rate, the scene had begged to be painted, as had the rest of her paintings that lined her bedroom walls and filled her closet.

One day she'd display them and show the world her visions, if she ever got the courage. Right now, her only desire was to paint. It fed her soul and eased her mind.

She stepped out of her sundress and threw on an old t-shirt just as the phone rang.

Oh, crap. Sofia checked the caller ID to make sure it was who she thought it was. *Restaurant De Mon Coeur* popped up on the screen.

She'd forgotten all about work again. *Again.* When was she going to get her head together?

"Hello?" she answered, and braced herself to hear French curse words through the earpiece.

"Sofia," her coworker and friend, Madeleine, said in a hushed tone. "André's on a tirade. Get down here now. It's super busy."

"Shoot. I'm so sorry. I'll be right there."

~ * ~

"I can't believe we've been waiting for twenty minutes," Grayson whispered against Rachel's ear. "We have a reservation."

"They look busy."

Gray drew in an annoyed breath and rolled his tense shoulders. Tomorrow at work was going to be hectic, and he didn't have time to sit around and wait when he could be preparing for his presentation. If he got this new account, there was no reason Linden wouldn't give him the promotion he needed to have a financially stable future with Rachel.

He glanced at her sitting next to him. Not too close and not too far. That was the way she liked it, and he couldn't complain. Rachel was a beautiful woman, but there were times when he needed his distance.

That would change after the wedding night, he was sure. After they made love for the first time, the connection, the passion between them would grow.

"I like that dress on you," he said, trying to find some compliment that wouldn't make her feel uncomfortable in his presence.

She brushed a hand over the peach silk hem running across her thighs. "Thanks," she said and gave him a glance. "I like your, um, tie."

Gray grinned at her. Her shyness was an adorable quality. Not being able to help himself, he leaned down and brushed his mouth against her ear. "Our wedding night is close," he whispered.

"Phillips?" A man in a tux appeared before them. "Party of two?"

Rachel stood quickly, the profile of her face a new shade of red.

"That's us," Gray said. He stood close to Rachel and placed his hand on the small of her back, hoping someday she'd get used to his touch.

~ * ~

Sofia finished buttoning up her vest and thanked the heavens the material was black. She'd forgotten to wash the vest and her matching black skirt since her last shift two nights ago. The baby-blue blouse underneath was straight from the dryer and slightly wrinkled. It would have to do. She was *so* late.

The kitchen was bustling like Sofia had never seen before. She slipped by the perspiring chef, who was cursing in French over a boiling pot of something.

"Bernard," he yelled at one of the prep chefs, who nearly dropped the knife from his hand.

"*C'est terminé?*"

"*Un moment,*" Bernard answered with a shaky voice.

Boy, was he in trouble, Sofia thought as she reached the wall where the time clock hung. Two years of working in the place, and she still didn't have a clue what they were saying, but their body language and tone said more than words ever could.

She pulled her time card from its slot and clocked in...forty minutes late. *Shoot*.

"Sofia," André shouted as he pushed through the door, his face even redder than the chef's. "You're late again."

"I'm sorry." She gave him her best innocent smile. The man was a sucker for a sweet smile and a blonde head of hair. One out of two had to work.

He growled under his breath. "One more time and you're fired. Go take tables five through nine."

"Yes, sir. Right away."

~ * ~

Gray pulled Rachel's chair out for her, but her attention was on the piano player seated twenty-odd feet away. She gave him a small wave as if she knew him.

Which would be impossible. The guy had tattoos crawling up his neck underneath his pressed white dress shirt. He was sporting a goddamn ponytail and smiling back at Rachel as he worked his fingers against the keys, playing a slow tune.

"You know him?" Gray asked, and guided her into her seat.

"Um, sort of. We went out once or twice a couple of years ago." Her voice faded as she spoke, but he heard every word.

"Really?" He sat across the table and watched as she continued to glance at the piano man, who probably got his last tattoo in a nine-by-nine cell from a guy named Snake. "He doesn't look like your type."

"My type?" Her brown eyes fluttered as if being cleared from confusion, then quickly veered up at him. "You're my type, Grayson."

"Huh." So, there was a side to his virginal bride-to-be he didn't know about. "You said you went out once or twice?"

"Well, three dates, but it was a long time ago." She clasped her hands together on top of the table.

"Maybe we should talk a little more about our past relationships. Sometimes I feel like I don't know you as well as I should. And we are about to be married. It couldn't hurt."

"I'd rather not. It's not a big deal." Her cheeks flushed as she made busy work of tugging the napkin onto her lap and straightening it, avoiding his stare.

Gray wondered what she was hiding. "It's important to me," he said. "I don't like surprises. You know that."

"You're being ridicu—" Her eyes narrowed as she glanced over Gray's shoulder.

"What? See another ex?"

"No, there's something wrong with the waitress. She's staring at us. Very strange."

~ * ~

Sofia balanced the glasses of water on the tray as she slowly walked up to the man who could only be *her* Gray and the woman he was with.

Maybe she was his cousin or sister or...or his maid.

Why would he take his maid to dinner, Sofe?

The tramp had a nice-sized ring on her finger. No way was he married to her. That wasn't possible. At no point in her visions did he ever wear a ring or speak of another woman.

No, when she closed her eyes and dreamed of Gray, they were completely in love. No other woman existed. It was only the two of them.

She stopped behind him. Inches away. If she weren't sane, she'd think she felt an unknown force luring her to him. Of course, this was the man who she would inevitably and passionately fall in love with. She knew that. How could she not be drawn to him?

One small step farther and she was standing beside him, looking at his strong profile. His clean-shaven jaw was clenched. His full lips frowned. His thick, dark lashes hovered heavily over his eyes, and his large hands pressed down on the table in front of him.

He made it obvious he was avoiding her as she walked up beside him. But why?

The water glasses on the tray Sofia held clinked together. She realized she was trembling.

"Are those ours?" the woman sitting across from him asked.

Sofia ignored her. Whoever the woman was wasn't important. She'd be out of the picture soon anyway. Trying to gain composure, she cleared her throat and remembered Nana's words from that morning.

He doesn't know you like you know him.

It wasn't fair. She couldn't call out his name, jump into his lap and kiss him like in her dreams. She was a complete stranger to him.

Which didn't explain his reaction when he crooked his head to peer up at her. His dark eyes widened and his lips parted.

"Who...?" He stood too quickly and bumped the tray she was holding.

Sofia didn't have a tight enough grasp on the tray, so it wobbled in her hands. One glass of water tipped over onto the table. It rolled and crashed onto the tile floor. The other glass took its time, almost in slow motion, as it toddled and leaned toward Gray.

"Oh, shoot." She watched the water splash up against his chest.

Smooth move, Sofe. Way to make a man fall in love with you.

She stood paralyzed for a moment, as did the rest of the restaurant, it seemed.

So here he is. My destiny. Now what?

She couldn't help but ogle the way his wet light blue shirt clung to the muscles in his chest. The way his shallow breaths lifted his pecs. Per her dreams she knew exactly how solid those pecs were to the touch. Solid. Powerful. That was Gray.

Yeah, she had it bad.

With all the courage she could muster, she met his gaze. Why would she be afraid of a man who was kind and loving, anyway? Who treated her with respect and compassion?

She noticed his Adam's apple bob, and looked up farther to see his face pale. She held back the urge to reach up and press her mouth to his. To taste him.

To love him.

"I'm sorry," she whispered as she met his searching eyes.

His gaze swept over her, but stopped at her name embroidered into her vest. She'd never felt more naked but, oddly, in a good way—in a heated, passionate, make-love-to-me-right-now way.

"You should be," he finally said, with the deep voice she knew so well.

"What?" Sofia shook her head out of its hazy state.

"You should be sorry." He flicked at her name on her vest. "Sofia, this is the worst service I've ever received."

"Excuse me?"

"How much do you get paid to work at a snail's pace?" He picked up the tipped over glass lying on the tray she somehow still held outright. "And drench the customer in the process?" He set the glass down on the table, making a clinking sound that echoed throughout the otherwise silent room.

Sofia peeled her eyes away from Gray to see that everyone within viewing range was staring at her, including his dinner date, who only had pity in her eyes. Pity for Sofia.

"Grayson," the woman whispered, "it wasn't her fault."

No, not my fault I'm in love with a man I'm only just

meeting, Sofia thought, before Gray's rough finger under her chin stole her attention. He guided her to look up at him.

"This was entirely her fault. She's intrusive and clumsy. What else do you have up to, Sofia? Are you trying to ruin my dinner date?" He sneered down at her. He actually *sneered*. His lips curled wickedly, as if she didn't mean anything to him and never would.

Her chest squeezed as she choked on a breath. Seriously? In all the scenarios that had filled her fantasies, she'd never thought her first meeting with Gray would go like this. Heck, she'd never dreamed he'd act like an arrogant, rude bully.

And for the first time in her life, rage filled her.

Not heartbreak. No, he didn't deserve that. Not with the way he was acting. The woman had called him Grayson, but the man from her dreams would never treat Sofia this way.

"Look," he said, and tapped his finger on her chin. "She can't speak either. Is she even really here?"

That was it. A person could only take so much ridicule. She swiped his hand from her chin with one hand and slammed the tray against his abdomen with the other.

It wasn't enough. He deserved more pain, so she stomped one of her Mary Jane's down on his foot as hard as she could.

"Fuck," he yelled, and inhaled sharply.

Good. Now maybe he'd wise up.

"Sofia," André shouted from behind her. *Oh, shoot*. Sofia twirled around to face the angry Frenchman.

"He started it," she said, and immediately wanted to kick herself for sounding like such a child.

"You're fired, Sofia. Clock out and leave."

"But—"

"There's no excuse for harming a customer. Leave. Now."

Gray's date stepped forward. "She's not to blame, sir. My fiancé is, I think, having a bad day."

"Fiancé?" Sofia spun back around at the word. She looked up at Gray. "You're engaged?"

He didn't answer, but the rigid expression on his face was enough of a reply.

Okay, now it was time for the heartbreak.

Sofia cheeks blazed. How could she have gotten it so wrong this time? The man she was in love with wasn't a jerk...and he certainly wasn't engaged to a beautiful woman.

"Of course not," she whispered, feeling defeated. "Only in my dreams."

"Your what?" He grabbed her forearm.

An extraordinary surge of heat rose through her body, and Sofia wondered if he'd felt it too. He closed his eyes for a moment and then opened them halfway, staring at her with a strange intensity.

"Grayson," his fiancée said, "what is wrong with you? Let her go."

Sofia wasn't afraid of him. She met his stare with an angry one of her own...which melted quickly when he leaned in and brushed his lips against her ear.

Her skin prickled at the mere touch, how his breath warmed her ear. Maybe he realized what a jerk he'd been and was going to apologize. She breathed in his familiar scent and reached her hand up to caress his cheek. Welcome him home.

He grasped tighter to her arm, pulling her hand back down to her side. "Get out of my head," he said in a low growl, and released her.

Before she could gather her wits and her pride to respond, he threw a bill on the table and guided his fiancée out of the restaurant.

~ * ~

Rachel stared out the window, apparently giving Gray the silent treatment for behaving so poorly. He'd been an asshole, he knew, but how else was he supposed to react when the woman from his dreams showed up as their server? When she stared at him with those striking blue eyes that dug into his very soul? When she dared him to kiss that silly, lovesick expression off her face?

She wasn't supposed to be real. She was a dream, and dreams couldn't threaten your future. They couldn't materialize in front of you and your fiancée and make you second-guess every decision you'd ever made.

But that was exactly what she'd done in a matter of seconds.

He gritted his teeth and clenched tight to the steering wheel. Shit. The mirage, the hallucination...the whatever you wanted to call her, named Sofia was not a part of his plan. No, not a woman who haunted him, stalking his dreams and making him want her more than he'd wanted any other woman.

To know she existed blew his mind. How could it be possible?

"I'm sorry," he said, trying to sound like he meant it. He reached for Rachel's limp hand and gripped her palm.

Sure, he was sorry for causing a scene, and even more regretful for being the reason Sofia lost her job. Not for a second did he like knowing he'd hurt her in any way, but he hoped it had worked. He hoped the woman hated him enough to make her stop torturing his mind. How she did it, he didn't know, but maybe now the dreams would end.

"Do you know her?" Rachel asked.

The question surprised Gray. Had he been that obvious? "I've never met her before," he said.

Even though he'd made love to the woman every night for the past month, kissed every inch of her sweet skin, he'd never actually *met* her in real life.

"Why do you ask?"

"The way she looked at you. It was odd. I see women staring at you all the time when we're walking down the street or eating out, but never like that."

"She was definitely a whack job." Gray cringed at his own words. When had he become such an ass?

"You looked at her the same way." Rachel wriggled her hand from his grasp and shifted a lock of hair behind her ear.

"Don't be silly, Rache." He didn't bother arguing with her. He knew the look. He'd seen it on Sofia's face. But he refused to believe he'd been giving it back. "She's no one to me."

Chapter Three

The oxygen masks hung above their lifeless heads. How many?

Sofia walked down the aisle, counting the slumping bodies. Just counting. That was all she could do. They were already dead.

She was able to hold back her sobs until she saw the child. A little girl. Maybe three years old, bent over a woman's lap. Sofia assumed the woman was her mother. They both had long black hair and pale skin. Blue lips.

God help me.

Air gushed from her lungs and a tight knot formed in her belly. *Be strong*, she told herself.

She needed to find out more if she wanted to stop this tragedy from happening.

It didn't happen yet. Not yet. There was still time.

She kept going. Tears slid down her face as she continued counting bodies, some of them blurry, some vivid.

Twenty, twenty-one...

One seat empty. Sofia glanced up and searched for the seat number, but there wasn't one. Anywhere. Maybe that detail wasn't important. Her goal was to try to remember every tiny clue. No telling when one item or element would connect with another after she woke. Her mind was clearer then. Not as foggy.

Confused.

Shoot.

She woke from the dream and stared up at the ceiling. Frustrated, she swiped the tears from her cheeks. Why couldn't she figure it out? How was she to save these people if she didn't even know who they were or where they were going?

So far, she'd gathered that the aircraft was a small commercial plane. Two seats on each side. How many people were there again?

Thirty-five maybe, plus the crew. She closed her eyes and envisioned it. The pilot had been dead, too, but the plane still flew. The whirring of the engines buzzed in her ears. That was all she was able to remember this time. Next time she'd have to try harder. She *had* to.

Just like she'd thought Gray *had* to pull her into his arms and instantly fall in love with her when they met.

Wow. She'd really fooled herself there, hadn't she?

How was the man she'd met at the restaurant the same person from her dreams? Her stomach turned painfully as she thought of how he'd treated her. Like she was a pest. Intrusive and clumsy, huh? *Ergh*. She fisted her hand and punched her pillow.

Sure, he was gorgeous. If Sofia hadn't dreamed of a man of his caliber loving her, she'd never have considered the possibility. But never had she guessed he'd act like a rude bully at their first meeting.

Get out of my head. The whispered, angry words were still fresh in her ear. But what had he meant?

Did he also have the gift?

Impossible. If he knew of their imminent love, he wouldn't have been cruel.

Not *her* Gray.

~ * ~

Gray sunk his toes into the cold sand and watched as she walked up the shore toward him, her white top illuminated by the moon. As she got closer, he could see her staring intently, sensually, seeming anything but innocent. Her rosy glossed lips peaked at the corners.

She wanted him...again. The woman was insatiable, and he loved that about her. What man wouldn't?

The weather was chilly. For the moment, anyway. Soon, he knew he'd be working both of them into a sweat. He spread out a quilted blanket onto the sand and waited.

She stopped in front of him and pulled her hair out of its ponytail. The honey brown locks fell across her slightly freckled shoulders.

Gray set the lamp down in the sand and smiled. "Out here in the open, Sofia?" he asked, teasing her. He'd make love to her in the middle of Time's Square if that's what she wanted.

Besides, not a soul could be seen across the foggy beach.

"Do you want me?" She slipped her white top over her head and let it fall to the ground.

Gray took in the sight of her plump breasts, covered by a lacy white bra. "Do you need to ask?" He leaned over and brushed his lips across her soft shoulder and up to her ear. "Always," he whispered. Goosebumps rose on her skin.

It was easy to love a woman who loved him back tenfold. He planted his hands on the curve of her waist, but before he could gather her body against his, she stepped away.

Gray eyed her curiously. What did she have up her sleeve now?

She laughed softy while she unbuttoned her jeans and slid them down. White lace panties grabbed his attention. She dipped her fingers down the sides of them, but didn't continue. The woman knew how to tempt him.

"Do you need some help with those?" he asked.

She smiled and shook her head. "Your turn."

"Ah. I see what we're doing now." He'd be more than happy to play along.

He tugged his arms out of his shirt and threw it to

the sand. Her eyes filled with hunger as she gaped at his bare torso.

Gray laughed. She did that every time, and he never grew tired of seeing it.

"No laughing." She smiled sweetly. "Just strip."

"Okay, okay, Miss Bossy." He began to unbutton his jeans, but remembered he hadn't put his boxers back on after the last time they'd made love that morning.

"Don't stop now." She kept her eyes on him while she finished peeling down her panties. A small patch of hair arrowed down her mound.

What better incentive, Gray thought, as he pushed his legs out of his jeans. He wanted her indoors, outdoors, on a bed, on an open beach—it didn't matter. Just as long as he was inside her.

Before he could make another move, she knelt down in front of him, wrapping her hand around his erection.

"Sofia," he said breathlessly.

Her pink tongue slipped out between those glossy lips and licked his tip.

Gray clenched his eyes shut as she took him in her mouth. Warm, soft and wet. She began to suck, letting her tongue have its way with him.

God, he was going to explode if he didn't make her stop.

"Wait," he said with a rough voice. "Wait, Sofia."

She drew back and looked up at him with glazed eyes. "What's wrong?"

"Nothing." He dropped to his knees in front of her. "Nothing at all." Then he clasped his hands around the back of her neck and crushed her mouth to his.

She accepted his tongue and tangled hers with it, deeply, seductively. Her fingers crawled up his abdomen to his chest, swirling around his muscles.

How did she know how and where to touch him?

How could he make her feel just as good? He reached down her back, unlatched her bra, and pulled the lace from her body. Then he cupped her heavy breasts and teased her nipples with his thumbs.

She moaned into his mouth.

Oh, he could do better than that. He skimmed his hand down her stomach, over her mound, and felt her moist heat. Her body stilled as he rubbed two fingers over her clit and inserted them inside her. Back out over her sensitive nub and slowly in again.

"Gray," she whispered, and dragged her mouth away.

"Where are you going?" He licked the outside of her well-kissed lips. "I'm not done with you yet."

"No, you certainly aren't." She sank down and sprawled back against the blanket.

Gray took in the exquisite view. The light from the lamp and the moon cast shadows along the curves of her cream-colored skin. She ran the back of her hand seductively along her stomach to her breast.

"I'm cold, Gray. Make me warm." She spread her legs for him, letting him see where he longed to be.

His mind grew fuzzy as he settled himself on top of her. Her hand guided his hardness inside her. She was wet and ready. Without much thought, he plunged forward into her, slick and snug. He fit perfectly, as if she were made for him.

He inched out and slid back in, listening as she hummed pleasure into his ear. Small, deep breaths flowed from her as he worked himself into her depths, like the ocean pushing itself onto the shore. Easy, slow, powerful. Crashing into her, becoming one and then pulling back, over and over.

Their skin grew damp as their bodies slid together in smooth, rhythmic motion. Gray enjoyed the feel of her breasts against his chest, the feel of her fingernails pressing into his backside as he drove into her.

When he reached her innermost wall, *that spot*, she called out his name and clenched down on him, sending him over the edge.

She moaned as he came hard. Filling her. Claiming her. Possessing her.

"Oh, Gray," she whispered into his ear, as he continued to pulse inside of her. "I love you."

~ * ~

Gray punched his hand into the mattress when he woke and found himself lying in his own wet mess again. Alone.

"Goddamn it," he yelled into the darkness of his bedroom. He leaped up and stripped the sheet from his bed.

The whole situation was embarrassing, humiliating. It tortured him. Made him...*fuck*, it made him feel lonely. Not whole. He had enough problems. The loss of his brother apparently hadn't been the last straw. Now he had this to deal with.

Lord only knew what *this* was.

The dreams were unpredictable, uncontrollable, and that was the last thing Gray wanted in his life. If he couldn't control it, then it controlled him.

He wouldn't stand for that. He trudged down the hallway and pushed open the laundry room door. Three fitted sheets already sat in the washer. He'd need to do a wash if he wanted something to sleep on tonight.

That was something he could manage. A clean sheet. Wash away the reminder of what *she* did to him. How she brought the dreams on, he didn't know, but he hoped it would stop before his wedding night.

He could imagine how Rachel would feel about him dreaming of another woman.

Rachel. She was the one, he reminded himself. She was a beautiful woman with a future in law. She was sure to *become* the ideal woman. Stable. Dependable.

A loyal wife, a dedicated mother, and a confident career woman. He'd have it all. *They'd* have it all. Then everything would be normal. No surprises to knock a guy off his axis. That's what he needed.

Gray started the machine and headed back to his bedroom. The clock on his bedside table read four in the morning. No point in attempting to sleep anymore. He needed to get ready for work.

He had a big day ahead of him...a life-defining day.

~ * ~

Rachel set the phone back down. She couldn't call Gray this early. He wouldn't be up. Besides, she had no idea what she'd say to him.

"I can't do this," she mumbled to herself. "You're perfect in every way, but I don't love you?"

Oh, her mother would like that one.

"Sure, I'll just call off the wedding a month before I'm supposed to walk down the aisle." See how much respect she'd get from her parents then. Probably enough for them to ask her to pay back every single penny they'd put into this ceremony, she was sure. Money she didn't have.

They were already paying for her education.

Not that Rachel wanted to end up as a lawyer, but it was their money, their trust in her and *what you could do if you put your mind to it*.

Those words. They were a mantra that ran through her mind relentlessly. "You could be so much more if you only tried," she said aloud, as she whipped the duvet off her body.

"I don't know about that." Grayson's voice filled the room. "You look pretty good as is."

Startled, Rachel stood straight up on the floor beside her bed and scanned the room. The door was shut, as it had been for the past five hours that she'd been tossing and turning. The moonlit room showed no sign of another human being.

"Grayson?"

No one answered. Not a sound. Just an eerie, cool breeze that touched the back of her neck and ran down her arms.

She shivered, and goosebumps erupted over her skin. Where the hell had that come from?

The windows were locked tight and the air conditioning wasn't running. "Grayson, are you here?"

Her alarm clock sounded off, shrieking its annoying buzz. She reached for it and pressed the snooze button. The green neon numbers blinked on the display.

Had there been a power outage?

"No, baby, it's not Grayson," his voice gusted into her ear, along with a chilled wind.

"Who?" Rachel turned quickly to see a man standing right behind her. She jumped back, bumped into the side of her bed, and fell back onto the mattress.

Oh my God. Hayes. It couldn't be. But there he was, flesh and blood, looking exactly like Grayson's identical twin brother, with hair to his shoulders, tucked behind his ears. He wore a worn t-shirt and jeans with holes in their knees.

All appropriate attire for a man who knew no boundaries—wanted no boundaries—a man who was always carefree...confident...sexy.

A man who had been dead for over six months.

"No. It's not you," Rachel said, more for herself than for the man before her. Hayes's death had been a complete surprise. A tragic halt to a vibrant, exciting life. Grayson had hated that his brother had been so frivolous, hated that he was a reckless thrill-seeker...and that he'd died in the same fashion.

A thousand miles an hour until I reach the end, baby. He'd joked about his antics, and Rachel had eaten up every ounce of his energy. He'd had more than enough to fill up any room he walked into. More than enough to share with her.

Rachel hated Hayes for the night they'd spent together the weekend before he decided to jump from an airplane with a faulty parachute. The fool had probably

40

never even checked to see if it worked in the first place. He'd loved the adrenaline rush of danger. He'd lived for it.

She supposed that was why she hadn't pushed him away that night he'd taken her virginity. She'd watched Hayes as he interacted with Grayson, how passionate Hayes was about life. She'd heard the stories of his adventures, and when he'd come to her that weekend while Grayson was away on business, an overwhelming desire had overcome her to feel Hayes's carefree spirit. To absorb it.

To be his next thrill.

And she had been, if only for a short while.

A smile spread across his face, showing a familiar dimple on his left cheek. "Have you missed me?"

"We buried you."

"I know. You cried for me." His smile faded. "Why haven't you told Gray about us? About our weekend?" He lifted his leg, resting it on the mattress beside her, and reached his hand out to her.

"No. No, no, no." Rachel inched back away from him. "You cannot possibly be him." She kept a baseball bat under the other side of the bed. If she could get to it.

"It's me, Rache. You know it is."

"Okay, so..." She was almost there. Just keep him busy. "You're a ghost?"

"Sure, why not? A ghost, an apparition, a spirit, an angel, or waves of energy that so far only you can see. Really interesting, I have to say, that the only person who *can* see me is the one person I want to see me. I guess that's the trick."

Slowly, she slid off the other side of the bed and bent down. No sudden moves.

He followed, crawling onto the bed. "You have no idea how difficult this has been for me."

"Oh, I can imagine." *Yeah, imagine him in a straightjacket.* How was she going to explain to Grayson that a man broke into her apartment, claiming to be Hayes Phillips?

So what if he looked like him, sounded like him, had that same damn dimple? Rachel had seen Hayes lying in that casket. She *had* cried for him and for their night together. She'd known it was in all probability a one-time deal, but she hadn't cared. He'd been the first man in her life to push her to her limits and keep on pushing. He'd dared to go there, and she'd rewarded him for it.

The man stopped in the middle of her bed and sat on his knees. "Rachel, you have to tell him about what happened between us. You can't marry him and let him find out on his wedding night."

"I don't know who the hell you are, but this is sick. It's wrong. You have to leave now."

"I fell in love with you that night. Did you know that?" He shook his head. "No, you probably didn't. I guess I forgot to mention that little fact."

Rachel's head whirled and pounded and wouldn't stop rehashing the details of the passion they'd shared. "You're not Hayes," she whispered.

"Gray's not the man for you, Rachel."

"You don't know what you're talking about." She felt the cold aluminum bat at her fingertips and grasped the handle. Keeping it clenched tight behind her back, she stood and faced the stranger.

He narrowed his black eyes at her. "What do you have back there? A gun? I'm already dead, sweetheart, remember? A big oops with the parachute and then splat?"

"That's not even slightly funny. And you can understand that your story is a little hard to believe, right? You don't look like a ghost. You look like a man who's sitting on my bed, uninvited. So either I'm dreaming this, or you're a complete stranger who has broken into my apartment, who I have to protect myself from."

In a blink, he wasn't there anymore. Rachel blinked again and then again.

There hadn't been enough time for him to hide. It was as if he'd simply disappeared. The same chilled breeze swept over her, sweeping her hair back off her shoulders and bristling her skin.

She shook her dizzy head and blew out a breath.

"A baseball bat?" His voice came from behind her.

Startled, Rachel spun around and lifted the bat up to her shoulder, prepared to swing. He stood there, laughing and clapping his hands. And he appeared...well, he appeared blurry. Like a television with a bad signal.

"You're...you're not..." She tried to think of the words, but was stunned by what was happening before her very eyes.

"What?" His smile crumbled.

"You're not all there."

He looked down at himself and waved a hand through his abdomen. *Through his abdomen*.

"Holy shit." She slumped to the mattress. The bat loosened from her shaky grip and landed on the bed behind her.

"This is weird," he said with a hazy voice. "Listen carefully, okay? This is important. Don't marry him. You don't love him. And he sure as hell doesn't—"

Then he was gone. Just like that.

"Hayes?" Rachel swept a quick glance around the room to see if he'd pulled the invisible act again. "Are you there?"

Nothing. She was alone—she thought so anyway.

What the heck had she seen? Hayes's ghost? A hallucination?

Oh, God, was she going crazy? She'd managed to put that night behind her, to forget about how Hayes had made love to her, so sweetly and with such adoration. She'd tried hard to forget the week before his death, the guilt of sleeping with him, and the debate in her head of whether she should break it off with Grayson so she could spend her nights with Hayes.

His funeral had decided that for her. Hayes had made the choice to jump out of the airplane. He'd made the choice, and when Grayson asked her to marry him two months later, there was no other answer.

How dare Hayes, hallucination or otherwise, tell her not to marry Grayson? As far as she was concerned, as far as her parents were concerned, a wedding would take place in one month.

Chapter Four

A day of job-hunting was ahead of Sofia. Only problem was she couldn't seem to force her eyes open. Heck, she didn't feel like getting out of bed, period. In fact, if sleep could guarantee she'd dream of Gray, the *nice* Gray, and not about dead people she couldn't save, then she would never open her eyes again.

"Get it together, girl," she mumbled to herself, while slipping out of bed and into her slippers.

Life doesn't happen with your eyes closed was one of mother's favorite sayings. But her mother had no idea just how much happened in Sofia's premonitions.

Love experienced for the first time, eyes closed or not, was so much better than anything she'd ever encountered. Life be damned if it couldn't catch up...and quick.

Her stomach grumbled, reminding her she hadn't eaten since lunch at Nana's house yesterday. Maybe a good breakfast would cheer her up and take her mind off of her whole good Gray/evil Gray situation.

"Yeah, right. Like that's going to happen," she said while walking down the staircase.

"Are you talking to yourself again?" Her mother stood at the kitchen doorway with a sweet smile on her face. Her tall thin frame leaned against the doorjamb as she held a bagel in one hand—gluten-free, of course—

45

and a glass of orange juice—undoubtedly organic—in the other hand. Her long, curly blonde hair was pulled back in a loose ponytail.

A classic beauty, Sofia had to admit. Natural. Hardly a dab of makeup and the woman still beamed with radiance. What was worse, the morning sun shone on her from the window, making her look like an angel, which was somewhat paradoxical, considering how her mother behaved on a daily basis. Not that she was evil, just a bit ornery, that was all.

Sofia smiled back. "Of course. It's the best conversation I've had all year."

"That's my girl," Laura said, and disappeared into the kitchen.

Sofia followed. She was hungry, after all, and what better time to talk about Mr. Lawrence's latest issue?

Her mother sat at the table-for-two next to the bay window. She seemed in deep thought as she nibbled on her bagel and drank her juice.

Sofia grabbed a cup of coffee and poured a couple scoops of her mother's fake sugar in, stirred it, and took a long, slurpy sip. *Mmmm. Boy, did it hit the spot.*

Now to find something decent for breakfast in this soy abundant, high fiber, low fat kitchen...

She opened the fridge and was overjoyed to see the pizza box from the other night still stuffed on the very bottom shelf, way back, where she'd left it. One piece of veggie pizza, extra cheese with jalapenos, sat inside. Yum!

She grabbed the piece and sat at the table, ignoring the way her mother eyed her choice of breakfast.

Living with her mother at the age of twenty-four wasn't something she was proud of. Nor was it something she planned to do for much longer. It was just... Her mom needed her. Sofia had found that out the hard way when she'd been admitted into a prestigious art school in New York after high school. Her freedom had lasted a year before she received a call from her crying mother, deeply depressed and heartbroken over a devastating breakup. The relationship had lasted two years, and he'd been the first man Laura had let into her life since Sofia's dad left.

She'd never heard her mom sound so hopeless, rejected again for something she couldn't control. Her psychic abilities were a part of her, and if men couldn't get that, she didn't want any part of them.

Long story short, Sofia left school to look after her mom. No matter the tough façade Laura Good tried to portray, Sofia knew how important it had been to help her through that break-up.

There hadn't been another man since, and Sofia hadn't had the heart to move out. *What could you do?* She missed school and being with people her own age who shared the same interests. But...her mom was more important.

"How old is that pizza?"

"A couple days. It's still good." Sofia picked at a jalapeno and changed the subject. "Herbert wants you to knock it off. Again."

Her mother smirked. "What the hell did I do this time to anger the uptight ass?"

Sofia caught herself rolling her eyes and stopped. It was a bad habit she'd been trying to break.

"I swear, that man doesn't like anything I do. Is this not my house to do with what I want?"

"It's yours, Mom." No point in pushing the subject. She'd relayed Herbert's message and now it was time to duck out before her mother got any angrier. For what reason, Sofia didn't know. With anyone other than Herbert Lawrence, she was a reasonable woman...for the most part.

Laura dropped her half-eaten bagel on her plate and blew out a breath. "You look tired."

"Kind of am." Sofia swallowed the bite of stale pizza crust she'd been chewing on. "Had another dream about that airplane again."

"With all the dead people?"

"Yep, and I don't have a clue what to do about it. It's not giving me much to work with."

"Well, you're not God, Sofia. You know that."

"Yes, I know, but if I can find out what the airline and flight number are, then I can do something to keep it from going up in the air." Sofia's shoulders tightened and burned, so she stretched her neck to release some of the tension. Tension she hadn't realized she'd been holding in, but what did she expect?

She dreamed about dead people night after night and now she'd lost her job.

And Gray, the only man she'd ever envisioned loving, was an arrogant jerk.

"You worry too much." Laura frowned. "You can't save the world and yourself at the same time."

"Well, I can try at least." Sofia set the pizza down, not quite as hungry anymore.

"What about that man you've been dreaming about?" Her mother grinned but avoided eye contact, a telltale sign that Nana had told her about Gray. Great. In less than twenty-four hours the news had already spread.

"I met him last night at the restaurant. He's engaged to be married to someone else."

"And?"

"And he's kind of mean." Sofia didn't want to get her mother riled. Men were the enemy as far as Laura Good was concerned.

"Well, of course. Testosterone can do that to a person, but was he good looking?"

Sofia stared at her mother, shocked. "Uh, yeah, you could say that."

"Then go get him."

"What?"

"Sweetheart." Her mother grabbed for Sofia's hand across the table. "You're a twenty-four-year-old *virgin*."

She whispered the last part as if it were some sort of crime.

"You don't know that."

Her brow rose. "Really. If this man from your dreams is the only man you'll ever feel comfortable giving yourself to, then for God's sake, go rape him if you have to."

"Mom. Just stop." Sofia pulled her hand away. This was *not* what she'd expected to hear.

"Okay, maybe rape is too strong of a word. *Seduce* him. You can't let these dreams rule your future. Why not take charge? Why not use it to your own advantage for once?"

"What if it's not that easy? What if he doesn't like me?" Just as the question left Sofia's mouth, she realized how absurd it was. At some point in the future, Gray would love her. It was only a matter of time.

"How often have your dreams been wrong?"

"They've always come true. Every one of them." Unless she prevented them from happening, like the anticipated murder of the elderly woman a few months back. Sofia was able to give enough information to the police to let them know it was *going* to happen, anonymously, of course.

Nana had told Sofia about what had happened to their ancestors when their gifts had been discovered. They were deemed witches and then executed. Times had changed, thank goodness, but society still wasn't quite ready to accept the types of gifts Sofia and her female family members possessed.

"Well, there you go," her mother said, breaking her thoughts. "Go get yourself laid. But be sure to be back by suppertime. I'm making a new recipe I found in *Woman's Day*." She gave Sofia a quick nod, stood, and put her dish in the sink. "If you need me, I'll be repainting the side of the house. What do you think of a tree full of plump, juicy purple plums? I heard through the

49

grapevine those are pretty popular in this neighborhood."

This time Sofia allowed herself a full eye roll. Obviously Herbert Lawrence had some sort of objection to plums.

"What? You think you're the only artist in the family?"

Before Sofia could argue, her mother was on her way out the front door. The woman wasn't going to stop until Herbert had a full head of grey hair, but Sofia wasn't going to concern herself with that today. She had other things to worry about.

Maybe her mom had a point. What would be the harm in hunting her dream man down to speed things up a bit? Well, other than Sofia getting her feelings hurt, big time. How long would he be a jerk? And for what reason?

There's only one way to find out, Sofe.

Without another thought, she threw away the rest of the pizza, rinsed out her coffee cup and headed to the laptop she shared with her mother. It sat on the large, dark walnut desk in the den, where the readings took place.

She settled into the black leather chair in front of the desk. A cold breeze ran up her spine. Her skin prickled, and she sat paralyzed for a moment. She'd never get used to that feeling—knowing a spirit was in the room with her. Sensing their presence happened quite often, since the ability to conjure up spirits was one of her mother's gifts. What better place for them to hang out and wait for their turn?

Thank goodness Sofia didn't have that particular talent. She'd seen enough of the deceased in her sleep.

Warmth returned to her body and the hairs on the back of her neck finally settled, so she continued with the task at hand—finding Gray.

Grayson Phillips, she typed in the search bar and hit enter. A vast list of websites popped up, but the very first one answered her question.

Linden Advertising, it said and underneath it read *Grayson Phillips, Creative Department*.

"Well, that was easy," Sofia said, wondering why she hadn't thought to do this before. "I found you, Mr. Phillips."

~ * ~

Gray switched on the lights to his office and maneuvered his foam poster boards through the door. All of his work for Bud B's Burger Restaurant's new "healthy food line" ad was carefully attached. One week's work, after Linden had shot down the PowerPoint presentation, saying *that's not how they did things around here*.

Linden was as old-school as they came. Gray wondered if the man would even own a computer if he didn't have to accept incoming email from clients. He also wondered how this place stayed in business if Linden refused to accept change.

Updating the technology was the first thing Gray planned to do once he got his promotion. Until then, he was stuck with these damn poster boards.

One week... That was all the time Linden had given him to find a way to make this crap seem tempting enough to eat.

Lord only knew how it would digest.

As always, Gray found it hard to believe in the product he was trying so hard to make appealing to other people. *Just as long as Bud B. likes it enough*. Then he knew Linden would have to give him the promotion to Director. Not that that job was any more tolerable, merely a step up the food chain.

If his life had turned out differently, would he even be here? Would he be striving to get a promotion in a career he was growing to loathe?

The answer was irrelevant. In a perfect world, Gray would be on a boat with Hayes, sailing along the California coast. That was what they'd been planning since they were in grade school, and they'd been well on their way to accomplishing it.

With their lifetime savings, Hayes had gotten on an airplane, met with a realtor, and with Gray's approval, purchased a two-bedroom loft in the San Francisco bay area. They'd planned on meeting there to start looking at sailboats...before Hayes died.

The world wasn't perfect, Gray had found out. It was downright cruel. Now he didn't want anything to do with that alternate universe, the one where it didn't hurt to think of a carefree life.

He set the boards gently against the wall to take another look at the finished product. The photos he'd gotten of the so-called guilt-free fast food were horrendous, so he'd taken it upon himself to design a few pictures to go with the whole ad campaign, which would plaster billboards all over Indiana and the rest of the continental United States. Hopefully.

Think positive, Gray. He didn't simply want this promotion; he needed it.

The door swung open as Gray leaned down to check out a small smudge he hadn't noticed before, and his colleague—the only competition for the promotion—walked in. Patrick Beaver had slicked back blond hair, a large white-toothed smile, and an impressive collection of pastel colored silk ties. He had a homely, nonthreatening-looking wife who brought in brownies every week and knew how to make small talk with Linden and *his* homely wife.

Yeah, Patrick Beaver was somewhat of a threat and anything but a friend.

"Phillips," he said with that idiotic toothy smile, "you ready for the big presentation?"

Gray stood to his full height and jutted out his chin. "Absolutely. Couldn't be more ready."

"Excellent." Beaver gave a nod as he arched his brow. "Is that it?"

"It is." Gray crossed his arms in front of him, daring him to say anything else.

Beaver yawned excessively and shrugged. "Good luck, then. You're going to need it. I've heard Bud B. isn't easily impressed." He winked and shut the door behind him before Gray could respond.

Nice tactic, fucker. It had worked. Patrick Beaver had successfully made Gray more nervous, if that were possible. He rolled his head from side to side to relieve some tension.

Get it together, Phillips. You can do this.

Just then, the speakerphone beeped and the creative department's assistant said, "Mr. Phillips, Ms. Rachel Spencer is on line two for you."

"Thank you, Sandy," Gray called out. This was odd. Rachel hardly ever called him at home, much less at work. Maybe something was wrong with the wedding planning. Hell, maybe she'd come to her senses and wanted to call it off altogether.

Gray held his breath and pressed the button that lit up line two. He didn't want to think about the reasons why he was more worried about being late for his presentation than the possible demise of his relationship with his fiancée.

"Rachel?"

"Hi, Grayson," she said in soft, shaky voice. "I know you have that presentation, but I really need to talk to you."

"It can't wait?"

"I'd like to talk about it now, if you don't mind?" She paused for a moment, probably waiting for Gray to give her his permission to go on, but he remained quiet, waiting to hear what she had to say next.

"Um," she continued. "I was thinking about Hayes."

"Hayes?" Gray hadn't heard his brother's name from her mouth since before his twin's funeral, and he sure the hell didn't want to hear it now, from anyone.

"You called me to talk about *Hayes*?"

"Yes." She paused again. "Maybe right now isn't a good time to talk about this after all."

"Maybe not."

"I'm sorry I bothered you at work."

"No bother, but you know that he's not exactly my favorite topic of conversation."

"I know. I'll see you this evening for dinner?" she asked, her voice still shaky.

"Yes, and be prepared for good news."

"Can't wait."

Gray hung up the phone and leaned on his desk. The clock on the wall said he had less than ten minutes to get to the presentation room and set up. Time to focus. He took another once-over at his boards and carefully picked them up. The speech and slogan he'd prepared rolled through his mind, but didn't have that punch they had the last time he'd read them.

Oh, fuck.

"Focus, Gray," he whispered to himself.

His phone beeped again as he reached for the doorknob. "Mr. Phillips, there's a Sofia Good here to see you," Sandy said through the speaker. "She doesn't have an appointment but she insists it's important. Would you like me to send her back?"

Gray clenched his eyes shut and tried not to get a mental image of her...all of her.

What the hell did she want from him?

Chapter Five

"Go right in," the perky blonde said to Sofia, as she pointed to a door flanked by two windows.

Gray was frowning through one of them as he shut the blinds.

That probably wasn't a good sign for what was to come. Too bad she couldn't have dreamed of this, so she could prepare herself.

What was the worst that could happen? Well, other than ruining her own destiny. She rubbed her clammy hands together, ignored the tight uncomfortable knot in her stomach, and briskly walked to the door, giving it two hard knocks.

He opened it right away and gestured for her to walk in. Sofia smelled his musky, smooth cologne as she brushed by him, since he hadn't given her much room to walk through. He looked impressive in his charcoal suit and striped navy and red tie. Sofia supposed it would have to be professionally tailored, since he was such a big guy.

Tall and muscled like an athlete. From head to... She shook the familiar naked image of him out of her head.

His office was typical with a desk, a computer, a small bookcase to the side filled with nonfiction marketing and advertising books, a picture of his stupid fiancée on his desk, and sadly, no windows to let in any sunlight. How depressing.

Fluorescent lights lit up the room, and Sofia wondered if this were partly why he was such a butthead. *A vitamin D deficiency could do that to a person, ya know?*

"What do you want, Sofia?" he asked.

"You're not very polite," Sofia muttered under her breath. She wrapped her arms around herself and looked anywhere but into his cold eyes. Poster boards were sitting against the wall decorated with sketches of weird looking hamburgers and French fries.

"Excuse me?" he asked.

"Did you draw those?"

"What do you want?" he repeated, not making any effort to answer her.

"I draw too. And paint."

His lips twitched to what might have been a start of a smile, but then flattened out again.

"Listen. I'm sorry if I was the reason you were fired from your job. Is that why you're here? Do you want some sort of compensation?"

"What?" She finally met his dark, gloomy gaze and saw only a stranger. "No, I thought maybe we could become friends, since we have something in common."

"Do you mean the dreams?" He leaned against his desk and crossed his arms, his eyes narrowing in on her.

Sofia crossed hers tighter. Two could play at that game. "Yes, I'm assuming you have them as well. Is that right?"

"I do, and I want them to stop. I'm getting married in a month, and I don't need or want to be dreaming of a woman who isn't in my future."

Don't roll your eyes, Sofe. If he only knew.

"How can I say this?" She pondered for a moment whether to tell him about her gift, but thought not. Gray didn't seem to be the open-minded type. But she wasn't sure how else to get her point across, or how she could convince him to spend more time with her so he could fall in love with her... If that were even possible.

"I've got a meeting to get to. Why don't you just tell me what I have to do to get rid of these dreams?" He edged toward her with his perfect lips pursed into a thin line. His hands fisted at his sides. Sheesh. Where inside him did the gentle man from her dreams exist?

"I can't get rid of them." She started to back away. Her hands itched to swipe the perspiration from her forehead, but she kept them at her sides.

"Can't or won't? What is it you want from me?"

"I, uh – " She found the wall behind her and stared up at him as he moved within centimeters.

Her heartbeat thrummed through her veins and pulsed heavy in her head. She couldn't think. The loving man from her dreams was so close, yet still out of reach.

Minutes passed, it seemed, as he stared at her with a cool dark eyes.

Finally, he lifted his finger and brushed it across her bottom lip.

Sofia froze, startled by his touch.

"Do you know what I do to you, what you do to me in these dreams?" A familiar spark of hunger flashed through his eyes, but other than that, it was difficult to describe the look on his face.

"Yes. I know exactly what we *both* do." She pressed her hand to his chest for two reasons – to keep him from getting any closer and to see if he, at least, felt like the man from her dreams.

He did. He was warm and *really* solid, and his heart beat ferociously under his crisp shirt. As he lowered his head down to her lips, Sofia inhaled his familiar scent. It was her Gray. And yet it wasn't.

His lips lightly brushed her mouth, and she closed her eyes, reveling in the possibilities.

Should she kiss him? Grab him by his neck and

force it? Was she going to fight for him? Was it worth it?

It was. She knew it was, but before she could do anything or say anything, his lips grazed her ear.

"Did you know?" He paused to pull in a breath.

"What? Did I know what?" Her fingers trembled against his chest as she forced herself to hold them still when they so wanted to touch every part of him.

"Did you know that you...that you had my cock in your mouth last night?" He whispered and stood motionless.

A sharp breath gushed from her lips at the bluntness of his words. Yep, she'd had that dream as well. The act had been loving and meaningful. Not a tawdry affair between strangers. Not like how he was treating her today.

Damn him. The only explanation for his behavior was he was trying to scare her away. He wasn't ready for her yet. But she was too stubborn to give up now. She wouldn't leave here without letting him know that he didn't break her.

"Did I like it?" She bravely skimmed her hand down to his noticeable erection. At least this part of him wanted her. In time he'd grow to love her. Fate would show them the way.

Before she could grasp him, he grabbed both of her hands and pinned them above her head. He pressed her body against the wall with his steely frame. His muscled leg slid between her thighs.

Her body reacted, both startled by the sudden invasion and thrilled to have him so close. Her legs trembled against his as her pulse thrummed. She licked her lips, waited for his next move. Would he kiss her?

A myriad of emotions passed over his face, none of them soothing. "Is this what you want, Sofia? Do you want me to fuck you? Will that stop the goddamn dreams?"

She tensed, mortified. Her stomach flip-flopped,

sick with disappointment. But she was *not* going to cry. She wasn't going to let him win. "I wish I could stop them," she said, gritting her teeth. "I wish I dreamed of a different man, a man who wasn't a piece of work."

"Then you have to stop them."

"I can't!" Her eyes burned with unwanted tears. Damn it.

"Why *not*?"

"Because I dream of the future, you ass. And apparently you do, too, now."

Well, that did the trick. He released her hands and stepped away, shaking his head. "Please, just leave," he said in a low voice, as he reached for the door handle. "I don't want to see you anymore."

"Fine with me." Sofia regrouped by sniffing back her tears and heading toward the door.

Maybe this would prevent her future with this...this jerk from happening. Maybe the dreams would stop now. Because letting him touch her again was the last thing she ever wanted to do.

But before she could yank the door open, he grabbed her arm and stopped her from leaving.

"Hey," he whispered softly, confusing her. "I'm sorry I made you cry. I didn't... I'm just sorry. But you're not the woman for me."

Sofia tore her arm from his loose grasp, but didn't dare look up at him. He didn't *deserve* to ever see her again. "I hope you're right," she said, and left.

~ * ~

With his pulse pounding at his neck, Gray watched Sofia rush through the lobby and hit the elevator down button repeatedly. She didn't look back when the doors opened and then closed behind her.

He'd hurt her. And, damn, seeing her shake, seeing her eyes tear up, had knotted something inside of him. His stupid fucking mouth. He hadn't expected tears. He hadn't expected to regret pushing her away. It was easier to pretend she was of no importance when she was simply a vision in his head. But each new second he spent with her in reality forced him to recognize she was more than that. Much more. She was a human being with feelings. And he'd purposely pulverized them.

Gray knew better than that. Even if she was a little nuts, thinking she could dream of the future, he should've handled the situation better.

Instead, he'd been cruel.

What the hell was wrong with him? What was he becoming? He'd never treated a woman that poorly. Truth be told, in the past he'd been considered the nice twin. Friends had gone to him when they needed a shoulder to lean on. They'd gone to Hayes to have a good time.

Now, neither of those men existed.

"Um, Mr. Phillips." Sandy stood in front of him with one of her penciled eyebrows vaulted dramatically.

Gray stopped and glanced around. He hadn't realized he'd walked out into the lobby toward the elevators. What was he going to do? Follow her?

Give in to the thoughts that had been flooding through his mind while he'd had her backed against the wall?

He'd almost lost control in his office. Her enticing sweet vanilla scent, her blue eyes staring up at him, her glossy full lips pouting, her hand on his chest lowering to feel his stiffening erection, the softness of her breasts as he pressed up against her—it was all Sofia in the flesh, not some dream.

Authentic. Tangible. Sensual.

Stop.

He had to think of Rachel. *I might be an ass, but I'm not a cheater.*

"Mr. Phillips?" Sandy waved her long artificial fingernails in his face. "Anybody home in there?"

"Sorry." Gray straightened his tie. "I was, uh,

thinking."

"I could see that." She slid a red fingernail down the seam of her low v-neck sweater. "That wasn't your fiancée, was it?"

"No." He didn't bother explaining. It wasn't any of her business. "Do you need something?"

Her lips curved coquettishly. Gray knew that particular smile quite well. It was the same one he'd gotten from numerous women who'd ended up in his bed over the years before he met Rachel.

"I do need something," she winked, "but it'll have to wait. You're late for a little appointment. Mr. Linden called while you were in your office with that woman. I didn't want to interrupt. The conversation seemed pretty heated."

"Oh, shit." Gray hurried to his office to grab his materials. The clock on the wall said he was fifteen minutes late.

Damn.

He picked up his boards, closed the office door behind him, and ran directly into Mr. Linden.

Mike Linden was a small man. Five and a half feet tall, and he couldn't have weighed more than a hundred and ten pounds judging by the way he dropped to the floor like a feather.

Gray apologized, and sweat beaded his brow. He held out a hand for Linden to take, but his boss proudly pushed it away and rose to his feet on his own. The small elderly man dusted off his suit jacket as he glared up at Gray.

"Phillips," he said, while sweeping back a lock of silver-streaked hair, "you screwed up."

"It won't happen again, sir." Gray hated groveling, but he *had* screwed up and needed to dig himself out of the hole he'd created. "Is Bud B. still here? I'll apologize to him myself. I'm sure he won't mind once he sees —"

"Nope." Linden put his hand up. "He left. He's a

busy man, and you making him wait put a dark cloud over this entire company."

"Then I'll call him and explain." There had to be some way. Gray couldn't simply give up.

"Don't you dare, Phillips. Luckily, Beaver stepped in and handled the situation. He'll be taking over the project."

It wasn't until then that Gray noticed his nemesis smiling smugly a few feet behind Linden. No way was this happening. In a matter of minutes, Gray had mucked up his chance to be promoted and this moron was reaping the benefits.

"You've got to be kidding me," Gray muttered.

"I assure you, I'm not," Linden said. "I had high hopes for you, Phillips, but if you can't even arrive on time to an important meeting, how can you manage an entire department?"

Beaver, over Linden's shoulder, lifted his eyebrows as if waiting for Gray's answer. The nerve.

Gray clenched his fists at his side and tried to ignore Beaver. The heat of anger rose up his chest. "You're saying not only do I not get the account, I don't get the promotion either?"

"Why don't we talk about this at a later time? You seem upset."

"No. I want to know now. I've worked my ass off for this company, and I deserve that promotion."

Beaver stepped to Linden's right. "That's highly debatable, Phillips," he said while shaking his head. "Mr. Linden saw for himself just how unreliable you can be." He smirked and silently mouthed, "You fucked up."

It was all Gray could take. If he was going to fall, he'd drag Beaver down with him. He tightened his fist and swung, hitting his colleague square in the jaw. And damn, did it feel good.

If only for a moment.

~ * ~

62

Papers flew across the driveway after Sofia stumbled over her own feet. Of course an afternoon shower had just poured through, leaving the ground wet and ruining all of her job applications.

"Just great." Sofia looked around at the damage and began picking up each piece, crumpling them all together into a sopping ball. Her entire morning had been wasted. Why, again, hadn't she filled out the applications while she was there? Oh, yeah, she'd wanted them to look perfect before she handed them back in, with her resume she'd designed on the computer attached. The template had cute pink swirls and... She sighed.

What about her life was ever less than disastrous? *Evidently, nothing.*

"Stop feeling sorry for yourself, Sofe." She tossed the applications into the trash before heading inside. If Sofia Good was anything, she was resilient. Strong.

Strong enough to stop rapes and murders from happening, and strong enough to attempt to peel the thought of never being loved by *that* man from her mind and her dreams.

However, she was not strong enough to deal with her mother and her grandmother talking about her as she walked through the door. Not today. The whispers echoed into the hallway from the den. They didn't even bother to stop when Sofia leaned into the room and cleared her throat.

Her mother held up a finger. "Sofia doesn't *need* a man in her life. She's got me."

They sat on either side of the large walnut desk, inclining toward each other as if that would stop Sofia from hearing their every word.

"Need a man? No," Nana said, "but she deserves a little happiness."

"You can stop now," Sofia cut in before they could continue. "I have no idea why you're discussing this, but it's pointless. *Sofia* doesn't need *or* want a man, especially

Gray Phillips."

Geez, it disgusted her to say his name aloud. She hoped she never saw him again, eyes opened or closed. As of this morning, he was nothing to her.

But then why did it hurt so much?

Maybe because this could be her only chance at love.

"Oh, honey." Nana stood up and held out her arms for Sofia. She'd obviously read her mind. "Come to Nana."

Dang it. Times like this she wished she knew her mother's trick to block Nana out. Her mother had learned it in high school, and it had something to do with envisioning someone naked. Was it Rodney Dangerfield?

"Sofia, don't do that."

"Sorry, Nana, but I'm really not in the mood to be read."

"I'll try not to, but I'm worried about you. I can see that he's hurt you."

"I'm fine. Really."

"If he's been having the dreams, too, then he'll come to you eventually," Nana whispered and rubbed Sofia's shoulders.

Now, how did she know that? No secret was safe in this family, not even the ones in her head.

"I don't want him to. In fact, I'm going to prevent it from happening. I can do that, you know. I can control my own destiny." And her mind. *Rodney Dangerfield, Rodney Dangerfield.*

"What happened?" her mother asked as she walked toward them.

"I don't want to talk about it, Mom. It's over and done with." Sofia willed back the unwanted tears forming in her eyes.

It was no big deal, she told herself. That relationship simply wasn't meant to be. That was all.

Her mother moved in and caressed her cheek. "Darn it. I never should have told you to go after him. Men are nothing but closed-minded nimrods. They're all testosterone-driven assholes, and it sounds like this guy isn't any different. He's not worthy of you, just like your father—"

"Laura," Nana interrupted. "Please, show a little self-control."

Sofia glanced from her mother to her grandmother and wondered for the billionth time how they could possibly be related. One short and overweight, the other tall and lean. Sofia was somewhere in between them, leaning more to the short and, okay, slightly chubby side—so maybe eating cold pizza for breakfast hadn't been the best decision. The only characteristic that truly bonded them was the blue eyes.

And, of course, there was the whole no-man-will-ever-love-them issue. Psychic powers weren't exactly on a man's list of top ten reasons to stick around.

Her mother was right. Who needed a man anyway? All Sofia required was a job and the two women in front of her.

"Sofia," Nana began in a cautious tone, "I'm going out of town for a week or two. An Amish family in Allen County needs a midwife for a difficult pregnancy, and I agreed to help. I was wondering, since you no longer have a job, if you could housesit for me and take care of Sam? Besides," Nana eyed Sofia's mother, who was fuming from being cut off and was most likely planning another desperate attack on poor Herbert to take the edge off, "it might be good for you to have some alone time away from everything."

~ * ~

Penny Jones pulled up to her home after driving from her daughter and granddaughter's house. She knew what she needed to do for Sofia.

Something she'd only done once before.

Something to help Sofia find her own true love, just as Penny had many years ago.

It had worked its magic then, literally. Now it was time to do it again. Sure, magic spells took a lot out of Penny, and she wasn't as young as she once was, but this was important.

She walked inside her home on a mission to bring her granddaughter happiness. She was determined to make it so Sofia didn't suffer the same bitter fate as Laura. She'd already picked out the necessary materials. Items she usually kept in her shed out back, along with all of her other magical goodies, were spread out on the floor. She sat down in front of them, close to the Earth.

Penny didn't practice witchcraft often. Her mother had taught her less was more. She'd taught the same to Laura, who decided for herself *and* Sofia that magic was not going to be a part of their lives at all. Their gifts were about all Laura could handle. Anything else was unnatural to her, abnormal.

Penny never argued, never undermined. Until now.

Each magnet lay out on the hardwood floor before her. One represented Sofia, the other Grayson Phillips. Penny closed her eyes and slowly breathed in and out, letting the energy rise inside of her.

This is interesting. A masculine voice vibrated into her head.

Penny opened her eyes and glanced around, but there was no one to be seen. "Hello?" she called out. It had been a mind she'd read, rather than an actual voice she'd heard. She could tell from the vibrations.

Can you hear me? he asked.

"Yes, but I can't see you. Are you a spirit, by chance?"

"I am. But you're not frightened?" He spoke this time in a deep and youthful tone.

"No." Penny chuckled. She'd heard her share of ghosts in the past. In fact, her late husband had spent a week on earth after he'd passed, before fulfilling his unfinished business and moving to the light. "No, I'm not frightened by you one bit. However, I am curious why you're here. Who are you and what is your business?"

"My name is Hayes Phillips, Gray Phillips's brother. I need to see to his happiness before I can cross over, and I think your granddaughter, Sofia, can help with that."

"Oh? How do you know of my Sofia?"

"She's the palm reader's daughter, right?"

"Yes, she is."

"Well, I've been watching her." He paused and laughed an infectious laugh. "Not in a weird way or anything."

Penny smiled. "That's good to know. Go on."

"You see, I was angry with the palm reader at first. I'd been to her a month before my death, and she'd told me to be careful. That's it. She hadn't warned me of my looming death. She hadn't even given me a hint. So, I brooded in their home, watching them, wanting to get even with the so-called psychic. But as time passed, I was more entranced by the daughter. She was sweet, innocent, and pretty in her own way. Not really my type." He chuckled lightly. "Definitely perfect for my brother, though. I began to think how lucky he would be if he were to find her. Then I remembered."

The young man stopped talking, but Penny continued to read his thoughts. He'd remembered how selfish he'd been, leaving his brother. And Rachel. He'd gone to see them after the spirit world had taken his body and saw the ring on her finger. They were engaged to be married, but neither of them was happy with the idea.

How could they be?

Penny nodded as she came full circle with the rest of the story. "I understand why you're here. We have the same goal then, don't we?"

"Yeah, I think we do."

~ * ~

Rachel braked hard, nearly hitting the school bus filled with children on their way home from school.

She'd been so consumed with her thoughts she hadn't noticed the light was red.

What was wrong with her? She was going to kill someone if she couldn't get it together.

Hayes. He was the problem. She couldn't get him out of her head. All night and all day during class, visions of the intimate time they'd spent together had manipulated her mind. Kissing. Wanting. Spreading her legs for him and letting him have whatever he desired.

Seeing him again had been agonizing. If the man in her room really had been Hayes, if his words had all been true, then he'd loved her. Who knew what would have happened if he'd lived to tell her? It wasn't fair to her, and especially not to Grayson. How could she ever go ahead with the wedding, knowing what she knew? After everything was said and done, she couldn't imagine letting Grayson into the space in her heart where only Hayes had been.

It wasn't right, and it had been ridiculous of her to ever think it would be.

The car behind her honked twice, letting Rachel know the light had turned green. She pressed the gas pedal and carefully continued home.

The phone call to Grayson this morning had been a pathetic attempt. As soon as she'd heard his voice over the line, she'd chickened out. Not only did she not want to hurt him any more than he'd already been hurt, she didn't want him to think poorly of her. She didn't want to see that look of disappointment she'd become so familiar with.

He hadn't always been this way. Remote and irritable. Before Hayes died, he was a kind, loving man. Rachel had loved that part of him. If only the passion had been there—the little thing called chemistry. Then she would've never slept with Hayes, and she wouldn't be in this predicament right now.

Her cell phone chirped on the seat beside her, and

she pulled off the road into a convenience store parking lot to answer it. No sense in adding another distraction to her already preoccupied mind.

"Hello?"

"Rachel, it's your mother."

"Hi." Darn it. Why hadn't she checked the caller ID?

"I can't talk long, dear, but don't forget to meet me at the bridal shop at five for your dress fitting. Olga has a tight schedule and doesn't like waiting."

"The dress fitting," Rachel repeated absently.

Seeing her wedding dress was the last thing she wanted to do.

"Don't tell me you forgot. How many times have I told you to write down appointments in the day planner I gave you?"

"I can't do it, Mom." There. She said it.

"It's a simple task that saves a ton of grief and keeps you organized, Rachel. I don't see what the big deal is. I've done it since—"

"I'm not talking about the day planner, Mom. I can't... I'm not feeling well. I can't make the dress fitting." Her excuse was only partially true. There wasn't enough courage in the world to tell her mother the real reason she wasn't going.

"Well, take some ibuprofen, have a short nap and meet me there at five."

"No. I can't make it. Not today."

"But Olga—"

"Tell Olga I'm deeply sorry, and I'll be sure to refer every bride-to-be I know now and in the future to her because she is such an understanding, caring, and highly skilled dressmaker."

"Well..."

Lying to her mother was never easy, and in the past, she'd avoided untruths at every cost. Today was the exception. "I have to go, Mom. I'm going to throw up."

A familiar chilled wind crept up Rachel's back and

underneath her hair before finally resting like a heavy hand on her neck.

Rachel snapped the phone shut and dropped it in her lap. "I'm losing my mind," she said through fresh tears.

"Let me find it for you." Hayes's deep voice filled the car, and Rachel felt an invisible but very tangible finger wipe the tear away.

Chapter Six

"Not every man is bad." Nana smiled sympathetically as she poured hot water from the teakettle into Sofia's cup. "Your grandfather was a fine man."

Sofia dunked her teabag up and down. Nana had insisted on making Sofia tea and a sandwich before heading off to help deliver the baby.

Agreeing to housesit and take care of the cat, Sam, had been an easy decision for Sofia. It wasn't as if she'd had any major plans or a job...or a boyfriend. Nope, she was free to sit up in this dark, scary house—out in the middle of nowhere without a telephone or electricity to charge her cell phone—for a long, *long* time.

First, she had to convince her grandmother she would be fine by herself. "Yeah, I sort of remember Grandpa. He used to give me candy when Mom wasn't watching."

"He did?"

Sofia ducked her head and took a sip of tea. "I guess you weren't watching, either."

"No, I wasn't." Nana paused, then shook her head. "The point, dear, is that good men are hard to come by, especially for women with gifts. Trust me, honey, reading your grandpa's dirty old mind on a daily basis wasn't the highlight of our married life." She sat down opposite Sofia and tapped her fingers on the table. "Although it was nice to know my husband still found me attractive after thirty years of marriage."

Sofia cringed. "What was the point again?"

"The point? Right. Sorry. What I'm trying to say is this Gray fellow may or may not be the man for you, but you're still young and you have a good head on your shoulders. You have plenty of time to find a man to fall in love with, and when you do, he'll be special."

"Thanks, Nana. You're right." The idea of being alone was becoming more and more appealing. Sofia loved her grandmother, but sometimes Nana was a little too optimistic.

Particularly when all she wanted to do was open the well-stocked liquor cabinet with the key that was hidden beneath the antique silver tray.

"All right, dear, I'll be going now. You remember how to use the stove?" Nana stood and rested her hand on her hip.

"Yes, I do." *The gas, no-electricity required stove.* Shoot. Forget about having microwave popcorn as a midnight snack, or heating up leftovers for breakfast. How did Nana live?

"Good. But don't use it while you're drinking, okay? I don't want to come home to a burned down house."

"Yes, ma'am." Her cheeks blazed. Mind read once again.

Nana pulled out the liquor cabinet key and slid it across the counter. "You're welcome to whatever I have, but don't get carried away."

Sofia nodded, avoiding eye contact.

"Heal your heartbreak however you choose, dear, but don't forget that I love you." Nana kissed Sofia's head as she passed by on her way to pick up her suitcase.

"Love you too." Sofia waited until the huge Buick left the driveway before she let a ragged breath.

Alone again.

~ * ~

Rachel locked her bedroom door and jammed a chair under the knob. How that would keep a ghost away, she didn't know, but she had to try something.

Ever since she'd arrived home, the chill that was Hayes had wrapped itself around her, encompassing her, not giving her a moment's rest. Still, she refused to acknowledge him, hoping he'd give up and leave.

"It's okay, Rachel. All you have to do is agree to talk to me." His voice breezed over her body, chilling it all the way to her ears.

God, it was freezing. She couldn't take it anymore. She grabbed a quilt off her bed and wrapped it around her body, but it was useless. She was just as cold, if not more so. As if she'd pressed him through her skin and into her bones.

"Go away, Hayes," she yelled, unable to hold her tongue any longer.

"That's my girl." He'd slipped behind her this time.

Rachel swerved around and spotted him leaning against one of her pink-painted walls. A smile of victory was on his face, revealing his dimple. She didn't know whether to be angry or overjoyed to be able to see him once again.

She gathered her wits and took a breath. "You have

to leave me alone."

His smile disappeared. "Not as long as you're planning on marrying my brother. Tell me you're not, and I'll be gone forever."

"Why don't you go aggravate him? Why me?"

"Trust me. I've been doing my work on him."

"Great. I'm glad to know you're creating havoc even in your afterlife. Why can't you let us be happy?"

"Happy?" He laughed. "Don't kid yourself. Neither one of you is happy, especially you. And you're not going to change that by marrying a man who doesn't love you."

The words hit Rachel hard, twisting a knot in her stomach. Down deep, she knew Grayson didn't love her, but it hurt like hell to have that assumption validated.

"Maybe he doesn't love me..." She ground out the words. "But that doesn't matter. He needs me. When you left him like you did, everything changed. He's not the same man he used to be. It's like he died inside when you died. I wouldn't be doing him any favors abandoning him. I'm all he has left."

"Don't you think I know that? That's why I'm here, sweetheart. To fix what I broke. I can't go on– " He raised his arms toward the ceiling and let them fall to his side. "I can't move on until you're both happy, or well on your way." He took a step forward, his gaze dark, pained. "And he'll never be content if he marries you."

"Thanks a lot."

"Only because he's not the man for you. You don't love him. Not the way she loves him." He mumbled the last sentence, but Rachel caught every word.

"Someone else loves Grayson? Who? Who are you talking about? Do I know her?" She pressed her palm to her chest. "Is he cheating on me?"

"No. The guy is too much of a goody-two-shoes to not be anything but completely loyal. I always hated that about him," he said, but smiled and shook his head. "Anyway, it doesn't matter who the woman is. Just know there's someone out there who's more his type."

"That's just great. Thank you, Hayes, for ruining my life from the grave. It's not like you didn't do enough damage while you were—" She stopped herself. "Just leave. Please."

"Look, Rachel, you'll find another man. Someone who will give you what you need, and considering how receptive you were to me the night we spent together, I'm pretty damn sure Gray's not that guy."

"Go to hell."

He laughed half-heartedly. "That's funny you say that, sweetheart, because seeing you about to marry my brother is hell enough for me."

"Grayson needs me—" Rachel started to say.

But he had already faded into nothingness and was gone just like that.

"Fine." She glared at where he'd been standing. "Leave me. That's what you're good at, after all."

The small room was quiet again...and warm.

Rachel had never felt so lonely.

The doorbell rang out from the living room. No doubt Grayson stood on the other side of the door, waiting to take her to dinner so he could tell her about the promotion he'd gotten to make the start of their marriage easier.

The marriage she would never be able to bring herself to enter. How was she going to tell him?

~ * ~

Gray stuffed his hands in his pocket and forced a smile on his face when Rachel opened the door. "Hi," he said, and stepped into her tiny apartment. He glanced around, looking from her flowery sofa to the rows of books she had lined on her bookshelf, to the burgundy rug on the floor.

But he couldn't make himself look into her eyes. Not after being fired from his job. How foolish he'd been, to punch his co-worker, and in front of his boss too. Luckily, Beaver had agreed not to press charges as long as Gray agreed to leave the building and never step within a hundred feet of it.

Stupid.

He'd come up with a backup plan, though. He'd get another job. A better paying one that didn't include him kissing anyone's ass.

"Grayson." Rachel's voice was low and careful, different from her usual false cheerfulness.

Intrigued, he met her stare. Her face was paler than normal, her lips were pinched together, and her red-rimmed eyes brimmed with tears. She was sad about something, which was rare. Gray hadn't seen her cry since Hayes's funeral, and never before that. The woman was good at controlling her emotions.

"You okay?" He reached for her but she stepped back.

"No. I'm not feeling well. Would you mind if I postponed dinner?" A tear ran down her cheek as she wrapped her arms around herself and shivered.

"What's wrong? Can I get you something?"

"No. I don't want anything from you."

"Okay." This was interesting. Since when did timid Rachel talk like this? "What's going on, then? Are you angry with me?" Maybe she'd found out about him losing his job.

"I'm not a virgin." She blurted it out so fast, Gray had to rewind and replay the words in his head.

Then it hit him. *She's not a virgin.*

He had to admit it wasn't a huge surprise. Especially after seeing the type of guys she used to date. He teetered on his feet before asking, "Was it the piano player from the restaurant?"

More tears streamed down her face as she shook her head, leaving Gray feeling uneasy. Warily, he took a step toward her, but she backed away.

"It isn't that big of a deal," he said. "It's not like it happened when we were together, right?" He watched as her body trembled. "*Right?*"

"I'm sorry, Grayson."

Oh. Huh. "Okay. When did it happen?" His mind was numb, and he couldn't think of anything else to say or feel. Should he be jealous? Angry?

Should he leave and never look back? His life plan was falling to pieces in the span of less than a day, and he had absolutely no control over it.

Rachel wept before him, pathetically. What the hell was wrong with her? The worst was said and done. He could forgive her and move on. That was possible. He had control over his own feelings, at least.

"You don't have to tell me," he said, trying to comfort her. Did he really want to know who it was anyway? "Nobody's perfect. Just say it was a mistake, and we can forget all about it." Some of his plan could be salvaged, at any rate. He could tell her about losing his job and they'd be even. It would all work out.

"I can't forget. I've tried, but he won't leave me alone."

"Who?" Gray tensed. If someone were threatening his fiancée, he'd kill him.

She sobbed. "It was Hayes. I slept with Hayes."

"My brother?" Gray's voice cracked as the air was sucked from his lungs. This couldn't be true.

"I'm so sorry."

He put a hand up. "No. Don't do that. Don't apologize to me. Hayes wouldn't have done that to me. Why are you lying about this?" Hayes might have acted like a fool all his life, but he'd had values and a strong loyalty to Gray. The brothers had made a pact in high school that they would never let a woman get between them. Ever.

You don't sleep with my girl and I won't sleep with yours. Gray clearly remembered the words they'd said on a handshake one night after a party where Christie McCrery had attempted to play them against each other. The evening had almost ended in a fistfight between brothers, until they realized how stupid they were being by choosing a woman over each other.

"This is bullshit."

"I'm telling the truth, Grayson. I understand if you want to cancel the wedding." She placed her freezing cold hand on his forearm.

He stepped away from her grasp, thinking her touch might tip the scales of his shaky balance. His sanity. Anger and uncertainty raced through his veins, making him woozy.

"Rachel, if any part of this is true, not only do I not want to marry you, I never want to see you again. And Hayes? My God. I can't believe it happened. You were never even alone with him."

"When you were away on business." She swiped at a tear. "He came over then."

"The weekend before he died? Is that when you're saying it happened?" His gut clenched. If his memory of Hayes could be any more distorted, she'd done her best to make it so.

With unsteady legs, he headed to the door.

"He wants me to tell you that he's sorry and that he loves you," she said before he could open the door.

Gray spun around. "What are you talking about?"

"He's here, Grayson." Her lips quivered. "He wanted me to tell you that."

For a moment, Gray believed her. His heartbeat sped as he glanced around the room a few times and, of course, saw no one. Either his ex-fiancée was playing mind games, or she was going nuts.

"Get some help, Rachel," he said as he walked out the door.

~ * ~

Gray stepped out of the elevator and into the hallway. The condo in downtown Indianapolis he'd purchased with Hayes five years ago was still his home. It seemed a lifetime ago they'd moved in. They were fresh out of college and ready to take on the worlds of business and women. Together, they were going to conquer both.

Too many memories.

Every day since the accident, Gray had told himself to sell the condo. Now that he'd lost his job and his

79

fiancée, he didn't see any other choice. He couldn't afford the mortgage for this condo and the San Francisco loft he'd bought with his brother not long ago. The loft had been purchased with the dream of sailing the coast with Hayes, but the plan had been buried along with his twin. Now, Gray had to give up a residence, and since the loft was mostly paid for, he would move there.

A fresh start. He had power over that.

He was ready to leave behind this city and every bad memory it held—sweet, beautiful Rachel, who wasn't so innocent after all. His loyal, fun-loving brother, who had been even more selfish than Gray remembered.

He clenched his jaw as he continued down the hall. Five doors down he stopped at his condo. His hands shook as he pulled the keys from his pocket.

Was it animosity or anguish surging through his body? They didn't deserve either. They were the ones who made the mistake, not him.

"Fuck you, Hayes." Gray slid the key into the lock, and as he did, a chill wrapped around his neck. He rubbed at it, paying it little attention, while he attempted to open the door. But the lock wouldn't budge.

He yanked the key out and made sure it was the right one, then shoved it back in. Still the key wouldn't turn. He grabbed the ice-cold doorknob and tried to twist it. Nothing. The building's central air system was probably cranked to the max again, but how would that jam his lock?

After several more attempts with the key, Gray finally gave up. He'd need to call a locksmith and hopefully they would be open and willing to help at this hour. His watch said eight o'clock, but it felt like midnight. It had been a long bitch of a day, and he wanted nothing more than for it to end.

The sooner, the better.

He pulled out his cell phone, but it was dead...and cold. "Fuck." He lost control, clenched the phone into his hand and punched the door with it. The phone screen cracked, and his knuckles throbbed with pain from slamming up against the hard wood.

"Problem, dude?" Gray's new neighbor directly across the hall stuck his blond curly head out the door.

What was the guy's name again? Gray couldn't remember. The young college-aged kid had moved in— probably on his parent's dime — about a month ago.

"Can I use your phone to call a locksmith? My lock is jammed."

"Ah, that sucks, dude. Come on in."

Gray followed the young guy into his condo. His place was smaller than Gray's place, or maybe it just seemed that way, given a pool table took up most of the living room, and there were clothes, pizza boxes, and beer cans spread out everywhere. The kid treated his condo like a dorm room.

But Gray didn't give a shit. His only goal was to get into his home, drop into bed, fall asleep...

And maybe dream of her.

The irony killed him. All he had left to look forward to was being with Sofia in his sleep, the same woman he'd pushed away. The woman who could make him forget everything with one touch.

"Here's the phone." The kid handed him a black cordless and sank into his beanbag in front of the big screen T.V.

"Thanks. Do you have a phone book?"

"Nah. Just 411 it. My old man pays for it."

Figures.

"What does your father do?" Gray asked out of curiosity.

"Who fucking knows? He owns a lot of shit, like, DashAir. You know, that airline that has the airplanes all painted like taxicabs. Lame, huh? Hey, but if you ever want to get hooked up on a flight deal, come see me, dude. My ex-girlfriend flew to Cali for like a hundred bucks or some shit like that."

Gray nodded, not wanting to pursue the conversation any further. He pressed the talk button and put the phone to his ear, but there wasn't a dial tone. He hit the button again and it beeped several times.

"Ah, sorry, dude. That means it needs to be charged."

"You got a cell?"

"Lost it this morning. My stepmom is supposed to be ordering me a new one. You can crash on my couch for tonight if you want."

Another chill struck the back of Gray's neck so hard, he couldn't ignore it this time. "No. I gotta get out of here." He hurried to the door, but stopped when a thought hit him. "You hear about any problems with the main AC?"

"Nah, dude. You?"

~ * ~

Gray dropped into his BMW and revved the engine. Thank God his car cooperated when nothing else in his life did. Maybe he'd go for a drive. He could find a hotel and straighten out everything in the morning.

Yeah, that was what he needed to do. Just find a bed somewhere and get some rest. If he had a friend left in the world he could go to them, but he had no one. Blood drained from his face at the realization. The emptiness left a hollow pit in his mind where numerous memories could hide, covered by a protective blanket of darkness. Memories he'd thought weren't worth rehashing. There used to be a time when friends were abundant. But after Hayes died, Gray had let all his friendships perish as well.

Why return their phone calls when all they wanted to do was tell Gray how sorry they were?

Well, he didn't want their pity.

Cold air burst from the air vents unexpectedly. Gray looked down at his hands that hadn't moved from the steering wheel, or had they? Had he turned the air on without realizing it?

God, he needed some sleep. He shut the controls off and rolled down his window. The sun had set and the summer evening air had a comfortable breeze. The aroma was pleasing as well. It relaxed him.

Vanilla.

Sofia.

He inhaled the scent and laughed. The woman bewitched him, and he had no idea why. She wasn't his usual type, but for some reason, as he drove down the highway, he longed for her. He wanted nothing more than to kiss her. Just kiss her.

Even though he'd done much more with her in those dreams.

Considering how he'd treated her and how she'd responded, Gray was sure he didn't have a chance in hell to make any of those dreams come true. Not now. She was furious with him, and he deserved every bit of her anger.

He drove aimlessly until he happened upon a detour that forced him to turn off his course, cutting down his chance to find a hotel. Damn. The need to lie down and close his eyes was overwhelming. He continued driving down side streets until he stumbled upon a new highway.

Hell, maybe it was karma biting him in the ass. If he believed in such a thing, the scenario he found himself in might make sense. He was the reason she lost her job, and she was the reason he'd lost his. He'd blamed Sofia for trying to come between him and Rachel, and he'd lost Rachel even before he'd had her. Tit for tat.

Another detour sign was up ahead, so he turned off this highway and onto another. Where the hell was he? The neighborhoods were dwindling.

Call him naïve, but he couldn't see Sofia ever intentionally hurting him. If she was the same woman from the dreams, she was nothing but loving and giving. She'd allowed him to be the person he once was in those dreams. He missed being that man. He missed having friends.

He missed her.

How could he yearn for a woman he didn't even know? A knot of regret caught in his throat as he realized he might never find the answer.

Gray ran into yet another detour and he eased off the gas. What was going on with these roadblocks? Damn it if he cared. He turned the only direction the concrete barriers allowed, off onto a country road.

He chuckled as he noticed he traveled down the

same path he'd taken on his bike ride the other morning. What the hell was he doing?

Driving to her house?

Lord knew it wasn't a conscious decision. Those detours had confused him. Not to mention, his mind was all in a jumble. He was a total mess.

For whatever reason, he needed to see her. Talk to her. Touch her.

Kiss her.

No, he couldn't do this. He'd hurt her enough, and she'd made it clear she never wanted to see him again. Plus, there was the whole issue of her thinking she could see the future. The last thing he needed was to get mixed up with a nutjob who lived out in the middle of Amish country.

A cute sexy nutjob with lips that begged to be nibbled.

Stop.

Going to see her was an all-around bad idea.

He pulled to the side of the road and prepared to make a U-turn. As he turned the wheel and made sure no other car was on the desolate road, the lights on the dashboard blinked and then shut down completely.

"You gotta be kidding me." He turned the key in the ignition, attempting to restart the engine, but it was just as dead as his cell phone had been. Just as lifeless as his neighbor's phone. Just as useless as his front door lock.

Aggravated, Gray let his head fall to the steering wheel. The freezing leather felt good against his throbbing head. Getting stuck out here in Amish country was the cherry on top of the shit cake.

He didn't have a cell phone to call for help. In fact,

he had nothing. No one.

Go to her.

The words breezed through heavily scented air, and Gray breathed it in.

Go to her.

Chapter Seven

The liquor and wine bottles were all lined up on the yellowed Formica kitchen table. Rows of them. Sofia had dusted and organized each one of them from largest to smallest. They were all ready to go back inside the liquor cabinet she'd already wiped down. She sipped the rest of her first glass of red wine and stared at the collection.

"Nana sure does have a lot of liquor."

She wondered for a moment if reading minds was somehow bothersome to her grandmother. Maybe getting drunk helped. Although she'd never seen Nana inebriated…that she knew of anyway.

The wine was starting to kick in. Sofia pressed her numb lips together and hummed. Anesthesia via Pinot Noir. She wasn't much of a drinker, that was for sure. One glass would probably do the trick to take the edge off. Perhaps.

"Perhaps not." She laughed and poured a little more into her glass.

A knock on the door startled her, and she set the bottle down with a clank.

Who the heck could that be?

The humongous old grandfather clock in the corner

said the time was just past ten o'clock. Sofia picked up one of the eleven oil lamps she'd lit as soon as the sun started to set and carried it to the door.

No peephole, of course and only one deadbolt. Did her grandmother think bad guys couldn't make their way out to the country? Sheesh.

"Who's there?" She pressed her forehead to the door and listened closely.

"Sofia? It's Gray." He cleared his throat. "Grayson Phillips."

Sofia jolted back a step as her lungs deflated.

Bad guys certainly could make their way out here.

But why? And *really?* Only one way to find out. She opened the door a crack to make sure the man on the other side was indeed Gray. The porch was dark, unlit, but the moonlight struck his strong profile. Shadows hit in all the right spots to make his perfectly angular face even more masculine and handsome. Yeah, it was him, all right. In all of his deceptive gorgeousness. The question was what was he doing at her Nana's house at this hour? At all?

"I know this might seem odd," he said. "But can I come in for a moment?"

"No." She slammed the door and held her breath, her heart thumping against her ribs. She'd made up her mind never to see him again—hence, stopping the dreams and a future with the jerk from happening—and this little invasion was *so* not helping.

"I know you're angry with me," he said through the door. "I'm sorry for the way I treated you."

A little too late, pal.

"Can I please come in? I promise I'll be nice."

Sofia glanced down at what she was wearing—pink stretchy shorts and a matching tank top, her usual pajamas. No way was he coming in.

"I know I don't deserve any of your time." He sighed. "I *really* need to talk to someone, and you're the only someone I want to talk to. The only one I can talk to."

Huh. He sounded miserable. Not mean miserable, like before. More like tormented miserable. Desperate.

Curiosity made her open the door again. Only a tad, though, so the light from the lamp would show if his facial expression matched the sound of agony in his voice.

It did. His dark brown hair was a mess, tousled as if he'd run his hands through it too many times. A streak of mud or grease stained his forehead. His blue dress shirt was unbuttoned and rolled up to his elbows. The white t-shirt underneath was stained with a smeared handprint.

"Why are you such a mess?"

"My car broke down up the road." He lifted his grease-covered hands. "I tried to fix it, but I don't have a clue what's wrong. I usually know my way around an engine but... Well, you get the picture."

"You were on the way here? To see me?"

"No." He answered without delay and took a step forward, standing only a few inches from the door. "Not at first."

Sofia pulled the lamp back in and heaved the door shut.

He stopped it with his foot. "Wait. My twin brother died."

~ * ~

Gray didn't know why he'd blurted that out, but it got her attention.

"Really? When? Are you okay?" She let the door fall open, revealing her curvy body covered only by a tiny pair of shorts and a tank top that didn't quite cover her navel.

God help him.

She made an attempt to pull her top down. The stretchy material snapped back up.

"Um." Gray gathered his senses. *Just one kiss.* She had to let him in if he kept hustling his sob story. She was sweet like that. Wasn't she? "It happened six months ago. I just found out my fiancée, no, ex-fiancée, slept with him a week before he died."

"You're kidding." She wrinkled her nose.

Adorable.

"No. She gave her virginity to him while I was away on business." He was pushing it, but the sob story was working.

"Oh, my gosh. You just found out today?"

Gray nodded. "I told her I never wanted to see her again. Then I drove home and found my door lock was jammed. I couldn't get in."

"Having a bad day?"

"You could say that." Gray leaned forward against the doorway and tried to look grief-stricken.

Yep, he'd officially lost all self-respect.

But it was working.

She pushed a lock of hair behind her ear and seemed to think for a moment. "Well, I guess you can come in for a drink. But then you have to leave."

"That's perfect." *Yes.* "Thank you."

She turned with the lamp in her hands, showing him her backside. Across one luscious butt cheek read the word "Sweet." The other read "Dreams." The fitting phrase caught his eye and made him chuckle.

She spun around. "Keep laughing and you can show yourself back out the door. My Nana bought these pajamas for me." She shrugged and added in a less confident voice, "She likes to shop the clearance racks."

"No. I like them. Really." He closed the door behind him without breaking eye contact. "Very appropriate."

"Sometimes," she mumbled, and led him to the kitchen.

Gray peeled his stare away from her for a moment to notice the many bottles that covered the table.

"I was cleaning out Nana's liquor cabinet. It was kind of dusty." She gestured to the cast iron double bowl kitchen sink. "Want to clean up?"

"Sure." He washed up and then pulled out a chair at the table and sat. Not until then did he realize the lights were out. Lord, where was his head? The only thing that lit the house were oil lamps bunched together on the wooden butcher block set in the center of the kitchen along with one or two hanging from the walls.

How odd.

"Pick your poison," she said, with her hip pressed against the table.

"What?"

"What would you like to drink?"

Without thinking, Gray handed her the bottle closest to him. "Did the electricity go out?" He wouldn't be surprised if he'd brought his bad luck with him. Or maybe this was part of Sofia's eccentricity.

"No." She smiled as she poured what appeared to be whiskey into a glass. In the low light, her lips looked soft, and her eyes glistened. "My grandmother, I call her Nana, believes that electricity and phone lines give her migraines. That's why she lives out here amongst the Amish."

"Interesting. So this is your grandmother's house? Is she home?"

"No, I'm house and cat-sitting for her." She set the glass in front of him and lifted her body up to sit on the butcher block next to the lamps. "Isn't it strange that you came here tonight? I mean, I don't live here. I live in Indianapolis with my mother. If you'd shown up here any other time, Nana would've opened the door." She laughed softly and continued. "Not that she would've minded having a hunk show up at her house."

"So you think I'm a hunk?"

Another laugh.

Gray liked the sound of it, a soft, sultry sound. Her laugh reminded him of a certain dream he'd had. Nothing was more exciting than playful sex. For the first time, he allowed himself to wonder if real sex with Sofia would be as thrilling as in his dreams. Now that Rachel was out of the picture, nothing and no one kept him from fantasizing, or acting out his fantasies.

He shot down the whiskey, keeping a keen eye on the fantasy in question. He was free to do whatever the hell he wanted and it felt great. He didn't have a job or a definite future with a woman. His *life plan* was a complete joke. Wasn't it amazing that the world wasn't falling down around him?

"What are you smiling about?" she asked.

"Sorry. I didn't realize I was."

"You don't have to apologize. I was just curious. It's the first time I've seen you smile, is all. I mean, aside from the dreams." She lifted her wine glass and sipped.

"I lost my job this morning," he blurted out.

Again. What was it about this moment here in time with her that made him want to reveal his life story? The good, the bad, and the ugly.

She whistled. "You sure had a heck of a day." Her body lengthened as she let her feet fall to the floor. She crossed the small distance separating them and poured him another round.

Gray let his gaze roam over her as she stood before him. Her rounded breasts stretched the cotton fabric of the pink top she wore. Her nipples were slightly erect. No apparent bra.

"The day's getting much better."

~ * ~

Sofia told herself it didn't matter that his fiancée was out of the picture. It didn't matter that he'd apologized and was being somewhat decent. It most definitely did not matter that he was sitting there, staring at her as if she were his last hope. Looking helpless with his tousled hair and the grease mark on his forehead he'd forgotten to wipe clean.

She ignored the desire to sit on his lap and make his bad day a whole lot better. She wasn't responsible for his happiness and she wasn't buying his sudden interest in her.

Determined to stay focused, she finished pouring the whiskey into his glass and retreated back to the butcher block, a safe distance away.

"Thanks for the refill."

"You're welcome." Darn. She'd forgotten she'd only invited him in for one drink. How was she going to send a drunken man out into the dark night without a way home? Why should she care?

He didn't care about her. He'd made it clear that morning in his office and at the restaurant when he'd gotten her fired.

He downed the drink and shoved his hand through his hair. "I really appreciate you letting me come in, Sofia. It says a lot about your character. You're a kind person, aren't you?"

Sofia shrugged. "Not everyone is a coldhearted jerk." As soon as the words left her mouth, she regretted them. The man had already been through enough today.

"Ouch." He brought his hand up to his heart, covering the smeared handprint.

"Sorry."

"Don't be. I *was* a jerk to you. And I'm sorry. If I could take it all back, I would."

She let his words soak in. They felt good to hear, she had to admit. But it didn't change a thing.

With empty glass in hand, he stood to his full six-foot-plus height and stared down at her. Sofia scooted back farther on the block, unsure of his next move. If he wasn't a man she'd gotten to know in her dreams, she might have been frightened of the lazy, sexual look in his eyes.

Instead, it ignited her. A surge of want dipped low inside, reminding her of what it felt like to make love with this man in her visions. To see him naked, running her fingers across his strong, lean muscles, sweating as he lay on top of her, driving his thick, hard erection inside of her until she —

Stop it, Sofe. She gulped and attempted to gain control. *Stop*. *It*. The only reason he was here was because he'd lost everything else. He hadn't intended to come here. To him, Sofia Good was the last resort. A substitute. A replacement to buffer his hurt pride, his busted ego. The dreaded rebound girl.

Too bad. Because she refused to be anything but someone's top choice.

To break his stare, she thrust the bottle of whiskey into his gut. "Here."

He didn't falter as he slowly took the bottle from her grasp, then finally poured himself another round. "Thanks." His dimple showed. "You know, this stuff isn't too bad."

"Glad you approve." She tried to avert her gaze but he was too close. And she just couldn't bring herself to tell him to move away. Not yet. Not when he smelled like the man from her dreams.

She sniffed again, rubbing her nose to cover her actions. The faint hint of musk aftershave and the night air. Despite the grease on his shirt, he smelled clean and...manly. Strong and welcoming.

Damn. Too much like the dreams. Yet the man before her had yet to prove to be anything like *her* Gray.

He set the bottle on the table, then turned toward her again, not giving her enough space to breathe steadily. The look in his heavy-lidded eyes made her wonder if he might lean in and kiss her...or maybe do more than that. But instead of ravaging her, he simply swiveled and stood beside her, leaning against the butcher block.

He sighed softly and looked down at his glass, swirling the liquid around, thinking about something. Up close, Sofia was even more convinced the man was way too attractive for his own good. For her own good, actually. She wrapped her arms around her belly to keep from reaching out and touching him.

Although she knew exactly how she wanted to run her fingers over his jaw to his chin, up to his powerful lips. Into his hair, ruffling it a bit more to make him look less like an uptight businessman and more like her sexy, kind, happy-go-lucky fantasy man.

The two couldn't be more opposite...which confused her on a number of levels.

"So," he said, breaking the silence and startling her. He looked at her from the corner of his eye. "You said you dream of the future? What's that about?"

Right. That. "Oh, well, yes. Sort of." She wasn't exactly prepared for that question. Having hidden that fact from most of the people who came into her life in the past for obvious reasons, she was used to avoiding the subject.

"Sort of?" He turned toward her with a look of interest. The hand that held his glass brushed against her thigh.

Focus, Sofe. Stay strong. "Not sort of. I do dream of the future, but I can change it. Prevent certain things from happening."

"Things like me?"

"Like murders, accidents, and horrible attacks on innocent people. And yes, I can prevent you from happening." She dared meet his gaze. His coffee-brown eyes were soft. The dimple on his cheek deepened as he grinned with apparent amusement.

"Have I been so awful that you've grouped me with your nightmares?"

"They're not nightmares. They're real, and they're going to happen if I don't stop them."

His grin faded to a frown as he brought the glass up to his lips and drank. The remoteness in his eyes returned.

"It's all right if you don't believe me. It doesn't matter what you think of me, now or ever, since I'm going to do you a huge favor and stop those dreams for you. All we need to do is say good-bye right here, right now."

He set the glass down behind her. "Maybe I should go if you're done with me, then," he said, but didn't budge. His dark gaze searched hers, waiting.

"Maybe you should." Sofia shot back at him, feeling proud of herself. If only for a moment. "Isn't that why you're here? To get rid of me once and for all?"

He chuckled uneasily and shook his head.

"Is something funny?"

"Funny. Ironic. Insane. All of the above." In a quick move, he was in front of her again, leaning forward and bracing a hand on each side of her.

"What are..." She couldn't finish the question. His face was so close to hers...his lips just a tongue-lick away. If she were a bolder woman, she'd do just that—stick her tongue out and outline the ridge of his sexy, fierce lips. Yep, a bolder woman might want to do that.

She swallowed. Time literally ticked by as the grandfather clock tick-tocked in the corner. The sound was usually soothing. Now it only emphasized the rapid beating of her heart.

"Do you want the truth, Sofia?" His eyes glistened in the lamplight as if he couldn't hold his secret back for another second.

She squelched her curiosity as best she could, then jerked a shoulder up and resumed breathing. "Sure. Go for it."

"Those dreams"—a fresh grin slowly curved his lips—"are all I have to look forward to. I don't want them to stop." He gave a short laugh. "And you know what?"

"You've lost your mind?"

"Possibly. Because I have no desire to leave here tonight." He brought a hand up and ran his knuckles across her cheek. "I don't want to leave here. Can I stay? I promise to behave myself."

Her skin sizzled under his touch. Geez, was he going to kiss her? No, he couldn't. Not tonight. Not ever. It just wasn't going to happen. She'd already come to terms with it, and now he needed to. Right?

"No," was all she managed to say.

"Please. I'll sleep on the couch. I'll keep my hands to myself."

"I'm still angry with you. You treated me awful."

"I know." His fingers traced her jaw, her neck. "I was an asshole. I don't deserve your kindness."

"You blew it." She shivered. Her head swirled.

"An unforgivable asshole. If you punched me in the face and told me to go to hell, I wouldn't be surprised." His voice lowered as he spoke, his gaze dropped and focused on her lips. "But you won't. Because you *are* kind. Because you'll take pity on me...and the bad day

I'm having. My car's broken down. I don't have anywhere to go." He met her eyes again. "Please, Sofia."

The room did another complete spin, but she tried to blink it away.

"We should go to bed." She blurted out the words and instantly felt the heat reach her cheeks. "Um...I meant *I* should go to bed."

And get away from you before I do something stupid.

Sofia stretched her arms out in front of her, simultaneously pushing Gray away from her. A safe distance. That was what she needed. "I'm exhausted."

"And a little tipsy," he added.

"No, I'm fine. I'm super fine. But you..." She dropped to the floor and felt the room spin around a few more times. Maybe she wasn't so fine.

She gripped the butcher block to keep steady. How was she going to get rid of this guy without feeling guilty for throwing him out into the darkness without a vehicle? Dang it. Why did she care? "You can sleep in the guest bedroom if you want."

"That would be great. Thank you." He stuffed his hands in his jeans pockets and smiled mischievously.

"But you'll have to leave first thing in the morning, understood?"

"No problem."

"Because I don't think—"

He put his hand up to stop her. "I know. I blew it."

~ * ~

Gray had to admit, Sofia's backside was starting to become his favorite part of her body, with the way her ass filled out those shorts. She led him up the narrow, dark wooden stairway, with two lamps hanging from her fingertips. *Sweet Dreams* stretched out with each step.

"I think Nana has a fresh toothbrush stored in the medicine cabinet. And I'll have to make sure there are fresh linens on the guest bed."

An orange cat zipped past at warp speed, nearly tripping Sofia on the top step.

Gray didn't have enough viable brain cells left in his head to react in time. His leg curved into hers and his pelvis pushed against her bottom before he could stop.

"Sorry," he said, and took a step back. Just in time. One second more, and she'd have felt his erection hardening in his jeans.

"My fault. I shouldn't have stopped short." She continued down the hallway. "Sam scared the bejeezus out of me. I really hate coming up here when it's dark. It's creepy, the way the old wooden floors creak."

Rapid thoughts of how he could comfort her ran through Gray's mind. Holding her in his arms, kissing her lips, making her forget about anything but him inside of her.

Keep your head together, Gray.

"It's funny, but I think I had more courage spending the night here when I was a little girl. I guess I was naïve to what horrible things can happen in the world." After a couple of steps, she spun around and pointed into one of the open door rooms. "This is the only bathroom. There are towels and whatnot in the small closet in there. Like I said, the toothbrush is in the medicine cabinet. And if you want to use the bathroom tonight for whatever reason, then take your lamp with you."

"Running water?"

"Yes. Fortunately, that doesn't give my Nana

migraines." She continued a couple steps to the next open door on the opposite side of the confining hallway. "This is my Nana's room. I'll sleep in here."

Curious, Gray stuck his head in the room. The window was open, letting the moonlight in and the breeze whip the white curtains about. The room was a fair size, big enough for a large dresser and the queen-sized bed covered with a checkered quilt. The walls were bare and white, like the rest of the house. The smell of burning kerosene filled the air.

None of it seemed familiar. He hadn't dreamed of this place. With Sofia. Actually, he hadn't recognized the setting in the dreams at all that he could remember. He'd spent so much time trying to forget them. Erase them from his memory.

Not that he believed in any of them—that somehow they were visions of the future. Gray considered himself open-minded, but some things were a little too hard to believe.

Sofia cleared her throat from across the hallway as she pointed to the last door on the left. "This is where you'll sleep. For tonight."

Gray followed her inside, encouraged with where things could lead. *Just one kiss*. It blew his mind that he hadn't had one dismal thought since he'd walked into her house. Not one recollection of all the pointless energy he'd put into his relationship with Rachel, or of how Hayes had betrayed him. No, his mind was captivated by the woman standing in front of him.

"Looks like the sheets are fresh." She ran her hands across the top quilt. It was identical to the other one. In fact, the rooms were mostly indistinguishable, except this bed was wedged up against the window. Not that Gray gave a shit about the furniture arrangement, when Sofia was crawling across the mattress on her hands and knees with her rounded bottom emerging from those damn shorts.

"Getting comfy?" He hoped.

"No. Geez. This probably doesn't look too good, does it?"

"Good doesn't even begin to describe it."

"The window's closed," she said, ignoring his flirtation. "I'm opening it so you won't be stuffy." She released the latch and began pushing up the window inch by inch.

Absentmindedly, Gray began getting ready for sleep, shrugging off his dress shirt and kicking off his loafers. It wasn't until then that he noticed the black mark on his shirt. No way was he going to ruin *Nana's* sheets with his filth. He slipped it over his head, ready to climb into bed and dream.

Hot, sensual dreams of Sofia. He'd get entirely undressed when she left the room. No point in wrinkling the only clothes he had to wear.

But it seemed Sofia was having trouble getting the window up to where she wanted it. She struggled, grunting and yanking.

"Wait." Gray crawled across the bed, feeling like an ass for not offering to help sooner.

"What are you doing?" Perspiration dampened her sweet face as she eyed his shirtless chest.

Holding back a laugh, Gray knelt beside her and grasped the bottom of the windowpane. "Helping," he said, and forced it up.

Wind gusted in and blew her hair off her shoulders. One piece stuck to her moist cheek so he swept it behind her ear.

"What are you doing?" she asked again, her eyes wide in what seemed like fear.

"Are you afraid of me, Sofia?" Had he been that awful to her?

"Of course not." She wrinkled her nose. "Why would I be afraid of you?"

Her tone wasn't convincing. Carefully, Gray cupped her cheek. Her skin was soft, speckled lightly with freckles. Beautiful in a way he hadn't noticed before.

A wary sigh heaved up her chest. Then she leaned into his hand and pulled in her bottom lip only to release it, wet and inviting.

Just one kiss.

Gray brushed his thumb over her lip, desperately wanting to erase every bad notion she had of him. What was it that made him want to be more to her than a *cold-hearted jerk*?

So much more.

Another gust of wind blew in, and she closed her eyes. Before she could open them again, he tilted her head up and molded his mouth to hers.

She gasped slightly, but didn't pull away. Her lips were supple and sweet to the taste. Like in his dreams, but better.

This was real.

He wasn't going to wake up and find her gone. To make sure, he grasped her waist and held her close. Faint whimpers muffled against his lips. He almost drew back, but her fingertips running up his arms gave him permission to continue.

Eager for more, he slid his tongue into her mouth. Her hips arched against his growing erection. Her hands glided over his shoulders and clasped onto his neck, nudging him down. Did she want him to take her? Now? Here?

He was a free to do whatever he wanted with whomever he wanted. For some reason, he only *wanted* to be here in this moment with this woman. From the way she was luring him toward the mattress, she desired more than just one kiss.

Gray wouldn't refuse her. He wrapped one arm around her for support. The other arm braced against the bed as he lowered her, kissing her thoroughly all the while. He wouldn't disappoint her like he had already. This time, he wouldn't give her anything less than his best.

~ * ~

Sofia was out of her mind. Or maybe it was simply cluttered at the moment. With how great he kissed. With how he looked and felt, half naked on the bed beside her...on top of her.

Oh, geez. What am I doing?

Lying down. That was what she was doing.

Running her hands over the lean muscles on his back. Intertwining her legs with his. Going mad over the way he was making love to her mouth with his tongue. He tasted so good, so...so *him*.

His hand sneaked under her tank top, and she jerked her eyes open. His touch, slowly sliding along her skin up over her abdomen, made her tremble with both desire and anxiety. He must have noticed her

104

nervousness because he peeked down at her through narrowed eyes.

They both took in a breath, but his hand kept traveling.

What could be going through his mind?

No, don't think about that, Sofe. Just let it happen. Enjoy it.

Had he done this with his ex-fiancée? Had he loved her? That gorgeous woman he was going to marry up until today?

"Wait," Sofia said, as his hand gripped where no man had ever touched her.

His thumb brushed across her pebbled nipple, sending chills down to where heat rose, surged. He pressed his jean-covered erection into that spot, against her heat, as if he knew how close to the edge she was, and wanted to propel her over.

It was working. She held back a moan by biting into her lip.

"Sofia," he breathed, obviously as on edge as she was. "Are you sure?"

Summoning the last of her sanity, she nodded and pushed against his solid chest.

"I'm sure." She couldn't do it. Sofia Good was *not* going to be his rebound. His last resort.

"Okay." He lifted off her and stood, exhaling and raking a hand through his hair.

"Sorry," she muttered as she hurried to the door.

"For what?" He followed behind her, grabbing her waist before she could leave. "Don't apologize." His voice was a whisper, his warm breath feathered along her neck.

Sofia sucked in a breath. Her body trembled. Geez,

he was going to think she was a prude...which of course she was. Didn't help that her cheeks were burning, which meant her entire face was most likely bright red. Here was the hottest man she'd ever laid eyes on holding her in an embrace, and all she wanted to do was run like hell to get away from him.

"I'm the one who's sorry." He kissed her temple and loosened his hold on her. "Goodnight, Sofia."

"Okay," she said stupidly, still mesmerized by what had happened, what could have happened—quite possibly her only chance to lose her virginity. And to fall in love. Because who wanted to be with a woman who had visions of the future, other than the only man she'd ever envisioned loving?

She backed out into the hallway, only stumbling once when she realized it was really dark.

"Here." He handed her one of the lamps. "Don't want you to be scared."

"Thanks. Um, goodnight." She started toward Nana's room. With each passing step, she could feel him staring at her backside.

"Sweet dreams." His voice was soft and playful, and followed by a sexy chuckle.

Sofia turned abruptly to respond with something witty and reproachful but couldn't think of a damn thing to say, so she stuck out her tongue.

Very mature, Sofe.

He laughed again. "Night, sugar. See you in the morning."

The man was nothing but trouble. Good thing he was leaving *first thing tomorrow*.

Wasn't it?

~ * ~

"You should be ashamed of yourself, Mom."

Penny looked at her daughter and sighed. "I just walked in the door, Laura. Can we save this until the morning, please?"

"No, we can't. I can't believe you went through with this."

"You know I only did it for her own good." Penny set her suitcase against the wall and sat her weary body down on the couch. The spell sure had taken a lot out of her. She wasn't as young as she used to be, that was for certain.

"What if she comes home and sees you here?"

"She won't be able to leave my house until—"

"Until what?"

"Until the spell is complete. Until they admit they're in love."

"Oh, shit." Laura paced a line in the carpet in front of the couch. "You are truly something, Mom. What gives you the right to interfere in *my* daughter's life like this? And lie to her about it? Shouldn't she be the one to decide whether she'll fall in love with this asshole?"

"Spare me the guilt trip, Laura. Look what you did to Hayes Phillips. You could have saved that boy's life, if you'd only told him his true fate."

"No!" Laura stopped and pointed a finger at Penny. "I am not responsible for these people's actions. That kid was going to jump off that airplane no matter what I said. I told him to be careful, but of course he didn't listen to me. They never do." With a red face, she stomped up the stairs, but turned once to add, "Besides, aren't you the one who told me when I started this business that I shouldn't play God? Being a little hypocritical, aren't we, Mom? And with your own family?"

Before Penny could respond, Laura disappeared upstairs. A second later, she heard the bedroom door slam shut.

Good. She didn't have the energy to argue with her stubborn daughter anyhow.

Surely, she didn't get that quality from me.

With a harrumph, she grabbed at her suitcase handle and started upstairs. She'd sleep in Sofia's room tonight. Being close to her granddaughter's things would give Penny a better feel for how the spell was working.

Penny had taken Hayes's word and read his thoughts that Grayson Phillips was a decent man. A man Sofia could love. A man who would return the love unconditionally, even with the knowledge that Sofia was "gifted."

As Penny lay in bed that night, she prayed for many things. She prayed Sofia would forgive her for lying and interfering. She prayed Grayson would treat Sofia right.

She prayed Grayson would never find out that Sofia's mother could have prevented his brother's death, and didn't. But mostly she prayed Laura would find a love of her own.

Because Penny was convinced no spell would be strong enough to push through her daughter's bitter heart.

Chapter Eight

Rachel rolled over onto her side and opened her eyes. The sun was rising and spilling soft light through her sheer pink curtains, reminding her of the night before.

She glanced down at what she was wearing. The red dress she'd worn the night Hayes had made love to her. She'd put it on just for him, thinking he'd love it. The memory made her want to slap herself silly. What type of awful person was she?

She'd known Hayes was going to come over to check up on her. He'd told her, whispered it to her when Grayson wasn't watching. Then she'd gone out and purchased this dress. This daring red dress. A color she'd never had the nerve to wear before for anyone else.

Now, her head throbbed from a hangover.

How many glasses of wine had she drunk before stumbling into bed? Who knew? Who cared? She didn't want to cry anymore. Her eyes were dry and crusted over with the tears she'd spilled the night before. Pathetic. Truly pathetic.

When was she going to gain some control over her life? Over her emotions?

Then, an invisible arm wrapped around her waist. The bed indented behind her and she felt his body encompass hers.

"You're so beautiful in this dress."

His voice cheered her up for a moment, before she remembered he wasn't really there. Not fully.

"Rachel, you have to know how sorry I am for leaving you. I promise you that you'll find love with someone who deserves you."

"I don't want anyone else. I want you." More tears found their way out and ran down her temple.

"Baby, you have no idea how good it feels to hear you say that. If I could change the past, you'd be damn certain I'd be lying here after a night of making love to you."

But he wasn't here. Just how long did she have with him now?

"How long can you stay? I mean, until you're able to move on?" She turned toward him and ran her fingers over his chest and neck and face. She couldn't see him this time, but she could feel every inch of him.

"I'm not positive, but everything's in motion. It could be any minute, hour or day." He kissed her forehead.

"Why can't I see you?"

"All my energy is going into being able to touch you and have you touch me. I can't do both, baby. I'm sorry."

"I don't want you to be sorry anymore." Rachel felt him wipe a tear from her nose. She wanted him closer. She wanted that night back.

"Can you make love to me?"

He chuckled and brushed his lips against hers. "It sure the hell feels like I can."

~ * ~

Sofia beat the eggs in a mixing bowl and turned the gas burner on low this time. She wasn't going to burn this batch. Nope. This one was going to be perfect. The bacon and sausage, however, were a little on the dark side and the pancakes, well, a couple of them were edible.

So what if she wasn't the best cook? It wasn't as if she were applying for wife-status. Not even girlfriend-ability. Because as soon as Gray got out of the shower and ate this breakfast – oh, yes, he was going to eat it after all the hard work she'd put into it – she was driving his fine butt out of here.

His nice, tight, athletic butt.

She'd had another dream of him. Just before dawn, she'd awakened in a sweat and couldn't go back to sleep. Knowing he was down the hall when she'd reached orgasm, alone in her grandmother's bed, was fairly humiliating. What if he'd heard? She was pretty vocal in her dreams, but had no idea if she revealed that in her sleep.

Thankfully, he was still fast asleep when she'd checked on him. He'd left his door wide open and was wrapped up in the white linens. Naked, with Sam the traitor cat curled up at his feet.

Not that she'd seen Gray's...manly component, only his thigh. Calf. Ankle. Chest.

The muscle line that curved down his stomach to his... *That* she did *not* see.

Quit being such a prude, Sofe.

"Morning." His deep voice rumbled over her shoulder, close enough for her to smell his minty breath.

She jumped and noticed the eggs needed to be stirred pronto. *Focus!*

"Didn't mean to startle you," he said, and casually slipped his hand onto her waist.

Like she was his girlfriend. Darn, why did it have to feel so good? Make her feel so secure?

"You've been busy." He settled his chin on her shoulder and eyed her most recent disaster. "It smells great."

"You are a horrible liar, Grayson Phillips."

"I would never lie to you, Sofia Good."

She stifled the urge to turn her head and see the

expression on his face. "Well, I guess I believe you, considering you only have a couple of hours tops to *never* lie to me."

"Getting rid of me so fast?" The warmth of his body disappeared, and Sofia slumped her stiff shoulders.

She watched from the corner of her eye as he walked to the other side of the kitchen and stared out the window. Silent and somber.

His dark hair was damp and curly from showering. His wrinkled blue dress shirt was untucked from his dark jeans and his sleeves were rolled up. The white t-shirt with the stain was partially crammed into his back pocket. Even ruffled, he was a gorgeous man. The dreams didn't do him justice.

Sighing, she plopped the eggs on a plate and carried them to the table she'd already set.

"This is kind of nice," he said, still looking out at the cornfields.

"What is?" She stood next to him and tried to see exactly what he was seeing.

"This." A cute grin pushed up the sides of his lips as he looked down at her. "I grew up in the city, so this is a treat for me. No noise. Just the sound of the grandfather clock ticking and you and me talking. It's nice."

"Oh."

The man didn't look like the country type, but who was she to argue? Maybe this was part of his recent crisis. What does a shrewd, controlling businessman with his whole big, glorious life planned out in front of him do when everything and everyone wilts away in such a short time span?

Well, he goes to see the desperate girl from his dreams and hopes she'll make him feel better, that's what he does.

"Hungry?" Sofia asked, suddenly realizing he hadn't broken eye contact.

"Yes." His gaze dipped down to her chest, making Sofia want to curb his hunger in a way that wasn't prudish in any shape or form. "Nana pick that off the clearance rack too?" He smiled with his whole face as he read the words on her chest.

"What?" *Good Lord*. What had she put on this morning? She'd been in such a haze, she'd simply thrown on whatever she'd stuffed in her duffle bag. "Please don't let it be the *Sweet Dreams Are Made Of These* shirt." The one with the hot pink words that spread across her breasts.

"It most certainly is."

"This is mortifying. Listen, I'm really not trying to lead you on. I saw a white t-shirt, so I grabbed it because white matches everything, right? My mom gave it to me as a practical joke. Honestly, I didn't think it was very funny, but I kept the shirt because I didn't want to hurt her feelings. Nana always teases my mom that the boob gene skipped a generation, but I never laugh. My mom is drop-dead gorgeous and she doesn't need boobs, really. And I packed this shirt, thinking I won't see another living soul for the next few days. Of course, now you're here, but I wasn't thinking this morning because of the dream I had of you last night. I just *couldn't* think. Of anything. I was lucky to put two and two together and get dressed. I don't even know if I remembered to put on underwear." She finally stopped rambling and took a breath.

"You dreamed of me last night?"

Nice, Sofe. Of course he would pick that out of all the babbling mess that had left her lips. She heaved out a breath. "Yeah. It was really no big deal." Her cheeks burned from the memory of how big a deal it actually was.

"No big deal? Am I not satisfying you in these dreams you're having?" His smile disintegrated into an indignant frown.

"Um." How was she going to get out of this one? He'd satisfied her completely, as always, but she didn't want to tell *him* that.

"Was it just last night that I failed you? Because the reason could be I didn't dream of you for the first time in over a month. Maybe there's some sort of—" He waved his hands. "I don't know what. Something's missing. I mean, if I believe in this seeing the future..." He let his sentence fade, biting into his lip.

"It was fine, Gray. What do you mean you didn't dream of me?" Could it be that her plan to get this guy out of her future was working? If so, why did it make her feel awful?

"Fine? I was *fine?*"

"You were brilliant, okay? Can we eat now?" Sofia slumped down into a chair. The food before her didn't look so edible anymore.

Why *couldn't* she have the hot guy?

Well, Sofe, because he's only here to mend his wounds. Then he'd leave and break her heart. The dreams never guaranteed he'd love her forever, did they now?

"Brilliant?" His smile lit up again as he sat opposite her. "Are you saying that to appease me?"

"No," Sofia said, solemnly. "You rocked my world. Again."

"Why do you look upset about it then?"

"I'm not upset. I'm hungry." She forked some cold eggs onto her plate, then into her mouth to prove her point.

He followed suit, filling his plate with everything she'd prepared. "So, you're not wearing any underwear?"

~ * ~

Gray rinsed off his plate in the sink. He hadn't had a full breakfast like that in a long time and he was stuffed. "Thanks for the grub, Sofia," he said, as she stood next to him. "It was delicious."

"A man who's easy to please? Or a compulsive liar?" She reached over the sink and turned the water on.

"I'll choose door number one. I didn't complain

about the hot water in the shower only lasting a minute and a half, did I?"

"Until now." She smiled at him. "Sorry about that. I should've warned you. Nana's water heater isn't very powerful."

"No worries. I needed a cold shower anyway, after the kiss we shared last night."

Her cheeks stained bright red for the third time that morning. He liked that she was easy to read. The blushed cheeks were a dead giveaway to what she was really thinking. Obviously, kissing him had affected her on some level.

Hell, he'd figured that out last night when she'd wrapped her legs around his hips, allowing him to feel the heat between her thighs. But the blushing showed it wasn't something she did often, if at all.

Just like in the dreams, she was completely innocent. And sweet.

She squeezed some dish soap into the sink and grabbed the plate out of his hand, nudging him out of the way.

He grinned, adding playful to the list of things he liked about her.

"Now, what kind of man would I be if I allowed you to do everything?" He nudged back.

"You wash. I'll dry."

"Fine with me." She laughed and tossed a dishtowel at him.

Gray caught it and swatted her jean-clad bottom with it – faded jeans that showed off her heart-shaped ass. He secretly hoped that snug white t-shirt would get a little wet while dishwashing. She wasn't exactly fashionable, but whatever she wore, she looked sexy as hell.

Shame she wanted him to leave. They could have a lot of fun together. Gray smiled to himself. Having fun hadn't been high on his priority list for a long, *long* time.

It hadn't been part of his idiotic life plan. However, the woman beside him inspired him in ways he hadn't imagined. Besides, he didn't exactly have much going on in his life now. He could put off moving to San Francisco for a month or so. Live off his savings, well, whatever was left of his savings after he paid back Rachel's parents for the chunk of change they put into the wedding that wasn't going to happen. Her heartless actions may be the reason the wedding was off, but he could see now that she'd done him a favor. Marrying Rachel would've been a huge mistake.

Now his life had no limitations. Maybe he could convince Sofia to go out with him a few times. Show her who he really was, and who he could be if given the chance.

Anything was possible.

"Sofia, can I take you out on a—" Before he could finish, the faucet made a clanking sound and fell off into the sink, spurting water straight up and onto Sofia.

Gray dropped to his knees and threw open the cupboard door. He spotted the valve that shut off the water and turned the knob until it wouldn't go around anymore. The sound of Sofia laughing hysterically brought him back up to his feet just as fast.

"What could possibly be funny?" he asked, but couldn't help but chuckle along with her.

Her shirt was drenched, more wet than Gray had hoped, but he wasn't complaining in the least. Underneath, a white lace bra sparsely concealed her ample breasts.

She slapped a hand on her thigh and continued her hysterics.

Gray chuckled. Her good mood was contagious. "What?" he managed to ask finally.

"Oh my gosh." She took in a breath. "Ever since I realized I was wearing this shirt, I've been looking for a reason to change."

At that, they both doubled over. Gray laughed more than he had in years. Not since his college days with Hayes. Sofia had a spirit and liveliness that reminded Gray of his brother. Hayes would've liked her, there was no doubt.

Hopefully, not as much as he had taken a liking to Rachel.

But that was a different story for a different time. Right now, all Gray wanted to do was be close to Sofia in any way she'd let him. If he wasn't going to be able to dream of her anymore, he'd need to step up his game in real life.

Taking a chance, he leaned in and dared to kiss the side of her lips.

She stepped back, halting the laughter altogether.

Damn. Undoing the damage he'd already done wasn't going to be easy. "Why don't I fix the faucet while you change?" That would give him a little extra time.

"You don't have to." She paused. "Are you sure?"

"It's no problem. I'm pretty good with my hands." He winked at her, and she blushed again.

Fourth time, but who was counting? "Your grandma have a tool chest?"

"It would probably be in the shed out back, but she keeps it locked up for some reason." She pulled out a set of about ten keys from a drawer. "One of these might open it. But you don't have to put yourself through all that trouble. I'll get it."

"No trouble at all." Gray grabbed the keys from her and waved her away. "You go change into some dry clothes."

He couldn't rip his gaze away as she sprinted from the room. Curvy hips, narrow waist and an ass that had him biting his lip. Shaking the desire ratcheting his body, he headed to the shed.

The mid-July day was warm, and there wasn't a cloud in the sky. The lake west of the house had a small pier with a rowboat attached. He wondered if there were any fish in the water. He hadn't been fishing since he was a kid when Dad took Hayes and him camping.

Living in the city didn't give Gray a chance to be by the water he loved. He wondered for a moment if he could charm Sofia into letting him have a couple hours out on that rowboat. She seemed determined to get away from him, though. *To stop her dreams of me from happening.*

He wasn't sure what to think about her claiming she dreamed of the future and had the ability to change the events she saw in her dreams. It was all a little far-fetched even for him to believe, and he considered himself fairly open-minded.

After everything was said and done, he couldn't deny there was something mystical about the dreams that had brought them together. Something he couldn't explain in any sensible terms. Something he wasn't ready to rationalize.

For once, he planned to go with the flow. Hayes would have been shocked.

The old wooden shed was indeed locked. The padlock wasn't very big, so one of the smaller keys might fit it. And if they didn't, Gray didn't think it would take much to simply lift the dilapidated door right off its loose, rusty hinges. He could screw it back on properly when he found the tool chest. Luckily, he didn't have to worry. The third key he tried worked. He carefully pulled the door open and walked in.

Sunlight shone through the many holes and cracked spots in the wood, allowing Gray to see what the shed consisted of. Very odd. Next to the lawn mower was some sort of altar.

Along the walls were shelves filled with bottles of herbs, oils, and some burned candles. He leaned forward to see if any of the bottles had labels, but none of them did. Moving on, he spotted a decorative saber knife

118

hanging on a nail above a shelf. Curious, he picked it up and gently ran his finger over the sharp, shiny blade. The handle was adorned with various colors of gemstones. Beautiful. He hung the knife back up. Just below was a silver chalice engraved with some sort of circular design.

Did the old woman perform rituals in here, or what? Freaky. A chill crept over his spine. He shrugged it off, then jumped when the cat appeared out of nowhere, jetting under and around his legs before shooting back out the door. *Freaky cat too*.

"Are you in here?" Sofia walked in and glanced around wide-eyed. She'd changed into a white cotton mini-skirt and a blue top with a moderately low V-neck that showed a sliver of cleavage. Her hair fell over her shoulder in damp ringlets. Damn.

He tried not to stare. "Do you know what all this stuff is?"

"Huh." She glanced around. "My mom always said Nana was a witch, but I thought she was kidding. Dang. She really does practice witchcraft. I had no idea." Her gaze landed on Gray. "Do you ever truly know a person?"

"That's an excellent question. I've been deceived by the only two people in my adult life I've ever gotten close to."

"Your fiancée and your brother? What were their names again?" she asked, while swirling her finger over the dagger's design.

"*Ex*-fiancée," he corrected. "Rachel, and my brother's name was Hayes."

Her nose crinkled as she wiped her hands together. "Well, Rachel and Hayes were fools, if only for a night."

Before he could reply she pointed to a rusted toolbox covered with cobwebs. "There it is. Let's get out of here."

~ * ~

Sofia ran her fingers through Sam's fur and watched Gray work on the faucet. It was a hot day, so he'd taken off his shirt and thrown it at her, chuckling after she gave him a dirty look.

And now he was shirtless. Half-naked yet again.

The muscles in his back and biceps flexed as he twisted the wrench. Sofia sighed. The man was a work of fine art to be observed and appreciated. *For sure.*

He turned his head to smile at her. "Hey, sweetie, can you get me a drink of water?"

Sweetie? "Sure, *darling*." Sofia snickered and jumped to her feet, sending Sam to the floor. She opened the gas-powered refrigerator she and her mother had purchased for Nana two Christmases ago to replace the old icebox. They were always on the lookout for appliances that didn't require electricity. Nana was getting up there in age, and anything that made her life more comfortable was a godsend.

Sofia pulled out a bottle of water and handed it to him.

"Thanks," he said, and chugged half of it down. "Hot day, today."

"Yeah."

A bead of sweat dribbled down the middle of his abdomen, into his jeans. She held back the urge to run her finger down the path and farther. To touch the muscles she knew so well.

Another sigh.

She seriously needed to get him out of here before she did something she regretted. Because even if this Rachel chick had crushed his feelings, there was no way he would be over her so quickly. Right?

"I think it's fixed. Just need to turn the water back on and test it out."

"Okay. Then I can drive you to your car. Or if you want, there's an auto-body shop I can take you to about ten miles away, and it has a tow truck."

"Whichever." He drank down the rest of the water and stooped to turn the sink valve.

"Super." She swallowed the rising disappointment building in her throat.

It wasn't as if she didn't enjoy his company. She did, so much so that she knew she would miss him when he was gone. Nevertheless, getting him away from her was for the best. For now.

Who knew? Maybe after his heart healed, he would come back to her and his reasons would be pure, less convoluted. She allowed herself one eye roll for that thought.

Yep, she was saving herself some serious heartbreak by saying goodbye, indefinitely.

Chapter Nine

"Always remember that I love you, okay?" Hayes showed himself to Rachel as he stood over the bed. His gorgeous body was still bare of any clothes. Just the way she liked him.

Rachel was ecstatic to actually see him. While they'd been making love, she'd blindly felt every inch of him. She'd had nothing but memories to sustain her.

"I love you too." She sat up and wrapped the sheet around her. "Do you have to go?"

He closed his eyes for a moment. "Sorry. Your mom is on the way up, and I have to check on some things with Gray."

"Can you come back?" Rachel sounded desperate even to her own ears, but she didn't care. She wanted to spend as much time with him as possible before he left her for good.

"I want to, more than you know, but I can't guarantee anything."

"But – " The doorbell rang.

"I'll try, but don't be sad if I can't. You'll find true love. I promise." He began to fade. "I love you, Rachel."

Then he was gone, before Rachel could tell him he'd be the only true love in her life. Before she could promise he'd be the last man to ever touch her body. She was certain of it. There'd be no other man. Ever.

The doorbell rang again, and Rachel threw on a robe. Her mother was the last person on heaven and Earth she wanted to talk to, but she needed to get this over with.

"Hi, Mom," Rachel said, opening the door.

"Oh, wonderful. You've been crying," Nora said, looking exasperated. "What can I expect this means?"

Not in the mood for a drawn out lecture, Rachel proceeded to what she thought really mattered to her mother. "I'll repay you for the wedding. The dress, the flowers, everything. Don't worry."

"I wouldn't be so hasty, dear. We can work this out." Nora pulled a lock of stiff auburn hair away from her Botox-enhanced forehead. "What is it? Is he having cold feet? Men always do that before a wedding. It's practically required."

"The wedding's not going to happen, Mom. I'm sorry."

"That's ridiculous. It's a mere few days away. To cancel now would be a crime against social etiquette. Now, you know better than that, don't you, dear? Think about all the people you'll disappoint."

Rachel's head throbbed. "I need to be alone, Mom. Could you please leave?"

"Here." Nora reached into her handbag and pulled out an envelope. "Show him these. He'll change his mind."

Rachel took the envelope. Anything to get the woman to leave. Stepping forward she backed her mom out into the hallway then clutched the doorknob.

"I'll wait for your answer. Don't fret, dear. He'll come around."

Rachel shut and locked the door after her mother left. Why did she have to be so stubborn? Better yet, why did she naturally assume it was Gray who was stopping the wedding? That *he* was the one with cold feet? She paced the living room until she remembered the envelope in her hand.

Probably was a bill from Olga the German dressmaking-monger. She opened it and pulled out two airline tickets with a sticky note attached. *For your honeymoon!* was written in her mother's handwriting, and right under it read *I already made reservations at Hotel Le Bristol. Grayson will love it!*

"Oh, Lord. Does she ever stop?"

Two tickets to Paris. Rachel hoped they were refundable, because how in the world would she pay her parents back for this? On top of the wedding that was *not* going to happen?

~ * ~

Gray followed Sofia out to her little blue hatchback. The paint was peeling, and one of the headlights was dislocated, hanging on by a few wires. The car had to be at least twenty years old. A literal death trap. Shit.

The driver's door creaked out a nasty sound as she hefted it open.

Hell, if he was going to get in a car like this, then he wanted to be in control. "Why don't you let me drive?" he suggested. "I know where my car is parked."

She tilted her head, smiling. "No. I'll drive. Just tell me where to go." She sank down in the driver's seat, happy as can be.

"I don't mind at all." He bent over her and checked out the interior. *Warped*. Springs sticking out of the upholstery. No detectable airbags. And no shoulder straps on the seatbelts.

Seriously?

She shoved him away. "You're not one of those guys who's uncomfortable with women drivers, are you?"

"Me?" He tsked. "Not at all." *Fuck*. Apparently having no other choice, he walked around the death-mobile and got in on the passenger side.

Her eyes twinkled with triumph as she gave him a sweet, innocent smile and started the engine. It died right away. Of course. What else would he have expected from this thing? She tried it again. Same thing.

"Crap. What's wrong with my baby?" She ran her fingers over the dashboard.

"Your baby? This thing is older than you are."

"No wonder he won't start—with all the negative energy vibes you're sending out."

"Tell me you're kidding."

She laughed and slapped his thigh. "Had you scared after seeing all that voodoo stuff in the shed, huh?"

The woman needed to be spanked. By him. "Why don't you pop the hood? I'll check it out."

"You are such the manly-man today, aren't you?"

Gray grunted overdramatically, and she laughed again.

He couldn't hold back a chuckle at how easy it was to make her laugh.

At the front of the car, he pulled the latch and lifted the hood. Surprisingly, it was pretty clean. The belts were all intact. The battery looked new. There didn't appear to be any fluids leaking anywhere.

Sofia stepped beside him. "See anything wrong?"

"Not yet. Did you have it serviced recently?"

"I have a friend who helps me out with that stuff. We do favors for each other all the time."

"A friend? Favors?" He didn't like the sound of that at all. Some asshole was probably trying to get in her pants. Before Gray could.

"Yeah, favors." She winked, swatted his butt, and laughed again. "You know what *I'm* talking about."

"That's not funny."

"It is funny, actually." Her hands planted on her curvy hips. "My friend's name is Madeleine. I paint pretty pictures for her apartment, and she keeps my car in tune."

"Oh." So he wasn't scoring any points in the charming department. What was new? He stuck his head under the hood again and poked around at a few things. "So you paint?" he asked, evidently too late. He turned to see Sofia walking up the porch steps and into the house.

Fantastic job, Gray. Way to woo the lady. Oh, well. At least he could attempt to fix her car and get out of her hair. For now, anyway.

~ * ~

After fixing lunch, Sofia peeked out the window. "He's still at it, Sam." She looked down at the cat who lazily purred at her feet. "I have a strange feeling you'll be sleeping with a hunk again tonight, you little traitor."

Sam sashayed through Sofia's legs and dashed out of the kitchen.

Gray had been working on her car all morning, only taking water and bathroom breaks. The poor man had to be exhausted and hungry.

"Hey, lunch is ready," she called out the window, and let the curtains fall.

Seconds later he walked through the door and into the kitchen. His hair was a mess and grease was smeared on his hands and t-shirt. He heaved out a breath, looking like he was ready to blow a gasket.

"I don't know what's wrong with that car. I'm sorry."

"It's okay." She shrugged one shoulder. "We'll figure something out."

"I don't get it. I'm not a certified mechanic or anything, but usually I can at least diagnose the problem. And as far as I can tell, there is absolutely nothing stopping that engine from turning over. You sure that battery is new?"

"Madeleine replaced it a month ago. Look, don't worry about it." Not able to help herself, she lifted to her tiptoes to press a kiss to his cheek.

His face softened and he reached out to touch her, but then glanced down at his filthy hands. "I look like a disaster, don't I?"

"Yes, you do." She smiled. "Wash up at the sink. I

made sandwiches."

"I think I'll need a fire hose to get all this off me."

"Worry about that after you eat. You have to be hungry." She poured him some lemonade and set it on the table by his plate while he cleaned up.

June Cleaver would be proud. Sofia had prepared club sandwiches with all the fixings on toasted white bread. And they didn't look too awful.

He sat down opposite her and eyed his plate. "Sofia, this looks really good. Thanks for making it."

"No problem at all." She waved a hand as if it had been a cinch.

"I was worried you were going to be mad about the car. I know you want to get me out of your hair."

"You probably don't want to be stuck here in the country, either. Right?"

"I don't mind at all, actually." He smiled and bit into his sandwich.

"Right. Because there's so much to do in a house with no electricity."

"I could think of a few things we could do." He waggled his eyebrows at her and took another bite.

Sofia's cheeks warmed.

"I'm kidding you."

She shrugged. "I know."

"How do you suppose we find a way out of here? I don't want to leave you stranded either. You know, I could walk down to my car to see if it decided to start working again. Stranger things have happened."

"How far is it?"

"About a mile, I think. Not too far."

"I see." An unexpected rush of panic swept over Sofia. What if his car *did* work? What if he left and she never saw him again? What if she were throwing away her only chance at love? Her head told her it was best to let him go, to see if he'd come back to her. Her heart was a little more selfish. A lot more worried.

"I think maybe you've had a little too much sun today," she said.

"You think?"

"Yeah. You probably want to shower and rest for a bit, don't you?" Boy, was she going to regret this.

"You wouldn't mind?"

"No. I mean, we can put our heads together and figure something out. There's probably not a good chance that your car would work anyway, right?"

"Probably not." He took another bite of his sandwich.

Sofia released a breath.

~ * ~

The sound of the shower ran through the pipes of the old house as Sofia dried the dishes she'd washed. She wanted to kick herself for being weak. And smile while she was at it. The idea of spending another evening with him soothed something deep inside of her. A need that ached to be quenched.

Anyway, the evening might be fun if she could just keep a lid on her never-ending desire to rip his clothes off and lick that deliciously shadowed line curving down his abdomen.

She waved a hand at her red-hot cheeks. Dropping her glazed over gaze, she caught a glimpse of a yellow mark on her shirt.

Mustard. Ugh. Why did she have to be so clumsy?

She pulled the shirt over her head and rinsed the mark off in the sink before it could set in anymore than it already had. Now she needed another new shirt to wear. Great.

The water had stopped running and she heard his footsteps cross the upstairs hallway to the guestroom. Quickly, she ran upstairs to Nana's room and rummaged for a shirt that didn't have any sort of print or silly slogan on it whatsoever. She found a teal tank top that she thought brought out the color in her eyes and slipped it over her head.

She hadn't exactly packed clothes to impress. Not that she needed to impress, but still. It wouldn't hurt to boost her confidence around the Adonis who used to make out with his Aphrodite fiancée.

She ran a brush through her hair and changed into panties that were a little less granny style. Again, just for the confidence boost. Her white skirt still appeared intact, amazingly, so she walked out into the hallway to make her reappearance.

Only, it was too quiet. There weren't any footsteps or creaking stairs or anything at all. He still had to be in his room because she hadn't seen him walk back down the hall while she was dressing. She tiptoed to the guest bedroom and peeked in to see his lengthy body splayed out on the bed. His eyes were closed. Sleeping? A towel wrapped around his waist, and his head rested on his hands. He must have been exhausted.

The way he lay there reminded Sofia of a dream. In it, he'd been freshly showered and stretched out on the bed next to her. She'd been bold and tugged his towel off him. His body was amazing, every part of it. She'd been craving him, as she did in all the dreams, and she'd leaned over and run her tongue over his hard—

Sam ran past her and jumped up on the bed, interrupting her fantasy, er, thoughts.

"Hey," Gray said in a sleepy voice.

"Hey. I was just...checking on you." Picturing him naked was more like it.

"Sorry. I must've fallen asleep." He shifted to his side and ran his fingers over the cat's fur. The towel gaped open at the slit, exposing more of his muscled thigh.

Sofia tried not to look. "That's okay. Go ahead and get some rest. I'll leave you alone."

"Why don't you lie down with me?" He shifted his hand from the cat to the mattress beside him and patted the bed.

Her entire body warmed as she picked at a flaky piece of paint on the doorframe. "I don't think that's a good idea."

"Just a nap, I swear. I'll probably want to hold you, but that's it."

Sofia's heartbeat galloped as her mind put out a vacant sign. As luck would have it, her courage disappeared as well. "I have to go do something," she mumbled, and hurried downstairs.

~ * ~

Gray woke to the sound of silence. Country life was so peaceful. He could definitely get used to this. The clock on the wall said it was a quarter after seven in the evening. Could that be right?

That was one hell of a nap. Too bad Sofia hadn't joined him.

He stretched and set his feet down on the floor, thinking how nice it was going to be to spend more time with her. The way things had transpired with both their cars had frustrated him, but he wasn't going to let it get to him. He wouldn't question the strange happenings that continued to draw him to Sofia.

And like Sofia, he wanted to keep a positive attitude, letting life take its course. He was going to drop the whole "life plan" crap and be in the moment. Forget about wanting to have control over everything that happened around him. What had that gotten him anyway?

Nothing but grief. Why not take things in stride?

Keep them simple, uncomplicated, enjoyable.

Hell, maybe he could show Sofia that he really wasn't a bad guy.

First, he had to find his clothes. He thought he'd dropped them by the bed alongside his shoes, which were sitting by themselves. He checked the bathroom, but they weren't in there.

130

Sofia wasn't in her room. Maybe she'd know what happened to them. He tightened the towel around his waist and descended the creaky stairs to find her fast asleep on the tiny, antique-looking sofa in the living room. A radio that closely resembled the one Gray had owned in the eighth grade was playing a soft jazz tune on the floor in front of the sofa.

He pushed it aside and knelt down over her curled-up body. Her head rested on a stiff, tiny pillow. She was stunning, even in her sleep. In a way he hadn't recognized at first meeting, but he was glad he did now. She had a sweet beauty he ached to touch. Gently, he swept his fingers over her, starting at her painted pink toenails, up her calf, over her curvy thigh, dipped into her waist, along her arms, her neck, and to her kissable soft lips. Her long, thick eyelashes fluttered open as he leaned down to press his lips to her cheek.

"Hi," she whispered and slowly sat up. "I thought I was dreaming of you."

The idea that the "dream Gray" got more action than the "real Gray" almost made him jealous. When were these supposed visions of the future going to start kicking in?

She stretched her arms and gave him the once-over. "You're probably wondering where your clothes are, huh?"

He laughed and leaned in for a quick kiss to her lips.

"Um." She brought her fingers to her mouth. "I washed them and hung them out on the clothesline."

"You did that for me?"

"I had to. You were looking pretty hobo." She smiled her sweet smile.

"Thanks, I think." He stood. "Out front or back?"

"Side."

The sun was going down when Gray headed outside in his towel. No neighbors anywhere in sight. Just lots of farmland. Hell, he could even dress out here. His clothes were hanging by clothespins from the single line that hung from the trunk of one large elm to another. He pulled on his t-shirt and inhaled the breezy, fresh scent of cotton. Then he quickly tugged on his underwear and jeans, which were still a little damp, but at least they didn't stink or make him look...hobo.

His chances of having Sofia in his bed tonight increased tenfold. "Thank you, Sofia," he said to himself.

He'd tried to get her there this afternoon, and she'd shied away. Which was a smart move on her part, because no way in hell had he only wanted that to be a nap session.

Not that he would've pushed her. Gray wasn't a man who hard-pressed a woman when she wasn't ready. Although the way she'd stared at him while he lay in bed led him to believe she'd considered joining him. It wouldn't be very hard for him to get her to open those curvy little thighs for him. If those dreams and his instincts were right, she was still a virgin. And if that was the case, he'd need to be careful with her.

Oh, hell. He wasn't doing anything with her if she didn't have any protection. Why hadn't *that* occurred to him until now? Probably because he hadn't bought a box of condoms since before Rachel.

Damn. It had been way too long.

Gray headed back inside and into the kitchen, only to see her bent over in the refrigerator. Her little mini-skirt hiked up. One more inch, and he could see heaven.

God help him.

"Lunch, I could do," she said. "Breakfast was a stretch. Supper will need a special visit from my guardian angel, I'm sure." She turned and kicked the refrigerator shut with her heel.

"Why don't I cook supper?"

"Huh. You cook?"

"Usually nuking leftovers in the microwave is my specialty, but I could probably throw something together.

132

It couldn't be that difficult."

"Couldn't be that difficult?" She glared up at him through thick, long lashes.

Oops. "Or I could just pour you a glass of wine and tell you how much I appreciate you making me breakfast, lunch *and* supper, you sexy goddess of the kitchen."

She quirked up one side of those pink, glossy lips. "Wine would be great."

Gray poured her a glass as promised and watched her throw a couple of chicken breasts into a frying pan after spraying it thoroughly with cooking spray. She put water to boil in a pot and pulled out a box of mac and cheese.

He stood out of her way, leaning against the butcher block as he poured himself a glass.

Anything to keep his mouth busy so he wouldn't say something idiotic. He'd always been amazed by the way Hayes could charm women. Hell, he'd charmed the chastity belt right off Rachel.

Gray hadn't even seen it coming. Little did Hayes know, he'd done Gray a favor.

Chapter Ten

Penny sat on the black leather chair, staring over the big walnut desk at her stubborn daughter. "If you don't want to do it for me, then do it for Sofia," she pleaded.

Laura strummed her plain bitten-down fingernails on the desk. She looked sleep-deprived and irritated all at once. Penny read mixed phrases of guilt, loneliness, and desperation pulsating from her daughter's mind.

The woman needed to get herself a man.

Penny blocked Laura's thoughts and concentrated on the task at hand. "You have the power. Hayes is there, watching them. Don't you want to know how Sofia is doing?"

Laura huffed out a breath. "Fine. I'll do it." After blowing out an exasperated breath, she began whispering in such a low voice, it was difficult to decipher the words.

Her face grew pale, and her eyes rolled back in her head. The murmured words grew faster and louder. "Hayes Phillips, I call upon you," she repeated over and over.

A blast of cold air shot through the room, and the young man appeared. He leaned against the bookshelf with his hands in the pockets of his holey jeans.

"This is what you look like?" Penny said. "Identical to your brother, are you?"

Hayes grinned. "He looks a little more respectable

than I do." His smile disappeared when he noticed Laura sitting on the other side of the desk. "What is she doing here?"

"She has the gift to call spirits. She's the one that brought you."

"I'll speak to you only," he said, dismissing Laura.

Laura stood. "Well, I guess my work is done here. I'll leave you two alone."

"Sit down," Penny ordered. Enough of the childishness.

With an eye roll, Laura sat back down.

"You want to know how they're doing?" Hayes asked Penny.

"Yes, that would be wonderful."

"It's happening slowly. They're attracted to each other, but she's wary of him, and Gray isn't exactly a smooth talker."

"Like you?" Penny raised her eyebrows at him for fun. He seemed like such an interesting fellow.

His thoughts were even more so. The name Rachel and her image vibrated passionately out into the room and into Penny's head.

He shrugged and continued. "I stopped planting Sofia's dreams in Gray's head. I'm hoping it'll make him miss her touch and force him to step up his game. He's got a problem with that. If he doesn't start laying on more moves, she might not think he's genuinely attracted to her. Because you all know how insecure she is, right?"

"My daughter is not insecure," Laura piped up.

"Of course she is, dear. Especially when it comes to men, since you've been feeding her bullshit that they can't be trusted."

"Well, they can't. And you're going to regret this, Mother. As soon as this Gray person comes out of his spell, he's going to leave Sofia heartbroken."

Penny ignored her daughter's glare and spoke to Hayes. "I was hoping this would all happen more naturally, but do you think the spell needs to be stronger?"

"And move it along faster? Couldn't hurt. I need to get this all done ASAP. My other project is getting a little overwhelming."

"Other project?" Penny was intrigued.

"The love of my life needs a new love of her life."

"Oh, well let me know if I can be of any help. And thank you for all of yours."

"Absolutely." He faded into nothing. "See ya."

~ * ~

A glass and a half of wine later and Sofia was feeling *pretty* good. She wasn't quite sure how Gray was doing though. He'd been quiet for most of supper and now he sat silently on the floor with his back leaning against Nana's sofa.

He'd insisted he'd break the sofa if he tried to sit on it. Sofia wasn't sure he was wrong. The man was big and the sofa was ancient and tiny. The two rocking chairs that stood in each corner of the room weren't too solid, either.

Feeling guilty, Sofia sat on the floor in front of him, carefully crossing her legs together to avoid giving him a show. She leaned back on her hands and eyed him. The dim light in the room made him appear serious and somber. What was on the man's mind? Maybe his ex? Maybe his brother? Had they been close? It was amazing that she'd loved him in her visions, yet she knew nothing about him in real life.

"What are you thinking about?" she asked, not being able to take the silence any longer.

"How much I want to kiss you again." The words slipped out of his mouth easily, as if they had been at the tip of his tongue.

And yet they were potent enough to warm her body from her scalp to her curling toes. Her cheeks burned, undoubtedly revealing how he affected her.

Trying to joke away her powerful response to him, she made a fish face. "What? You want to kiss these lips?"

"Among other things."

Change the subject fast, Sofe. She reached across the floor for the radio and pulled it in front of her. "Do you like music?" She switched it on to a station where Blondie sang *The Tide Is High*. As long as there wasn't a crooning love song playing or anything with sex or kissing in the lyrics, she should be safe.

"Sure. What about you?"

"I like to listen to it while I'm painting. The genre sets the mood. Like, when I want to paint something sexy and smooth, I listen to jazz. When I want to paint something edgy and dark, I listen to hard rock."

"What do you paint?"

You. "Whatever's on my mind. Things I'm passionate about."

"Like what?" He pushed on. "What did you paint last?"

You. "It's kind of personal."

"Oh." His forehead crinkled. "Will you show me sometime? I mean, if you decide you don't want me out of your life forever."

"I'd love to show you," she said. Stupid honesty sneaked up on her way too much.

"Good." He smiled, genuinely. Stunningly.

For a moment, Sofia wondered if it would be a horrible idea to forget her inhibitions. Just for one night...or forever. She controlled her destiny. The only problem was she couldn't control him. What if she let herself fall in love with him, only to dream of him dumping her?

She sighed. Now that would suck.

The song changed to a hip-hop tune, and Gray chuckled lightly.

"What?"

"It's embarrassing to admit this, but Hayes and I

used to break dance to this song in high school."

"You used to break dance?"

"Yeah. We'd practice like crazy on the weekends. We'd tear apart cardboard boxes and lay them out in the driveway. Smoother surface, you know? And we'd try all these crazy stunts until we finally got it right."

"That is so cute." Sofia tried to picture Gray spinning on his head. Hmm.

"You wouldn't think it was cute if you knew the reason why we did it."

"Which was?"

"To get laid. The girls loved it."

"Really? Well, I have to see some moves." She teased. "Maybe I'll love it too."

"Not gonna happen. It's been over ten years since I've even attempted it."

"Come on. Please?" She gave him her best pouty face.

"What do I get in return?"

"Um." Sofia thought back to her high school years. "I'll do the splits. Or try to, anyway."

His eyebrows arched. "Deal."

"Cool." She stood up and helped him clear a space in the middle of the hardwood floor.

He stretched his arms and his legs. "If I pull something, you'll have to nurse me back to health."

"You got it."

"Don't laugh."

"What if it's funny?"

He gave her a stern look while kicking off his loafers. "I'll try not to laugh."

"Okay, we had these routines that we made up. We had no idea what these moves were called; we just did them. First, we both did this." He did a handstand and brought one hand up. "Holy shit." He flipped over onto his feet. Barely.

Sofia clapped, mainly because of the way his biceps

and shoulders flexed. And it was nice to see him having fun.

"I used to be able to hold myself up longer, but I'm a lot heavier now."

"What did you do after that?"

He grinned. "Is this going to get me laid?"

"We already made the deal."

"Oh, hell. Okay, then I'd lean over and Hayes would do the leapfrog thing over my back. Then we'd line up and do a couple moves." He shuffled around, brought his knee up and jerked his arms around.

Sofia held her hand over her mouth to keep from laughing. He looked adorable.

"And then," he said breathlessly, "we did a backspin." He ran in a circle and fell into a spin on his back for about half a second, ending it by posing on his side, facing the other direction.

"Okay. Go ahead and laugh now."

She let out a giggle. "Gray," she said as he stood to face her with his arms crossed, "you are such a good sport."

"Hell, no, I'm not. I feel old and I think I have bruises on my back now."

"Oh, poor baby."

"Don't 'poor baby' me." His gaze dipped to her chest and back up again. "We made a deal."

~ * ~

Gray's body ached, but he was certain the pain and humiliation would all be worth it. That was, if she ever followed through with her end of the bargain.

First, she *had* to get a drink of water. Then she *had* to use the bathroom. Then she *had* to change into some shorts, which happened to be the little pink ones. God help him.

On her last pass through, Gray grabbed her by the shoulders. "Get it over with, Sofia."

"Oh, fine." She glowered. "After I pour some more

oil in that lamp. It's running a little low."

"Nope. You've procrastinated enough."

She scrunched her nose. "I may not be able to do it anymore."

"Try."

"Oh, fine." She got down on the floor and stretched out her legs in front her. With her hands, she hoisted forward and eased back, propping her body up. She was only a few inches from the ground. She bounced up and down a couple of times, stretching out her muscles and finally completing her splits.

A growing hard-on pressed against his jeans.

"I did it," she screamed, and jumped to her feet and into his arms.

"Yes, you did." He wrapped his arms around her, glad to have a reason to be close. Vanilla. She smelled like sweet vanilla... Or like the cupcakes his mom used to bake for his birthday every year. He'd almost forgotten that memory.

She backed away and clapped her hands, still excited, and Gray instantly missed her warmth. "Todd Beltman can eat his heart out," she said. "I bet he can't do the splits anymore. I bet he's fat and bald now. I ought to look him up."

"Who's Todd Beltman?"

"Freshman year in high school, I tried out for the cheerleading squad and made it. Everything was going great until we started doing lifts. Coach Perry paired me with Todd, and Todd said right there in front of everyone in the squad that he didn't think he could lift me. He thought I was too fat to be a cheerleader."

"*What?* Were you a big girl back then?"

"Roughly the same as I am now, only about two inches shorter, five pounds lighter." She looked like she was about to burst into tears at the mere memory. "I was so embarrassed, I quit and never tried out again."

"Sugar," he said, thinking the endearment suited

140

her, "the guy was probably afraid to touch a hot girl."

"No, he was right. I was too big. I would've crushed him. He was a tiny little guy, and I was this—" She blew up her cheeks and spread her arms out.

"You're out of your mind." Gray grabbed her hand and gathered her close. "And so was that fucker, Todd. We really should look him up. I'll lift *him* up and throw him across the country for hurting your feelings."

"I don't know. I've always been a little overweight."

The woman was insane. He let his gaze fall over her lush body. Curves in all the right places. No way in hell was she too heavy to pick up. To prove his point, he grabbed her by the waist and lifted her with ease.

She gasped slightly, grabbing at his shirt. "What are you doing?"

"Showing you that Todd what's-his-face was a lying little bastard." He lifted her until her head brushed the ceiling. Then, slowly, he lowered her, letting her slide against his body.

When he didn't put her down right away, she wrapped her legs around him and held on tight. She clasped onto his neck, bringing them face-to-face.

Gray shifted his arms. One cradled her bottom, keeping her up, while the other curved around her back, crushing her soft breasts into his chest.

"You can put me down now," she said, breathless. Her lips were within licking distance.

"Not until you kiss me." He grinned at her.

"You have no idea how tempted I am. But I can't. I—"

Gray covered her lips with his to shut her up. He didn't want to hear any excuses. He wanted to be the man in her dreams, the one who could touch her anywhere and everywhere. Make love to her any way he wanted.

To keep her from shying away, he backed her into the wall. Then he slid his tongue into her mouth and flicked it across hers. Luckily, she accepted it eagerly, moaning softly and raking her fingers into his hair.

The heat from her sex pressed against him. Closer. He wanted to be closer.

Feel every part of her.

His free hand found the hem of her tank top and slipped up underneath until he found her breast. He pushed her lace bra up and massaged the plump and supple flesh. Her nipple budded at his touch.

She squirmed against him and began to slip down the wall. Gray lifted her back up, supporting her bottom. This couldn't end yet. There was so much more he wanted to do with her.

He paused from kissing her to whisper, "Can I take you upstairs?"

Don't ask, just do it, you fool. This had been his downfall with many girlfriends in the past. He never pushed them, never wanted to take advantage of them. In the end, they'd moved on to guys who did push them.

Sure, he didn't have a condom, but he could think of about thousand other ways to please them both without protection.

"I'm not ready for that yet," she whispered back and dropped her legs from his waist to the ground, fixing her bra and top in the process.

Damn it. "Right." He fisted his hands at his sides, trying to ignore how his body burned with unspent desire and how his cock ached for release. But it was damned difficult, considering he'd gotten so close.

She stared up at him, the blue of her eyes only a thin ringlet around her pupil. "Thank you for making me feel better about the Todd incident."

Ah hell. The woman was after his heart.

"Thank *you* for reminding me there are memories of Hayes that I love and cherish. Those have been kind of hard to come by lately."

Her eyes welled up. "Oh my gosh. You must still be grieving over losing him. I'm so sorry. Were you two pretty close?'"

"Yeah. He's been my best friend since birth...and my worst enemy at times as well."

She stood up on the tips of her toes and pressed a kiss to his lips. "It'll get better, I promise."

"I think it just did."

~ * ~

Sofia finished showering and changing into her favorite light green nightgown. It had spaghetti straps and was silky and sleek against her skin. She ran her hands over her hips and felt truly sexy for the first time in her life. The change probably had to do with there being a hot guy downstairs who made her feel like she was something more than a short, overweight wannabe cheerleader. *So* much more. He was sweet for sticking up for her against her worst high school memory. It made her wish she'd met him back then.

Sighing, she pulled her sketchbook from her duffle bag and sifted through the pages. Her own personal homage to Gray. How humiliating would it be if he found it? Even worse, if he were to see the numerous paintings that filled her bedroom at home. Sofia Good: Dream stalker extraordinaire. *Why, yes, Gray, I did spend hours upon hours sketching and painting you, even before I laid eyes on you.*

Not good. She stuffed the sketchbook back in the bottom of the bag and scrounged for a new pair of panties. All that was left were her high-cut cotton briefs. Comfortable, but not sexy at all. She really needed to do laundry, but how embarrassing would it be to hang out your underwear for the world and Gray to see on a clothesline?

No way.

She opted to wear none for tonight. Nothing was going to happen, but it was fun to feel a little naughty. To know that with one slip of his hand, he would realize she was completely bare underneath this lightweight nightgown.

He'd only have to hike it up and straddle her on his lap... *Stop it, Sofe. Stop. It.*

Twenty-four years without knowing the touch of a man was starting to warp her mind. Sure, she could've given into a man's advances on one of the several dates she'd been on, but when she had visions of the men falling in love with someone else, the idea always lost its flavor. Of course, she didn't have that problem with Gray. In her dreams of him, he loved *her*, and no one else.

She let out a breath and put a brush through her damp hair.

"Sofia." Gray's voice jolted her, his low tone resonating deep in her belly.

She resumed normal breathing, then swerved to see him standing at the door with his hands braced against the doorframe. She really needed to remember to start closing and locking the door.

Or not.

His shirt was off again and he was wearing jeans that hung low on his hips, revealing muscles that trailed to places she'd yet to see in real life.

"Hi," she managed to squeak.

"Am I interrupting?"

"No. Not at all." She dropped the brush on the dresser and watched as he sat on the edge of the bed.

"So." He rubbed his palms on his jeans, looking like he might be as nervous as she felt.

Sofia licked her lips and pressed her hand to her belly, the area that wouldn't stop quivering. Her silky nightgown suddenly seemed weightless.

"Sofia," he said again, but she didn't mind the repetition. She loved how he said her name.

"Yeah?"

He reached out and grabbed hold of her wrist. His dark eyes coaxed her toward him as he gently tugged her over until she stood in between his thighs.

144

"I wanted to say goodnight." His hand settled on her hips, drawing her against him. Heat permeated from his body...or maybe it was the warmth rushing up her chest to her cheeks that caused her to feel feverish.

"Okay." Oh, boy.

"*And* because sometimes words escape me, I wanted to make a point to tell you how beautiful I think you are. Inside and out."

She gulped. "I, um...thanks."

His hands, broad against her hips, slid to the outside of her thighs and back up again. He must have noticed her lack of underwear, because he bit into his bottom lip and repeated the action.

Sofia was pretty sure her heart stopped beating. Not since Leo Wendle pinched her ass in the hallway in the seventh grade had someone acted like they appreciated God's big, old, huge gift to her backside. And Leo Wendle had been an acne-faced pervert with premature facial hair.

This was *so* much better.

"I think," she managed to say, "that you're beautiful too. I mean, handsome, not beautiful. Cause you're a guy. A man, really." *Just stop talking.*

"I hope you can forgive me for treating you badly when we first met. It might sound like a cop-out but after Hayes died, my life tilted off balance, and I went a little crazy trying to get back in control. Then the dreams happened, and as you know, I had zero control over those."

"But you didn't have one last night. Maybe they're gone now, so you don't have to worry about that any longer."

"I don't worry. Not now anyway." He teased her lips with a soft kiss. "I'm ready for the future."

Before Sofia could ask *exactly* what he meant by that—because sometimes she thought she needed a sledgehammer over her head to understand men—he stood up and said, "Goodnight, Sofia."

Really? No more kisses? No more touching? She watched him walk to the door, but couldn't stand letting him leave without...*something*.

"Wait." With a leap and a small sprint, she reached him and stood on her tiptoes to kiss him one more time. "Goodnight, Gray."

~ * ~

Gray tossed and turned in his bed. *Go to her.* The words played over and over in his head. She was only down the hall, lying in bed, wearing that silky little nightgown with no panties.

God help him.

He wanted her like no other woman he'd ever laid eyes on. The urge to slide into bed with her, lie on top of her, wedge himself between those thighs and enter her— hell, his erection pulsed at the mere idea. Why hadn't he been more assertive in her bedroom? He could be lying with her right now, naked, having already made love to her.

Making her his.

But he just couldn't hurt her. No protection, no sex. And honestly, Gray didn't think he had enough sense in him to stop at a little harmless fondling. Sofia had been smart to turn him down earlier.

Not that Gray wasn't safe. He knew he was free of any STDs, but he couldn't risk getting her pregnant. She was too good a girl. She deserved more. More than an unemployed asshole could give her.

Go to her.

Fuck. He threw the sheet off his naked body and hurried downstairs to get some ice-cold water to drink, or pour over his head. When he reached the kitchen, Sam hissed at him from on top of the butcher block, causing Gray to jump back. What was wrong with that cat?

She leaped down and raced up the stairs.

After Gray's heart started beating again, he searched

the refrigerator for a bottle of water but couldn't find any. Tap water would have to do. He opened the cupboard for a glass...and noticed a large box of condoms?

What the hell? He picked them up and saw that a sticky note attached. *For Sofia*, it read with a heart drawn next to it.

Nana was his new best friend. Strange that a grandmother would leave an economy-sized box of rubbers for her virgin granddaughter, but who was Gray to judge?

Forgetting about the water, he made his way back upstairs, attempting to throw a plan together in his head. Should he crawl into bed with her and hope she didn't kick him out? Should he *accidentally* trip in the hall, making enough noise she would wake up and see if he was okay? *Yeah, that would be real smooth, Gray.*

She'd want to have sex with him then, wouldn't she?

He lay back down on the guest bed and opened the box. Rows of condoms fell on top of his chest. It'd been a while since he'd seen one of these. He'd never even considered buying any when he was with Rachel.

He'd thought he could wait until they were married, but now that he was wiser about the whole issue, wasn't the real reason because he hadn't loved her? Hadn't desired her enough to push it?

Unquestionably, he'd had more passionate feelings about Sofia in the past forty-eight hours than he'd had during his entire relationship with Rachel.

Sure, the dreams probably helped those feelings along, but knowing now what he didn't know then, he was damn glad he was here instead of making the worst mistake of his life. He *hadn't* loved Rachel; it was obvious to him now. But did he love Sofia?

A low, hollow scream echoed down the hall and into the bedroom. Gray sat straight up, the hair rising on his neck. Sofia?

He jammed the condoms back into the box and set

them underneath the bed before rewrapping the sheet around his waist and running into the hallway. Sofia walked toward him, shaking and in tears.

He gathered her into his arms. "What's wrong? What happened?"

"Oh, Gray. I have to stop it."

"Stop what?" Damn, he'd do anything to help her.

"The airplane." She wiped the wet streaks from her face, only more brimmed in her eyes. "It's going to crash, which really doesn't matter because they're all already dead. Every one of them. Even the pilot. There must have been a problem with the oxygen in the cabin. Maybe the plane flew too high or too low or both. Maybe there's a crack in a window somewhere and all the air depleted from there. Or...or they all passed out before the oxygen masks fell. I don't know. It's just flying through the air with nobody at the wheel. What should I do?"

She wasn't making any sense. Had she had a nightmare?

"Relax and try to breath, Sofe."

"I can't go back to sleep. It hurts too much to see them, knowing I can't help." She gulped for air. Her crisp gaze held secrets Gray wasn't sure he wanted to know about.

Regardless, he wouldn't tolerate her being in pain, helpless against her own dreams.

"What can I do?" He kissed her forehead, wanting to comfort her in any way possible.

"Hold me."

Without question, Gray took her hand and guided her into her bedroom. She climbed onto the bed ahead of him and sat, waiting for him.

He gestured to the sheet wrapped around his waist. "I'll put something on."

"It's okay. Just lie with me."

Gray stretched out next to her, keeping the sheet over him while he enfolded her in his arms and held her

148

close. This unknown emotion filled him. He ached for her, wanted to be with her, and couldn't imagine never seeing her again.

Did he love her?

She rested her head on his bicep and met his gaze. A worried expression scrunched her forehead.

He pushed a lock of hair behind her ear and kissed her lips. "Did you have a premonition?" he asked—for the first time, believing that it might be possible.

"Yes. People are going to die if I don't help them. I don't know what to do." A tear fell off her cheek and onto his arm.

"Don't cry, Sofia. We'll figure it out together, okay? I'll help you as much as I can."

"You will?"

"Yes." He'd do anything.

"Thank you." She let out a sigh of relief and closed her eyes.

Chapter Eleven

Gray attempted to breathe steadily as she lay next to him. Trying to sleep was pointless, he'd realized, oh, about an hour or so ago. Not with her body curled up against him. Her nightgown had ridden up, revealing the lower half of her backside, which pressed against his erection.

Just a thin sheet separated them.

He tightened his fists shut to keep from touching her. Otherwise, he'd get carried away.

She wiggled and shifted again, turning her body around to face him.

He relaxed his stiff muscles, welcoming the small relief. But then he noticed her lips curl into a sexy smile. The white of her teeth glistened in the dimness of the room but her eyes were closed. Smiling in her sleep? Hmm. Interesting.

"Sofia?" he whispered, to see if she was awake enough to answer him.

"Mmm. I like that." She flattened her hand to his chest. "Feels so good."

"*Sofia?*"

"That feels even better."

Holy shit. She was dreaming. With the sensual way she was talking, he hoped it was of him. He kept listening, to be sure. What else was he going to do? Wake her up?

Nah. Not yet.

"Of course I want you, Gray. I always want you." She scooted closer and slid her leg over his hip.

Okay. This was looking up.

She laughed softly. "Feel me. See for yourself."

Deep breath.

"Mmm." She curved her leg higher, boosting her nightgown up farther.

Hell, he'd been good long enough. Only so much a man could take.

Just one touch, that's all. One touch.

Then he'd carry her to her back to her bed and leave her to her dreams. But first…

He slid his hand up her thigh, slowly. Upward more. Just a little more. His palm slid over the unbelievably soft flesh of her ass. And he couldn't help but caress her. Feel her.

She moaned again and rolled her hips forward, forging her moist heat against his cloth covered erection and away again. Definitely no panties. That was just not fair.

"Sofia," he whispered, wanting her permission to continue. "Please, baby." He pushed the sheet down some. If it happened again, he'd be able to feel her. Just feel her. That was all.

She panted softly, taking in small breaths. "Yes. Please."

Was she coming? *Oh, hell.* He exhaled.

Take her. Love her. She's yours.

"Sofia." His body shook with need as he gripped her hip and pulled her to him. "Damn, I want you."

Carefully, he angled her onto her back, taking in the sight of her. His hands shook eagerly as he edged her nightgown up her waist—*keep going*—past her plump breasts and then over her head.

Her body was incredible. Creamy white with the

151

moonlight shining down through the window.

The need to touch her overpowered any rational thought. He brushed his fingers along her thighs, across her mound, along her stomach. All soft, supple skin. Beautiful. Her nipples pebbled as his palms grazed over her breasts. He stopped to massage her, leaning over to run his tongue —

"Gray?"

He glanced up and noticed her eyes were open. She tried to sit up, but Gray lodged himself in between her legs.

"Sofia, I want you." No asking this time. He nudged himself against her heat.

She reached up and cradled his jaw. "Was I dreaming?"

"Not anymore. This is real." Not waiting for a reply, he kissed her lips, deep and long.

Her lips softened yet she trembled underneath him. She was nervous. He understood that. This would be her first time. And like the dreams, she'd give herself to him. He'd take her, make her his.

Not able to control himself, he grazed his lips down her neck to her breast again. Licking and tasting her, he savored how goddamn wonderful it was to have her, tangible flesh and blood. *Sofia*.

Her breathing quickened. Her fingers slipped through his hair.

This was going to happen.

He reached underneath the bed and pulled out a condom. She clasped her legs together when he skimmed it over himself.

"I'll be gentle," he said softly. Easing her knees apart, he wedged his body on top of hers again.

To make sure she was ready for him, he slid a finger inside of her. She was drenched. He slipped in another finger, preparing her as much as he could. Her lips quivered when he kissed her again, but she said nothing.

A wary but lustful look covered her face.

She loosened some, so he withdrew his fingers and guided himself inside of her. Inching in, stretching her.

~ * ~

Sofia tried to breathe. Her pulse rocketed while her heart rioted. This was happening. He was making love to her. And she wasn't dreaming this time.

Oh, wow.

Her fingers curled into his shoulders, bracing for pain but getting something different. Sure, the fullness of him entering her hurt a little, but her desire overrode any major discomfort. Nothing she couldn't handle. It only hurt the first time, she remembered from the dreams.

What she didn't quite remember was the squeezing in her chest or the fluttering in her belly. The feel of his bunched muscles under her fingertips. The way his naked hips fit between her trembling thighs. His chest against her breasts. All the sensations rolling over her, through her.

All of them *real.*

He slowly eased forward inside her, deep, deeper. His breaths were steady by her ear as he halted. "Tell me if it hurts too much."

"Just take me, Gray," she whispered. "Take me."

He peeked at her from the corner of his shadowy eye. A warning, it seemed. "If you say things like that, I might come before I'm done with you."

Sofia bit her lips shut and wrapped her legs around his hips.

He pushed in another inch.

She clenched her eyes shut.

"Are you okay?"

"I'm a big girl. I can take it," she said through gritted teeth.

He kissed a sensitive spot on her neck, then nuzzled his nose there. "You're incredible and so goddamn sexy."

Sexy? That made it kind of worth it. She focused her

thoughts off the pain and on how he was working that sensitive spot on her neck below her ear—the way he'd taken her hands and pinned them above her head—the way his perspiration-damp chest pressed and slid against her responsive nipples—and the way his muscular body felt between her legs.

She loosened for him more, letting him in all the way. All of his magnificent thick, hard length...

"*Sofia*. You feel amazing." He maneuvered to the spot that always made her orgasm in the dreams and slowly edged up and down against her. The pain was now mixing with pleasure. Deep, building pleasure.

"Oh, Gray," she said on a breath.

"Is this the spot?" He pushed up on his hands and smiled, all the while quickening his movements.

"God, yes," she cried, and the warm, wonderful buildup intensified, spiraling, erupting. Nerves she'd never felt before tingled and sizzled. Muscles tightened then went limp. Sweet, lazy limpness.

A few more thrusts and Gray gave way, falling onto her body.

Sofia wrapped her arms around him and held him close, spreading kisses across his cheek and jaw. Her emotions exploded, bursting free from where she'd kept them bundled up and hidden.

Love, want, need, devotion, loyalty—it was all for him.

And it was too late to go back now.

~ * ~

The aroma of bacon woke Sofia. Or was it Sam licking her toes? Either way, she opened her eyes and saw she was naked, with a white sheet partially wrapped around her body.

A little purple wildflower sat on the pillow beside her. He must have picked it from the patch growing by the house. How cute was that? She twirled it between her fingers and inhaled the scent.

154

The memory of what had happened the night before played in her head. Some parts she rewound and watched again.

It was happening. Last resort or not, she'd let him take up residence in her heart. A huge penthouse suite with a glorious view.

Nice analogy, Sofe. Does the door to this penthouse have a deadbolt on the outside, just in case he decides to vacate?

Sofia found her nightgown somewhere amongst the tangled bed sheets and slipped it over her head. She stripped the bed and remade it with fresh linens, deciding to wash everything since they'd made a mess.

She'd finally lost her virginity. Her mother would be happy about that fact, but probably not so much when she found out her daughter was falling head over heels.

A zillion other worries and doubts zoomed through her mind as she showered and dressed. But the worst was thinking about how Gray was going to react this morning. Would he regret sleeping with her? Would he want to get the heck out of Amish country, and fast?

Only one way to find out. She brushed her hair and teeth, put on a little makeup and lip-gloss, grabbed the laundry and headed downstairs. She set the laundry basket by the basement door to do later.

The air in the kitchen was smoky when she walked in. The windows were all open and he was at the stove, busying himself over a frying pan.

Sofia stifled a laugh. They had something in common, huh? She walked to the butcher block and lifted herself up to sit and watch. He was wearing his t-shirt and black boxer briefs, looking darn sexy with his disheveled morning hair and unshaven face.

He shot a grin at her, shut the burner off, and transferred the pan full of eggs to the other side. "I guess it's not as easy as I thought," he said, and turned to greet her. He wedged up between her legs and cupped her cheeks. "How are you feeling this morning?" he asked, but didn't wait for an answer. His lips locked with hers, drawing her in for a deep kiss.

She didn't protest in the least. In fact, she wrapped her legs around him and slipped her hands up under his t-shirt, curving them around his defined muscles. Her stomach flittered with delight and relief. This was her man, to do with what she wanted! It was hard to believe her dreams were all coming true.

Sort of.

"Gray?" She pulled away and caught her breath.

"Yeah?" He slid his tongue along her bottom lip. "I could kiss you all day long."

Sofia sighed blissfully. "After breakfast?"

"After breakfast what?"

"After breakfast you can do whatever you want to me, all day long."

His lips quirked up into half a smile. "I like the sound of that."

So did Sofia. Any doubt she'd had the day before had vanished from her mind. Only one nagging detail kept her from skipping breakfast and heading back up to the bedroom.

She dropped down from the butcher block and strode over to sit at the table. "Did you ever have the dream where you took my virginity?" she gathered the nerve to ask.

Gray set a plate in front of her and bunched his forehead. "Yeah. Why do you ask?"

"I didn't, um, reach orgasm in that dream, but I did last night. Don't you think that's odd?"

He sat across from her and smiled proudly. "No, I think it was beautiful. Because of those dreams, I knew exactly what you liked and how to please you. It was incredible, and now I can honestly say I am a true believer that I was dreaming of the future."

"But it was different. Everything was different. Do you remember? It was supposed to happen somewhere

156

else."

"Well, you said you could change the future, right? Maybe we're taking a different course." He shrugged and bit into his eggs.

"Do you think?" She nibbled her lip, fearing the worst. She remembered he'd told her he loved her in that dream, too, but he hadn't last night. What if they were going too fast? What if she'd given herself to him too soon? What if they weren't supposed to meet until much later? The only reason they were sitting there together at that moment was because they'd recognized each other from the dreams.

"Do you want to go out on the rowboat later?" he asked, changing the subject. "Want some orange juice?" He lifted the pitcher, a weak grin on his face.

"Why not? And yes." Maybe he was just as anxious as she was?

Probably not possible.

He came around and filled her glass, then leaned in and kissed her cheek. "Don't worry," he whispered.

Sofia forced a smile on her face. She couldn't push him away now. Protecting her heart wasn't an option. No matter what had happened or what was going to happen, she knew one thing was certain—she'd fallen in love with Grayson Phillips before she'd ever met him.

~ * ~

Penny sat on the couch and rested her eyes, attempting to avoid the migraine that was undoubtedly beginning. If only she could make a spell to get rid of these things. Then she could live closer to Sofia and Laura.

No. Too much time with these girls would put her in the grave sooner than she liked. It was better for everyone to love them from afar. As soon as this love spell business was all settled, Penny was heading back home, and she was going to finish knitting the last sweater. And maybe think up a strong enough love spell for Laura.

Her daughter was one hundred percent pure sour grapes. However, she hadn't always been that way.

The doorbell rang throughout the house, but Penny didn't budge. Laura would get it. It rang again a moment later. Where was that woman?

Penny rubbed at her temples and could feel Laura's thoughts from not far away.

Why won't he just go away?

He? Penny was intrigued. She stood and walked to the entryway. Laura was leaning against the door to the den with a frown on her face.

"Who's at the door?" Penny peeked out of the peephole and saw a distinguished looking middle-aged man. "A man?"

Laura put her finger to her lips and shushed her.

Penny read her mind and an image of a naked Rodney Dangerfield popped into her head.

She cringed. What disrespect.

To get even, Penny unlocked the door and opened it. "Hello? How can I help you?"

The gentleman seemed bewildered. "Um, I'm looking for Ms. Good."

"Which? Laura or Sofia?" Penny read his mind. He didn't have a clue who was whom, but he pictured Laura, her blonde hair shining in the sun, smiling.

"Uh, the older one, please."

Isn't he a charmer? "You want Laura. Just a moment, Mr.?"

"Lawrence. Herbert Lawrence. I live next door." He was upset about Laura painting the wall with plums. Good grief.

"Ah. Nice to meet you. I'm Laura's mother, Penny."

He nodded. Nope, not one ounce of charm. No wonder Laura didn't want to open the door.

"Laura," Penny called out. "Mr. Lawrence is here to see you."

Laura appeared from behind and swung the door open all the way. "Thank you, Mother," she said, gritting her teeth. Rodney Dangerfield was doing naked cartwheels in her mind.

After giving Laura her best stern look, Penny backed up into the hallway and listened in. The two murmured back and forth in angry voices, but Penny kept her attention on what was said underneath. Herbert thought Laura's skin looked soft and wanted to touch it. Laura thought the grey in his hair was kind of sexy. Herbert's feelings were hurt that Laura kept pulling these pranks on him. If she'd only settle down for once, maybe he could gather the courage to ask her out. Laura was scared to death that he was going to ask her out.

Laura slammed the door on him, stomped back into the den and slammed that door as well.

"Are you happy, Mother?" she yelled from the other side.

The wheels spun in Penny's head. Oh, she was happy all right. Her daughter wasn't such a helpless case after all.

Chapter Twelve

Sofia followed him into the guest bedroom. Nervous. Sex in the light of day was *much* different than sex by moonlight. He was going to be able to see *everything*. Every flaw. Why had she opened her big mouth earlier, saying he could do whatever he wanted to her? Was she so naïve not to realize he'd want her naked in the bed?

Oh, boy.

"Come here." He sat on the edge and pulled her to him. His hands slowly slid up her skirt to her panties. The granny panties, for the love of Pete. How humiliating. She really needed to do laundry...and buy some less pathetic underwear.

He didn't seem to notice as he caressed her inner thighs and stared into her eyes with unadulterated lust.

Holy cow. Her hands trembled slightly, she noticed, when she placed them on his shoulders.

His strong, broad shoulders, firm to the touch.

The man was perfect from head to toe, which was why she was still standing there. Seeing *him* naked in the daylight was so going to be worth it.

As though reading her thoughts, he tugged his shirt over his head and tossed it to the ground. "Your turn."

Removing her top wouldn't be a problem, she supposed. Her breasts were one part of her body she was proud of. She pulled her shirt over her head and was happy to see she'd put on the sheer white lace bra today.

At least there was that.

Gray seemed pretty happy about it too. He brushed his thumb over her nipple until it was hard and slid his tongue across the lace.

Heat rushed down from her stomach to slide between her thighs.

He reached around her back, found the latch to her bra and unsnapped the material. The pretty lace thing dropped to the floor and the warmth of his hands replaced it. He massaged, kissed and suckled, arousing Sofia so much that her knees almost buckled underneath her.

"Why don't you lie down?" he said gruffly.

Sofia shook her head, not ready yet. She raked her fingers through the hair at his temples and leaned her forehead against his.

He began to unbutton her skirt. Five buttons, thank God. This should take him a bit.

She sucked in her stomach as her nerves quaked and her body shivered.

"Why are you nervous, Sofia?" He stopped at the third button and settled his hands on her hips. "What's wrong?"

She gulped down. "I'm not as thin as what you're used to, am I?"

His sexy, dark gaze rolled over her. "Trust me, sugar—if I weren't crazy, in-over-my-head attracted to you, I wouldn't be undressing you right now, I wouldn't have made love to you last night, and I wouldn't get a hard-on just watching you walk down the hallway."

"Oh." That was nice to hear. But... "You can agree, though, that you'd still be with *her* if you hadn't found out about her sleeping with your brother, right?"

"Probably."

"Oh." Not so nice to hear.

"But I'd be miserable because I wouldn't have the smart, sweet, incredibly sexy woman from my dreams in my arms. If I'd only known you were real, Sofia. Had I realized that it were really possible to be as happy as I was in those dreams, I would've left her and I would've found you. I promise you that."

A tear brimmed and rushed down her cheek, and she swiped at it. Why was she so emotional lately?

"But you haven't seen me naked in the daylight yet," she warned.

"I have, over and over again, and I want to see you again if you don't mind."

Sofia imagined he was right. He had seen her multiple times. Just not in granny panties. She finished unbuttoning her skirt and slid it and the panties down at the same time.

There. That was that.

Then she dared look into his eyes to see his expression. They were heavily lidded as he slid his hands over her waist and down her hips to her thighs and back up again.

"So goddamn sexy, Sofia," he said huskily. "I want you." He looked up and met her eyes. "Can I have you?"

She nodded. He could have whatever he wanted, if he kept calling her sexy. Her body, her heart, whatever. Anyway, she loved the guy, and in such a short time. As if her emotions were running on overdrive when it came to him.

Full speed ahead without brakes. Just a sputter now and then, when her insecurities got the best of her.

She followed his lead as he climbed back on the mattress and pulled her on top of him. She straddled his hips and felt him grow hard underneath his boxer briefs.

Instinctively, she pressed her heat down against him, wanting more.

He groaned and tugged his boxers out from under her. "Now I can feel you. Do it again."

Sofia was wet, she could tell by how easy it was to slide against him, almost allowing him to enter her at one point. Which wouldn't be a bad thing. She'd been on the pill since she was sixteen. Her mother had insisted on it. *Just in case some asshole wanted to get frisky*. Sofia wouldn't end up pregnant and alone.

Gray seemed to be enjoying how she worked her body. He bit into his bottom lip, and his hands grasped tightly to her waist.

Sofia took delight in having the power to please him. She leaned over, pressed her breasts against his chest, and brushed her lips against his.

They kissed slowly, seductively, as he lazily brought one hand up her back until it was bracing the nape of her neck. Then he deepened the kiss, doing with his tongue what Sofia knew he wanted to do with his erection.

Why make him wait? The tip of him was right there, ready to enter. It teased as he prodded up against her. Sofia decided to take it a step further, and maneuvered around until the head of him slipped inside of her.

"Sofia." He exhaled. "Baby, I need to put on a condom."

She slid down farther, taking him as far as she could. No pain this time. Just warmth that flowed through her body. She sat up slowly, bracing her hands against his chest and inching him the rest of the way until she was straddling him again.

He closed his eyes and inhaled some steady breaths. "This feels really good. Please tell me you're protected."

Sofia nodded. "The pill. I'm on the pill." She pushed off him slightly and sat back down.

He groaned.

"Did I do that right?"

"Oh, yeah. But do you mind if I get on top?"

The manly-man act again. Wonderful. The man had control issues, for sure. Wants to drive her car. Wants to drive her. "What if I want to drive?"

He stared at her like she'd lost her mind. "Trust me, I won't disappoint you." He sat up and gripped onto her backside. "Hold on."

Sofia wrapped her arms around his neck and decided to go along for the ride. He flipped her over onto her back and immediately thrust deep inside of her. She gasped and felt instant and surprising bliss.

One of his hands was still on her bottom and the other braced against the mattress beside her head. He withdrew halfway and glided back in several times in a steady rhythm. Warm pressure built inside her. On the brink of release, she pressed her head against the mattress and gripped his shoulders.

"There's one more place I want to show you." He gripped her calf and eased it over his shoulder. "My flexible little cheerleader."

"You got to be kidding me." She moaned, relishing in the impossible tightness, how he filled her completely.

Gray kissed her lips and whispered, "Come for me."

At his words, she cried out his name, pouring out her pent-up desire, a raging fire burned from her belly to her toes. And he reacted, jerking, filling her with his warmth.

He fell on the bed beside her and pulled her into his arms. "Not disappointed I drove, are you?"

Sofia shook her head, taking delight in the aftershocks.

~ * ~

Gray held her limp body in his arms for several minutes, happy he was able to please her to the point of exhaustion. If she asked for more, he'd give it to her. He'd give her anything.

He loved her. It had to be love. He was drawn to her, wanting to spend every second with her. And in such a short time. Three days ago, he wouldn't have believed this was possible, to care this much for a woman. But here he was, heart wide open and filled with what could only be love.

How could it be?

He didn't want to question his heart; it felt so right. Yet he couldn't tell her. What kind of man falls in love with a woman in two days?

Well, he had to admit the dreams had helped. He knew her, everything from what made her scream with pleasure to what made her laugh. That kind of closeness he'd never had with a woman. He was able to be himself, not the man his brother's death had forced him to be, but the real Grayson Phillips. The woman in his arms had put the paddles to his chest and enlivened his dead spirit.

She sighed heavily underneath him. "You're my hero, Gray," she said in a little girl voice.

Laughing, Gray propped himself up and kissed her lips.

She blushed and smiled cutely. "Are you hungry?"

"Starving."

~ * ~

Rachel crossed her arms and tapped her foot. "Where have you been?" she asked Hayes, who also had his arms crossed as he stood in the middle of her living room.

"You can't sit around in your apartment all day, Rachel. It's not good for you. What are you thinking?"

"I was waiting for you. I thought you were coming back."

"I never promised that. I said I would if I could."

Angry and desperate, she held her hand to her chest, wanting to ease the ache. "We don't have much more time together. Where did you go? Who's more important than me?"

He shook his head. "You know I have to take care of Gray. I hurt him and I want to fix it."

"You hurt me too. You left me, Hayes."

"I know." He reached out, but seemed to change his mind. "But I can't change the past. I can only attempt to make the future better."

"For Grayson?" Rachel let go of the tears welling up

165

in her eyes. "Is he with that waitress?"

"Yes, but you don't need to worry about that."

"I knew it." She tried to keep her hands from shaking. "Did he fuck her?"

"Rache, why do you care?"

"He was going to be my husband. I was going to spend the rest of my life with—"

"Because I wasn't here," Hayes yelled, startling her. "If I hadn't died, he never would've proposed to you, and you never would've accepted."

"But you did die," she yelled back. "Grayson was all I had left, and you took him from me. Now I have no one." Her legs grew wobbly, and she collapsed onto her knees. *How absolutely pathetic.* But if she couldn't have Hayes, what was the point of ever getting up?

He knelt beside her and disappeared as he wrapped his arms around her. "You have *you*, baby. Don't ever forget that. You're too good to be trapped in a loveless marriage. Life has too much potential. And you..."

Rachel felt him lift her chin with his finger and kiss her lips. She savored the nearness, the honey taste of his lips, the soft yet firm caress.

He released her too soon and reappeared before her. His eyes were reddened. "You are too beautiful and intelligent and sweet to sit inside this apartment and act like life is over. If you really want someone to love you, then love yourself, baby. You deserve that."

His words stung. Was he right? In her heart, she knew he was. She couldn't remember the last time she could look in the mirror with pride, knowing she was the woman staring back at her.

"Will you promise me something, Rache?"

She nodded, swiping the tears from her face.

"Do something for yourself with no one else in mind. Not Grayson, not me, and most definitely not your parents. Make it special. Make it count. Something you'd never give yourself in a million years. Can you do that?"

"I could try."

"Good." He stood and helped her to her feet. "I love you, Rachel. You can always hold that in your heart. I can't give you happily ever after, but you can find it on your own."

"Hayes?"

"Yeah?" He held her close. She could tell he was struggling to be all there for her because of the way his body trembled.

"I love you too. I always will."

"I know. I have to go. Don't forget your promise to me."

He faded slowly from her touch and her sight.

Then he was gone.

Rachel let the last tear fall from her cheek. That was it for crying. She'd be strong. She had to be. For herself.

The white envelope her mother had left her was sitting on the coffee table. She picked it up and glimpsed inside at the plane tickets.

Something she'd never do in a million years? Oh, yeah, this was it.

~ * ~

Gray helped Sofia into the boat. She shook out a blanket and dropped down with the picnic basket and her sketchbook. There was only one seat for the rower, so Gray sat there with a fishing pole he'd found in the basement. He'd try some bologna for bait, like his dad had shown him many years ago.

He glanced at their surroundings. Trees lined over half of the lake's bank, but it seemed most of them were removed or didn't grow on this half.

Only a few stood, shading the water. It was beautiful all the same.

The skies had patches of clouds here and there. No major threat of rain. They'd have a couple of good hours out on the water, at least.

The boat seemed like it'd had its day. The red and

white paint was chipping and some parts of the wood were splintering. But the boat was sturdy, and the water looked tempting. Speaking of tempting, Sofia had on a white tank top, no apparent bra, and khaki shorts she'd changed into after they'd showered together. Originally, he'd wanted to take her right back to bed to satisfy the growing need to have her as close as possible. To hold her and make love to her until they couldn't stand it anymore. Sofia convinced him otherwise, reminding him of the boat and what a fun time they'd have.

He still wore his jeans and that was it. Sofia had insisted on washing his clothes again. They were hanging on the line next to some bed sheets and a couple pairs of her panties she'd blushed about after he'd noticed them.

"Okay, Captain Phillips, I'm ready." Sofia pulled a large pink-flowered floppy hat out of the basket and stuffed it on her head. She looked adorable.

After launching the boat away from the dock, Gray grabbed the oars and started rowing to the middle of the lake. He couldn't help but wonder if in an alternate universe, he'd be out on the ocean with Hayes in a much larger boat. They'd drink beers and fish, not caring if they caught anything because they'd be laughing at a stupid, pointless joke—the best kind—and having the time of their lives.

Of course, now Gray would want Sofia to be there to laugh along with them. She'd fit in perfectly with her down-to-earth sweetness and sense of humor.

Snap out of it, Gray. Hayes isn't coming back.

But he did have Sofia. "You ever come out here before?"

She glanced at him from underneath the ridiculously large brim. "When I was a kid. I used to visit Nana during summer break, and she'd send me out here if I started whining about being bored. The Amish kids would come over and swim with me. There were tons of them, and they all seemed to be related in some way. The

168

girls, for the most part, just stared at me as if I were some sort of specimen to analyze and whisper about. The boys were bolder. They stripped down to their underwear and jumped right in. Needless to say, I had more fun with the boys. Actually, I had my first kiss out here."

"Really? Tell me more." If only to hear the sound of her voice.

"I was twelve, just starting to fill my training bra, if you know what I mean. His name was Elijah, and he was sixteen. He was *really* cute, despite the bowl haircut and suspenders."

Gray laughed. "I can't believe your first kiss was with an Amish kid."

"What's so funny? He had game like you wouldn't believe."

"What did he do? Woo you with his horse and buggy?"

"No, he cornered me in back of the shed."

"Hmm." Gray didn't know how to respond to that. His shoulders tensed at the thought of how naïve Sofia must have been at the age of twelve. He pulled the oars in and laid them out behind him. "Did he do anything else besides kiss you?"

She smiled up at him, the shadow from the hat covering her face. "Jealous?"

"Of you getting taken advantage of by a sixteen-year-old Amish kid? Where was your grandmother during all this?"

"Taken advantage of? Please. He kissed me. That was all. And maybe brushed his hand against one of my boobs accidentally on purpose. It was all innocent."

"Did it happen more than once?"

"No." Sofia sighed and slumped down. "That night I dreamed of him making out with this girl named Johanna. She hated me. The little twit used to call me *Fancy Nancy*."

"So you dumped him?"

"More or less." She shrugged. "I spent the rest of my time here locked in the guest bedroom. I hate my dreams sometimes." Her eyes grew wide and she grasped his knee. "Not the ones of you, of course. Those are my favorite."

Gray leaned forward and brushed his lips over hers. "I could see that last night."

She rearranged her hat and sat back on her bottom.

"What was up with the other dream? The one that frightened you?"

Frowning, she glanced down at her sketchbook she'd placed in her lap. "There's nothing I can do yet for that vision. I can only hope I figure it out before all those people die."

"How often do you have these sorts of dreams, where you feel obligated to help?" He pinched off a piece of bologna he'd retrieved from the picnic basket and baited the hook of the fishing pole.

"Depends. Sometimes nightly, sometimes once a month." She opened the sketchbook and put her pencil to it. "Doesn't that make you want to run screaming from here?" A half-giggle stopped short.

"Is that what other guys have done?" Gray had wondered why she'd remained a virgin into her twenties.

"No, they never got the chance to." Her hand whipped across the page, but she held the book at an angle so Gray couldn't see. "You're the only one who's passed the dream stage. I usually find out a man's not my destiny before the second date, before they've had the chance to find out about my little *gift*."

He cast the line into the water, pleased with where it had landed. "Do you think I'm your destiny then?" The question slipped off his tongue. Although he wasn't sure he wanted to hear the answer.

She looked up for a second and then back to her drawing. "Time will tell, I suppose."

Chapter Thirteen

Sofia peeked up at him again, taking in another detail. Today was the first time she was able to sketch him in person and not just from memory. He was such a gorgeous creature. All tanned muscle and broad shoulders against a tree-lined lake setting. This would be her favorite sketch to paint thus far, she was sure of it.

His stomach muscles clenched each time he cast the line, she noticed. *Good idea washing his clothes, Sofe.* She gave herself a mental pat on the back.

"What are you drawing?" he asked.

"You." What was the point in being shy now?

He smiled and set the fishing rod in a secure spot. "Can I see?"

"Nope."

"Please."

"Okay, but only a peek." She turned the book around to show him the *current* sketch.

He grabbed it from her with ease.

"Gray!" She reached for the book, but he held her back with one hand.

"Hold on, sugar. I want to see." His dark eyes roamed over the almost-complete picture. "This is really good."

"Thanks. Can I have it back now?"

"Why? What else is in here?"

"Nothing." Just evidence of her obsession with him. No biggie. She grabbed for the sketchbook again, but he held it high out of reach. The boat rocked underneath them, and she panicked and gripped the sides.

"If it's nothing, you wouldn't mind if I have a look." He flipped the page.

"I –" She had no words. Warmth rushed to her cheeks. What a bully he was.

"You what?" He sifted through the rest, narrowing his eyes at certain things.

"What do you think? I'm embarrassed."

"Why?" He stopped at a page that must have caught his eye. "You have talent, Sofia. I love this one the best. The passion. The details. It's amazing." He handed the book back finally.

Sofia blew out a breath and warily peeked down at the one he'd chosen. It was the both of them in a naked embrace, their bodies entangled together in a bed sheet.

His finger edged her face up to look at him as he knelt down before her. "I didn't mean to embarrass you. I hope you're not, because I love them. Every one of them."

"And what if I said I had paintings of them as well?" Sofia decided to throw it all out there. Every bit of mortifying honesty. "Lined up in my bedroom and in my closet."

"I...I'd say I was extremely flattered." If she didn't know any better, she'd think he was doing the blushing now.

"And?" Scared out of his mind? Wanting to get a restraining order?

"And I love that you want to draw me. It tells me a lot."

"Like?"

"It tells me you thought about me. And I hope it means that you wanted me. Maybe possibly that you might...love me." He waved his hand to get the last two

172

words out and then cocked his head. "Of course I could be wrong."

Sofia panicked and asked the first question that sprang to mind. "Where did you get those condoms anyway?"

He flinched, then exhaled and sat back on the bench. "In one of the cupboards above the sink area. Your grandmother must've left them for you. It had a note that said they were for you."

"Nuh uh. Are you kidding me?" This was interesting news and something to take her mind off the love comment. He'd hit the bull's eye on that one. There was no chance she'd admit it, though. She could vividly picture his alarmed expression if she were to blurt out what she really felt about him. *Oh, Gray, I fell in love with you before I even met you. I want to marry you and have your babies.*

No. Not gonna happen.

"Why do you think she left those for you?"

"Gosh, I don't know."

Probably in case her dream man showed up, but how would Nana even fathom that was a possibility? Ergh. The women in this family were too unpredictable. Sofia had some tough questions lined up for Nana, especially after seeing all the witchcraft stuff in the shed.

He cast the line out again and stared out at the water. "Were you seeing anyone else?"

"Me?" She let out a laugh. "Remember, I'm the girl who can't seem to get to a second date."

His shoulders visibly relaxed as his dark eyes swept over her. This was one of many times she wished she had Nana's mindreading powers. The emotions that shifted over his face seemed to run the gamut. If he'd just pick one, she could read him better.

Ah, well.

"A sandwich would hit the spot, right?" She opened the wooden braided picnic basket and pulled out two peanut butter and jelly sandwiches on wheat bread.

"Thanks." Gray took the sandwich and bit into it.

Sofia handed him a paper cup filled with milk from the thermos. He finished his sandwich and drank the milk down without a word. She nibbled, watching him warily.

"Tell me about your childhood," she said.

"Are you sure there's fish in this lake?"

She shrugged. "Were you a happy boy? Did your mommy give you enough hugs?"

"You said your *Nana* has the lake stocked every so often."

"I said my Nana *talked* about getting it stocked every so often. Did you and your brother get along?"

His shoulders bunched up again. "Am I wasting my time then?"

Uh oh. Sofia scooted up and wedged her body between his thighs. "I'll tell you if I'm wearing underwear or not, if you tell me about your childhood."

He dropped the pole behind him and slid his hands around and down the curve of her butt. "How about we skip all the talk and you show me?"

The idea was tempting, but… "No, Gray. I want to know more about you."

A drop of rain landed on his nose, and he looked up at the sky. "Thank you, God," he said, overdramatically. "We better get back to the dock."

"After you tell me."

"Sofia, we don't want to be out on a lake during a rainstorm."

"It was one sprinkle, you wimp. Tell me. Please."

"Fine." He took a breath and began his rant. "Hayes and I didn't fight much, but if my mom were alive, I'm sure she'd say different. She loved us, but I think sometimes she wanted to wring our necks. She passed away after a long bout with breast cancer when I was fifteen. My dad was about sixty years old at the time. He'd

174

had us late in life, but he kept up his health until we left for college. After, he seemed to fall apart, and passed away when I was nineteen. Hayes and I were devastated, but we knew he'd had a long, happy life, so we were able to get through it okay."

Some more rain dropped down around them, but Sofia didn't care. The man had been through hell. "And then you lost Hayes. How awful for you."

"I don't want your pity. I want to see you naked."

"That's not funny, Gray." More rain splattered on them and the lake around them. Water dripped off her hat and down her back.

"I'm not laughing." He drew her close, crowding her breasts to his chest. "I don't want to talk about all that stuff. I don't want to think about it. I just want you for as long as this thing between us will last. Do you understand?"

For as long as this thing would last?

Sofia nodded, her chest knotting painfully. She understood perfectly.

~ * ~

By the time they reached the dock, the rain was pelting down. Gray tied up the boat while Sofia grabbed her picnic basket and sketchbook. Water drenched her white tank top, revealing her dark nipples. The wet fabric outlined her plump breasts, making him ache to touch her.

He met her gaze, and she didn't seem pleased with the ogling. She clasped the sketchbook in front of her and ran toward the house without looking back.

Now that Gray thought about it, she hadn't glanced or said a word to him since they started rowing back.

Idiot. What the hell had he said wrong this time?

He left the fishing pole and followed her through the yard, stopping short to grab the clothes off the line. Everything was soaked again. He flung them over his arm and ran up the porch, leaving the sheets. The clothes could dry on the bench under the porch roof, he thought, and threw them down one by one in no specific order.

The sound of horses clopping down the street surprised Gray. Why would anyone take a dead-end road to this house unless they were planning on visiting? The horse and buggy turned off the road and onto the dirt lane. The horses trotted up, pulling the thin wheels of the carriage through the dips and loose stones.

Gray grabbed his t-shirt and tugged it on as the man in the buggy called the horses to a stop.

An Amish man wearing a brown shirt, black pants and suspenders dropped down onto the ground and jogged toward the house. Water dripped down the plain black hat that concealed most of his face.

"Hey there," the stranger yelled, and stopped at the top of the steps, barely out of the threat of rain. He stood eye-to-eye and width-to-width with Gray.

"Can I help you?" Gray straightened his back and shoulders. It wasn't often he met a man his own size.

"Penny Jones home?" He had a slight accent Gray couldn't quite describe. Measured and lifted toward the end, maybe? A thick beard covered half of his rugged face. And his shifty blue eyes shot Gray an inquisitive look.

Penny Jones must be Sofia's Nana. "No, I'm afraid she's not. Can I help you with something?"

"Well, who are you?" The man had no manners.

"Grayson Phillips. I'm a friend of Penny's granddaughter." Gray stuck his hand out, but the man ignored it.

"Sofia? She here?"

He knew Sofia? "What's your name?" Dickhead? Gray hadn't come across many Amish, usually only passing them up on the road. They kept to themselves for the most part and Gray had liked it that way.

The door opened and Sofia lurched out. "Elijah?" she asked, eyes wide. She'd changed into dry clothes, jeans and a V-neck top that showed way too much skin.

Elijah? The first kiss guy?

The man removed his hat and put it to his chest. Gray noticed his shifty gaze do a onceover...of *his* woman. Weren't these people supposed to be humble? Righteous?

Apparently not this guy.

"Little Sofia. Can't imagine what you've been up to all these years."

Gray wanted to knock the teeth out of his smile.

"Not much. You got married." Sofia reached up and felt the man's beard. "To Johanna?"

Gray did remember that little fact—single Amish men were clean-shaven and married men grew out their beards, but why did she have to touch him?

A low chuckle wheezed from his hairy mouth. "No. I married Joe's Lizzie. Remember her? She prided herself on those peanut butter cookies. Always brought them out to the lake over yonder and teased the boys with 'em."

"Right." Sofia pushed a damp lock of hair behind her ear and gave Gray a lightning fast glance. "Do you want to come in? I can put some coffee on."

Please, for the love of electricity, say no.

"Well, suppose I can visit for a spell. Until the rain lets up some." He jerked his head to the horse and buggy. "Picked some tomatoes for your grandma. Saw her at the market the other day and mentioned she was wantin' some fresh tomatoes."

Damn it.

"Oh, that sounds yummy. Go grab them and bring them in. I'll start the coffee."

They each parted ways, leaving Gray standing on the porch like an ass. A neglected ass. He stalked inside to where Sofia was pouring water into a teakettle.

"What's going on, Sofia?" he whispered into her ear, after bracing his hands on her waist.

"I'm making coffee. What do you think?"

"Why are you mad at me?"

"I'm not," she mumbled, and set the kettle on the burner.

"Kiss me, then." Gray leaned in, but missed her lips as she wiggled away from him.

"You're all wet. Why don't you towel-dry upstairs?"

He backed off, but decided against leaving Sofia alone with Dickhead. He sat at the table and watched as the guy strolled into the kitchen with a basket full of tomatoes.

Sofia took them from him with a smile. Cute and innocent. Gray adjusted himself in his wet jeans. He'd taken that innocence from her last night *and* this morning, and he'd be doing it again if it weren't for the intrusion.

Dickhead sat opposite Gray at the table, boring a hole into Sofia's ass with those shifty eyes. Nothing was innocent about this religious man.

"Where's your wife?" Gray asked.

"At home with the children."

Sofia brought over two coffee cups and thumped one down in front of Gray, set the other gently in front of Dickhead. His gaze searched her breasts now. Why didn't she notice and slap him upside the head? She poured coffee into each cup and sat down at the third chair, facing the window.

"Where is Penny today?"

"She's helping as a midwife for the, um, the Zook family over in Allen County. Connie Zook, I guess, is having a difficult pregnancy."

"Zook? I don't think I'm familiar. Did Penny leave in a hurry?"

"I don't think so. Why?"

"She's very friendly with my Lizzie. I'm surprised she hasn't mentioned it."

"Oh. That is surprising." Sofia strummed her fingers on the table. Her gaze roamed everywhere but to Gray.

178

Elijah took a sip of his coffee and nodded. "You two a couple?"

"Yes," Gray said loudly, his answer almost covering Sofia's "No."

No, huh?

Elijah raised his eyebrows and set his coffee down. "Well, I better be headin' off now. Tell Penny I stopped by." He tipped his hat back on and swaggered to the door.

Sofia walked with him. Gray followed.

"Oh, and let Penny know that salve she made for Lizzie's cut worked. Healed real quick."

"I will." Sofia gave Gray another flash of a glance. "Wait, Elijah. Are you going by Tom's Auto Shop, by any chance?"

"S'pose I could. Why? Havin' vehicle troubles?"

"Yes. My car isn't starting, and my friend here, his car is stranded down the road. He needs a tow truck."

Gray's chest pounded. His pulse beat against his temples. She was trying to get rid of him. But of course she was. According to her they weren't a couple.

To hell if they weren't.

"Down this road?" Elijah asked. "Didn't see any cars coming up. Sure it's still there?"

"No," Gray spoke up. "It's been a couple days. Might've been towed away by now."

"Too bad." Elijah made a tsking sound with his cheek. "Want a ride out to Tom's anyway? They've got a phone over there."

Sofia graced him another glimpse, her eyes unreadable. "Why don't you go?"

He shook his head. He wasn't going anywhere without her. "Thanks anyway."

~ * ~

Penny's head throbbed as she lay on Sofia's bed. A streetlight beamed through the sheer curtains. But it wasn't the electricity that pained her this time. She grasped the magnets together in her palm and squeezed.

Sofia resisted. For whatever reason, her granddaughter fought the spell. Was it doubt and distrust that plagued the young woman's heart?

Penny clasped the magnets to her breast. If she could give Sofia her strength, she would. There wasn't much to give. The spell was more powerful than any she'd ever conjured. She only hoped Grayson could handle the intensity. The emotions he must be feeling. The magnet that represented him sucked in all the energy while Sofia's struggled to reject it.

"Love him and he'll love you back," Penny whispered.

A painful spasm erupted at her temple, and nausea swamped her. This was an awful episode, possibly the worst yet. She leaned over and vomited into the pail she'd set by the bed just in case, then wiped her mouth with a tissue and carefully lay back down.

"Mom?" Laura stuck her head through the door. Her curly blonde locks fell off her shoulders. "Do you need anything?" she asked softly.

Such a sweet girl.

The pain was too overwhelming to answer. It was best to rest as still as possible.

Laura sat down on the bed and took Penny's hand. "Mom, should I take you to the hospital? I'm worried."

Penny closed her eyes. The throbbing was relentless.

Her daughter's mind spun into panicky overdrive, but Penny was too weak to block it out. Too weak to make everything better.

Through the pounding at her temples she heard Laura pick up the telephone.

"Herbert, hello. Yes, this is Laura. Laura Good... Can you come over?"

Penny wasn't sure if it was thoughts or speech. Her mind was blurring. Nothing was clear.

"I need your help. There's something wrong with my

mother."

Chapter Fourteen

Sofia shut the door behind Elijah. The room was silent except for the pattering rain on the wood-paneled house, the ticking of the grandfather clock, and Gray's unavoidable presence behind her.

"Why didn't you go?" she asked, still holding onto the door handle. "You had the perfect opportunity."

He didn't answer, forcing Sofia to face him. His damp white t-shirt clung to his every muscle, and his chest rose up and down with each steadied breath. His eyes were darker than ever with dusk settling upon the house.

Her attraction to him was undeniable. Her love for him was heart-and-soul-consuming, to say the least. But at what cost?

"What do you want from me?" she asked. "Sex? For as long as this *thing* will last?" She mimicked the words he'd said while they were on the lake. Eye-opening words that made her question every second she'd spent with him. "Maybe I failed to mention this before but I'm not —"

"Do you feel this?" He gestured between them. "Or is it only in my head?"

She didn't respond, afraid she understood exactly what he spoke of. The bond that drew them together. The one she'd been fighting off and on for the past couple of days. It grew stronger with every passing moment.

"I need you, Sofia. I *can't* leave here."

She fisted her clammy hands. "Of course you can leave. Whenever you want. In fact, why don't you leave now?" She attempted to turn the doorknob, but it wouldn't budge, ice-cold under her fingertips.

What was going on?

Swiftly, he was on her, backing her against the door. His thigh pressed between her legs, and his hands braced against the door on either side of her head. "You won't get rid of me that easily."

Sofia gulped and felt his mouth against hers. She parted her lips for him, and he pulled her bottom lip through his teeth, teasingly. A battle roared inside her. He couldn't simply take control of her. She wouldn't allow it.

"Back up," she said with force, surprising herself.

"You're kidding." His husky voice rumbled against her lips.

"No. Back up."

He did. Slowly.

"It's not only in your head," she admitted. "I feel this too." She repeated the same gesture he'd made moments ago.

He let out a breath, sounding much like relief. "Then let's go upstairs and quench it. Let's make love until we're both satisfied."

"That's just it, Gray. What if I don't want it to go away? What if it hurts me that you *do* want it to go away?"

"Not go away. Just tame it. I *ache* for you, Sofia, ever since the first time I walked in this door. Being with you, getting to know you, has stirred something in me. And it's not letting up."

Where was a white flag when she needed one?

Focus. She'd give him what he wanted, but she'd do it her way. Besides, she wanted him too. The inner depths of her yearned for him. His kiss, his touch, his rough voice when he whispered in her ear.

He followed as she walked into the kitchen, watching her with those sensual, predator eyes, waiting for her next move. She leaned against the butcher block and bumped her butt against the edge a few times. Pretty sturdy. This could work.

"Take off your clothes," she said. "They're dripping all over the floor."

His lips turned up into a slight grin. "Yes, ma'am."

The man wasn't an imbecile, obviously. He yanked his t-shirt over his head and flung it at her. She spoke too soon. Biting back a smartass remark, Sofia laid the damp shirt across the back of a chair, then turned to close the window curtains.

Gray nudged up beside her, throwing his jeans over another chair. Which meant...?

She sneaked a peek from the corner of her eye.

Oh yeah, he was naked and his manly component was wide awake, standing at attention.

His lips brushed against her ear. "Ready for my next order, ma'am."

"Er, um, why don't you stand over there?" She pointed over to the kitchen sink.

"Will I be washing your dishes?"

She shook her head. Boy, did he know how to rattle her.

He chuckled quietly as he made his way to the sink. Sofia's heart sped. She'd never seen this side of his body before. Broad shoulders curved down into a lean waist and lower to his nicely shaped butt. Not too big. Not too small.

Was this man perfect in every way?

The ache Gray mentioned earlier settled deep in her belly, forcing Sofia to hope this *thing* wouldn't end any time soon. Despite her fear.

~ * ~

184

Gray felt much better now that at least *he* had his clothes off. He'd always been comfortable in his own skin. He worked hard biking and lifting weights, keeping his body in shape, and at this moment, it was paying off. The blush on Sofia's face assured him his ache would be quenched soon. He leaned against the counter with his hands behind his head and waited for her next order.

Service with a smile was his motto tonight.

True, Gray didn't usually take orders very well, but this was different. His point was proven when she stood in front of him, sultry blue eyes staring up through her thick eyelashes.

"Now, take off *my* clothes."

He inhaled sharply. Thank God he wasn't on a horse and buggy in the rain right now with the creepy Amish guy. He'd had no intention of leaving Sofia. Not until this overwhelming urge to touch her and to love her subsided. If it ever did.

Hell, he didn't know what the future held, but as he slipped her shirt over her head, he couldn't imagine it would be possible to stop the momentum of this relationship. He removed the rest of her clothing and waited for the next command, hoping it would be a good one. His cock was growing impatient.

She backed up against the butcher block. "Can you lift me up here?"

Ah, her demands were becoming questions. Was her confidence diminishing? She had a problem with that, didn't she? Lord knew why. She was a beautiful woman.

"Anything you want," he said, and boosted her up by the waist.

Once his hands were on her warm skin, it was difficult to let go. He slid them up to her breasts and caressed her soft, plump flesh. "I can't decide which I love more, your breasts or your ass."

She cradled his jaw and edged it up to meet her eyes. "Fuck me." Her voice was so low and heated, it took a moment to grasp what she'd said.

Then it hit him...deep down in his groin.

She leaned back on her hands and spread her legs for him, all the while daring him with her eyes. The confidence was returning. Damn, he liked that.

Gray ran his hands back down to her waist and jerked her forward to the edge of the butcher block. If she wanted to be fucked, that was what he'd do.

She gasped but quickly gained composure, clasping onto his shoulders and bracing her legs around him. "You're such a bully."

He chuckled. "Would you rather I carry you upstairs and make slow, gentle love to you?"

She shook her head. "I want it hard and I want it here."

His balls tightened. "Are you wet for me?" Gray slid a finger inside her and brought it out to lick. "Just right."

Her legs trembled against his hips. "What are you waiting for, then?"

Without further delay, Gray grabbed his pulsing erection and guided it into her, driving in until he backed up against her innermost walls.

Her hands clenched down on his shoulders. "Again."

He withdrew halfway and thrust in once more.

She bit into her bottom lip and closed her eyes. "Faster."

Gray grasped her thighs to hold her up. Then he began pumping her hard and fast. She was taut and slick, fitting every inch of him perfectly.

She panted and flung her head back, holding tight to his neck now, contracting against him with each push. Her juices dripped down to his balls.

She was coming.

He quickened his pace, and she moaned, throwing her head forward to rest against his shoulder. The tips of her nipples bounced against his chest.

It was more than he could take. "I'm going to fill you up," he warned her, and managed two more thrusts before releasing deep inside of her.

"Oh, oh." She dug her fingernails into his shoulders and jerked against him.

Gray's knees almost gave out, but he held strong. He took some breaths to gain back control.

Sofia heaved out a sigh and lay back against the butcher block. "You're dismissed," she said with a huge smile.

He chuckled and pulled out of her, but he wasn't done with her yet. The ache settled into his groin again as he watched her breasts rise and fall. Unable to restrain himself, he bent down and licked the sweet spot between her thighs.

"Gray?"

~ * ~

Rachel hung up with the travel agent and smiled. She'd managed to change her flight plans without a problem. The sooner she got out of here, the better. Hayes had been right. She needed to gain back her dignity. Her *self*.

She couldn't allow her mother to change her into a person she didn't want to be, a person Rachel didn't even like. It was past time to grow a backbone.

True, she didn't know who the *real* Rachel Spencer was. Her likes, dislikes...her talents and passion, but wasn't it about time she found out? What better way to start than to get away from life as she knew it. She could start from scratch with a one-way ticket from Indianapolis to Denver and then Denver to Aspen. She'd always dreamed of living in the beautiful Rocky Mountain town of Aspen. Ever since she'd visited when she was a little girl. Now she'd get the chance.

Since the last seat on the small plane had gone to her, fate had to be on her side.

~ * ~

Sofia tiptoed naked downstairs and into the kitchen with a lamp at her fingertips. Gray had finally fallen asleep, and she hadn't wasted any time putting clothes on. Her body still quivered from his relentless lovemaking and kissing and licking. He'd been meticulously thorough in pleasing her, up until he crashed from exhaustion.

The evening had been pure ecstasy, but now she could barely walk. Every inch of her body was sore. Not to mention her breasts. He'd found his favorite part of her body, all right.

Now she was in search of hot tea and a couple of ibuprofen to relax her enough to get some sleep. She wanted to be able to curl up against his warm, firm body and fall into a decent slumber.

She filled the teakettle with water and set it on the lit burner, then jumped when she felt Sam brush up against her leg.

"Hey, girl. Where have you been all day?"

The cat meowed.

"Hiding from that nasty storm, you say? What a smart kitty."

Another meow.

Sofia got the hint, opened a can of cat food and dropped it into Sam's dish. The cat didn't touch the food. Instead, she hopped up onto the butcher block and swatted her paw toward Sofia.

"What? You saw that earlier? Don't tell Nana, okay? She's not too fond of people making a mess in her kitchen."

Sam hissed and swatted again.

"What's wrong, girl?" Sofia took a step toward the cat, but stopped short when a chill breezed across her arm.

Shoot. She knew that phenomenon quite well. A spirit was here. But why? Sofia didn't know how to conjure them. She was pretty certain Nana didn't have the ability either. Although it seemed Nana had a few surprises up her sleeve...or in her shed.

Sofia ignored the presence. What else could she do? Say hello? Ask if it wanted some tea?

She reached to open the cupboard door and noticed a sticky note attached to the front. "Where did you come from?" The note hadn't been there earlier in the daylight, and now the darkness made it difficult to read. She snatched the paper and brought it to the lamp.

Sofia, You fill me with happiness. I love you with all my heart. ~Gray

Oh, wow. She held the note to her bosom and sighed.

He loved her.

But when had the sneaky devil had the chance to leave this note? Maybe she *hadn't* noticed it earlier. Strange that he wrote the sentiment down rather than tell her. Hearing the words from his lips would mean so much more...

She shook her head. It didn't matter. He loved her. That's what was most important. She loved him, too, and couldn't wait to tell him. And hear the words back. Grabbing the lamp, she sprinted as fast as her sore body would take her up the stairs, down the hall, and into the bedroom.

Gray was sprawled out on his back. His chest barely moved. He looked so peaceful, Sofia couldn't bear to wake him.

Oh, well. There was always tomorrow. She stuffed the note in the side pocket of her duffle bag and joined *her* man on the bed. His arm instinctively wrapped around her when she laid her head on his chest. Pure heaven. She had no doubt that in his arms was where she wanted to spend the rest of her nights.

~ * ~

Sofia opened her eyes and realized she was in the airplane again. She walked through the aisle, listening to the forlorn whirring of the engine as they glided through the air. Out the windows, she was able to see clouds. This was the first time she'd been able to see anything other than haze in the sky. Anxious to get a better look, she leaned over the two men wearing polo shirts, khaki shorts and sandals with socks underneath.

A fighter jet flew nearby. *What the heck?* Two pilots wearing helmets with those microphone thingies attached peered over at the plane. Their lips moved, and Sofia wished she knew what they were saying.

She supposed they were wondering why everyone was dead. Maybe they were worried about where this plane would land once it ran out of fuel, since no one would be able to land it safely. Or maybe the plane would crash before it ran out of fuel. Too many scenarios and none of them good.

Sofia glanced at the terrain below.

Mountains. They were headed into a mountain range where people might or might not have homes and a family, dogs and cats, schools full of children.

Could it be that Sofia was responsible for more than just the lives of the people on this airplane?

Ergh. She couldn't think about that. *Focus, Sofe.*

The fact that they were flying over a mountain range was at least one clue.

She looked down at the middle-aged man her knee was pressed into. "Sorry. This is really important."

What did it matter, Sofe? He's dead.

"Not if I can help it," she reminded herself.

The man was wearing a leather band watch on his wrist and the hands were moving.

It worked.

Sofia grabbed his arm and checked the time.

Twenty minutes after five. Good. This was good. She was gathering more info. She'd have this solved in no time. Rejuvenated, she searched for more clues. She closely inspected each person as she continued to walk down the aisle. What she was looking for, she had no idea, but something would poke out at her. It had to.

Seat twenty, twenty-one...

Twenty-two wasn't empty anymore. No, it certainly wasn't. The woman from the restaurant sat there. Sofia almost hadn't recognized her at first. Her face wasn't the porcelain shade she remembered. Her skin was blue, tinted with death, frozen in time.

Dear Lord.

Sofia clamped her hand over her mouth as her stomach revolted. No, no, no. Her legs faltered and she stumbled back a few steps, bumping into the seat behind her.

How could this be? It didn't matter. Now more than ever she needed to stop this plane from flying.

She had to save Rachel. Gray's ex-fiancée.

Chapter Fifteen

Penny kept her eyes shut tight as she lay in the hospital bed with Laura and Herbert sitting nearby. They'd been whispering small talk for the past hour, and Penny had no intention of interrupting.

Her migraine had settled down after the doctor ordered her MRI, gave her medication, stuck an IV in her, and admitted her into a room to sleep for the night. But Penny knew none of this had cured her.

Her true champion had been Hayes.

He'd come to her and told her of his plan to concoct a love note for Sofia and sign Gray's name. Hayes had been certain this would bring Sofia around. Obviously, it had. The migraine was gone, and Penny felt renewed. Ready to take on the world.

But not yet. Sometimes it was best to let the world spin on its own axis while you sat back, relaxed...and listened a little more closely.

"Thank you for all your help, Herbert," Laura said, for the third time since they'd sat beside Penny's bed.

Penny had closed her eyes and faked sleep the instant she'd heard them walk into the room.

Not until now did she allow herself one peek, only to notice Herbert held her daughter's hand. He squeezed her palm and smiled. A warm, gentle smile.

Laura didn't pull away. Tears welled in her beautiful eyes. "You were the first person who popped into my head to call."

Penny did a mental cheer.

"I'm glad you thought of me," Herbert replied. "I was convinced you didn't like me."

"I do like you." Laura wiped a tear from her cheek. "I suppose that's why I've treated you so poorly."

"Oh." Herbert bunched his forehead.

"But I'm sorry. I really am, and I promise I'll try to be nicer from now on."

He smiled again. "That would be wonderful. And I'm glad to help. If there's anything you ever need or want, feel free to call me...or come over."

"Thank you," she said a fourth time. A blush colored Laura's cheeks and she glanced Penny's way, forcing Penny to shut her eyes.

Which was fine with her. She'd seen enough to allow herself some real sleep. Just for a bit. A mother's work had to end sometime.

~ * ~

Sofia lurched up in bed and searched for the clock, taking a moment for her eyes to adjust.

Come on, come on. Okay, it was past eight in the morning. She'd slept in too late. *Dang it.* She threw a robe on and noticed for the first time that Gray wasn't in bed with her.

"Gray," she called out, probably a little

hysterically. "Gray!"

What the heck. This was important, and she needed his help.

Quick footsteps padded down the narrow hallway, and he appeared at the bedroom door with a toothbrush in his mouth, wearing nothing but his boxer briefs. "What's wrong?" he asked, wide-eyed, mouth full of toothpaste.

"You're not going to believe this." Sofia stuffed herself into a pair of panties and then jeans. "But humor me, if you can. We need to find Rachel. I dreamed she's on the plane."

Sofia didn't bother looking at Gray's expression, knowing this would shock him more than anything she'd shared with him yet. She dropped her robe, snapped on a bra, and tugged on a faded Indianapolis Colts t-shirt. Gray's footsteps creaked back to the bathroom, and Sofia's heart dropped into her stomach.

Undoubtedly, this was where he came to his senses and realized having a psychic girlfriend wasn't the best idea. Maybe he finally understood that life would be much easier if he simply found a woman who didn't have dreams that woke him in the middle of the night. Maybe the tramp would know how to make eggs without burning them too. Not fair at all.

She shoved her feet into a pair of tennies, grabbed Gray's note, kissed it and stuffed the paper in her jeans pocket. She'd always have the memory of the last couple of days with him.

The hallway was empty and so was the bathroom. He must've high-tailed it out of here.

She stopped in at the bathroom to tie her hair back into a ponytail and freshened up some. Rachel wasn't going to bother opening the door for a wild-haired waitress who reeked of morning breath, especially one who predicted death in the near future, perhaps as early as today.

This wasn't going to be easy, but what other choice did Sofia have? She needed to find out the flight number and destination, at least. Then who knew what?

She bounded down the stairs, scaring Sam at the bottom. The cat shot into the kitchen and jumped onto the butcher block. Sofia followed.

Still no sign of Gray. *Shoot.* He could've at least said goodbye. Or... *I'm sorry it won't work out between us. Forget about the note I wrote you last night. I didn't realize you were psychotic.* Who knew her mom had been right all these years? When the going got crazy, men left. That's what her dad had done anyway.

Tears stung her eyes as old memories surfaced.

Stop it, Sofe. Concentrate on the task at hand.

She sniffed back the tears, poured Sam some dry cat food, more water, and made her way to the front door. She strode outside...and ran into Gray who stood, fully dressed, on the porch.

He grabbed her shoulders and peered into her eyes. "Are you sure it was her?"

Sofia nodded and blew out a breath of relief. He hadn't left her. Not yet.

"And she was dead? She was on the plane dead?"

"Yes. She sat in the seat that had been empty in

all the other dreams."

"I need to know for sure because I can't take my new girlfriend to my ex-fiancée's apartment and throw this all in her face if there's any possibility it's not true. You can understand that, right?"

His new girlfriend. The words warmed Sofia from the inside out. "I'm positive it was her, Gray."

He wiped at a tear Sofia hadn't realized had trailed down her cheek. "Okay," he said. "Let's find a way out of here."

~ * ~

Rachel woke up with Hayes's heavy arm wrapped around her waist. She didn't bother trying to find him with her eyes, knowing he most likely wasn't visible. The mere thought of it left her feeling empty and alone.

"Morning," he said, and held her close. "Are you better today?"

"Than yesterday? Yes, much better than yesterday." She'd been at her lowest the day before and never wanted to go there again.

Although her heart still ached. She knew she'd lose Hayes soon, at any moment. "What if?" A thought sprang to mind and began to rush out of her mouth, but she stopped it.

"What are you thinking, Rache?"

"What if...what if I were to die? Could I be with you then?"

"No." He reeled away, deserting her.

Rachel turned onto her back and winced at the angry look in his eyes. "It was just an idea."

"Don't think that way. You need to live, baby. Your life is important to many people, and soon it'll be important to you again. You can't give up."

She sat up. "But what about you? Won't you miss me?"

"Of course I will, but I have to move on. I can't stay in this limbo forever."

"Move on where? Where will you go? Why can't we do it together?"

"Rachel, please don't say that anymore. You have to live. I can't tell you how essential that is."

"But— "

"You won't be able to find me if you end your life. I'll have crossed over, and you'll be stuck."

"Where, Hayes?" His riddles were beginning to frustrate her.

"I can't say. I don't even know myself. All I know is I'm driven to help Gray, and now I understand why I've come to help you too. It's so clear to me. You have to live. You have a journey ahead of you. You're going to go on and do great things." His dark eyes gleamed with intensity.

"Like what?" Rachel couldn't imagine. She'd thought herself powerless to do anything *great* since the day she was born. She was simply Rachel Spencer, eternal student, loving sister and obedient daughter of Tim and Nora Spencer. That was all.

"Live and love yourself for as long as this world will allow you, okay? Tell me that you'll do this for me. Make me proud."

"You'll be watching?"

"Yes. But I don't know what passage lies in front of me."

"Heaven? Does heaven exist?" Rachel reached out to touch him, but he began to fade.

"I love you, Rachel. Be strong and live."

"Hayes? Don't go yet." She grabbed at his arm, but there was nothing tangible to grasp. She fell forward onto her bed.

~ * ~

Gray kicked the hatchback's bumper, causing half of it to fall to the ground.

"Gray!" Sofia swatted his arm.

"Sorry. I'll pay to have that fixed," he muttered. The damn thing still wouldn't start, and it irked the hell out of him.

"Fine. Just don't kick my baby anymore. This car is practically a part of the family. I've had it since I was sixteen."

"Maybe it's time for an upgrade."

"Don't get grouchy with me, Grayson. Your stupid car is probably sitting in a junkyard right now."

Gray clenched his jaw at the thought of that. He'd paid a shitload of money for that BMW only a year ago. That car better not have a scratch on it.

"Let's go find out." He grabbed her hand, and they started up the lane to the road.

She didn't resist like he thought she might. Instead, she kept a steady pace at his side. "You think the car might still be there?"

He shrugged.

"Why are you mad at me?"

"I'm not." He was frustrated. His mini-vacation in the country with Sofia was ending. Time to get back to the real world. Well, as soon as they found Rachel. Not that his ex-fiancée was going to believe a word Sofia said. He imagined her reaction would be somewhere between appalled and annoyed. All directed at Gray, of course, for bringing his new woman into her home.

If Gray didn't trust Sofia, he wouldn't bother. In fact, he'd have left as soon as she'd told him about this mysterious coffin-plane flying through the sky.

But he did trust her, and he loved her even more. Which meant Rachel needed to be saved, along with the rest of those poor people. How had Sofia dealt with this enormous responsibility her entire life?

She remained quiet for the first quarter mile down the road, holding tight to his hand and chewing at her lip.

"It's not my fault I have these dumb visions."

"I know." Gray glanced down at her again. Redness rimmed her eyes. *Damn.* He hated that he'd upset her. "And I'm not mad at you. I swear I'm not."

She nodded and dropped her head to watch the dirt road in front of her. Gray slowed his pace so she could keep up. It was all he could think to do. He was the first to admit he hadn't a clue when it came to women. They were an anomaly to Gray. Had been for his whole life.

Hayes would know what to say to cheer her up. If only Gray had an inkling of that charm and understanding of women.

Tell her you love her.

No, it wasn't time for that yet. Maybe later on tonight, after they'd saved the day. Gray would take her to his place. They'd shower and make love. He'd order in some Italian, light some candles, play some music. *Then* he'd tell her how he loved her from the very depth of his soul.

Maybe she'd say it back. If she loved him. There was no telling.

At least ten minutes passed before Sofia spoke again. "Are we getting close to where your car should be? It's pretty hot out here." Her cheeks were pink from the sun shining down on them.

Gray surveyed the flat road ahead of them but saw nothing for what seemed miles and miles. "The car's gone. It would be down this way somewhere, but I don't see anything on the horizon."

Just a long road in front of them, a cornfield to the right, and an Amish cemetery to the left. Plain wooden slats marked the graves, and a white picket fence surrounded the area. Eerie.

Gray's parents and brother were buried side-by-side at a well-kept cemetery in Indianapolis. Their stones were upright, large, and made of granite. Gray had seen to it they'd gotten the best. Although he hadn't visited them since Hayes' funeral. He'd been too stubborn. It was time to do that again soon.

"Look," Sofia said, and poked him in the ribs.

His gaze followed to where she was staring. A horse and buggy drove down a road perpendicular to the one they walked. "Hey," Gray called out twice, but either they couldn't hear him or they were ignoring him. Probably the latter.

From his minute knowledge of the Amish, he understood they were aloof and mostly didn't want to have anything to do with non-Amish people, or the English, as he had heard it said before.

"Assholes," he muttered, definitely grouchy.

"They're not assholes, Gray. They're just careful. You're not exactly a small man." She shaded her eyes with her hand. "What should we do?"

"Where's your boyfriend live?" As soon as the words left his mouth, he bit his lips shut.

"Are you talking about Elijah?" She glared at him. "He has a wife, Gray. And children. I'm sure his family would not appreciate you saying—"

"Sorry." He cut her off. "I shouldn't have said that, but the guy *was* checking you out like you were piece of prime rib yesterday."

"He was not." Sofia shoved against his stomach. "Elijah may have been a little bit frisky as a teenager but he's a grown man now. A grown *religious* man."

"Right. I forgot. He must be a saint of a man with an angelic family living amongst all these virtuous people." If Gray could've been more sarcastic, he would've.

Sofia set her hands on her hips. "What are you trying to get at?"

"I'm sorry to break it to you, sugar, but men are men no matter what clothes they wear or vehicle they drive. If we see a woman as attractive as you, we're gonna look."

"Even if you're married?"

Time to shut up now, Gray. "Some men more than others," he mumbled.

She rolled her eyes at him. "I don't know where he lives, but the closest house that I know of isn't too far away. We'll have to walk to the end of this road, turn right and it's, I don't know, a mile or two down that way."

Gray surveyed the area again. "Why don't we cut through this cornfield to save some time?"

~ * ~

Sofia inhaled the sweet scent of the corn and tried not to think about the note in her pocket that Gray hadn't mentioned all day. Darn him.

He'd been grumpy and quiet, and Sofia wished he'd say the words she desperately wanted to hear. Unless, of course, he didn't believe them anymore.

She heaved out a sigh, and Gray gave her a brief glance before setting his focus toward their trek through the paths of the enormously tall cornstalks. His manly-man decision to cut through the stupid cornfield had gotten them lost, Sofia was sure. They'd been walking for at least an hour.

Why hadn't she taken one of Nana's many wristwatches to check the time? Who knew if the airplane would go up today, tomorrow, or a week from now? The only clue Sofia had was that it would happen around five o'clock.

Gray stopped short, and Sofia bumped into him. "Fuck," he said, and shoved his hand through his hair. "This is nuts."

"What?" She peeked around his waist and saw what caused his cursing. Broken, crooked stalks appeared where they'd once been. "Are we going in circles?"

"It appears so, Sofia," he grumbled. "Which doesn't make a damn bit of sense because according to the sun, we've been going the same direction this whole time." He shivered and spun around. "Did you feel that?"

"Feel what?"

"The cold air."

Sofia wiped a bead of sweat from her temple. "No cold air over here. Are you feeling okay? Want to take a break?"

"Just for a minute. I need to think." He snatched his wrinkled dress shirt from his back pocket, shook it out on the ground, then gestured for her to sit.

He may be a grump, but at least he was still a gentleman.

Sofia dropped to her bottom, and he sat down next to her. His hands trembled as he wrapped them around his knees.

"Gray? What's wrong?" She inched up to him and cradled his jaw. His skin was cold to the touch.

"Nothing. I'm fine." He eased her hand away and set it on her lap.

"What's going on with you? Are you feverish?"

"I said I'm fine, Sofia," he snapped, and met her eyes. "Sorry. I just get this feeling that...never mind." He pressed his thumb and forefinger to the bridge of his nose and clenched his eyes shut.

"What, Gray? You're starting to scare me."

"I don't mean to... I'm sorry." He opened his eyes and reached for her. "Come here, sugar. I need you."

Without question, she allowed him to pull her onto his lap. She'd do anything to make him feel better.

Their lips met, and he slipped his tongue into her mouth as if he hungered for her. Nothing was cold about his lips. They were quite warm and tasty. As were his hands as they slid up her shirt, finding her breasts. He squeezed her flesh, and Sofia inadvertently let out a whimper against his mouth.

"Did I hurt you?"

"Just a little sore from last night. It's okay."

"No, it's not. I never want to hurt you. Are you sore here too?" He gently rubbed between her thighs.

"Sort of. Nothing a hot bath won't take care of."

"I was too rough last night. Should've been more careful with you."

"No, you were fine. It was wonderful, Gray. Especially after I found the note." Sofia couldn't hold her tongue any longer. "I love you too."

"I love...what? What note?" He bunched his forehead seeming genuinely perplexed.

"The note you wrote me." The words rushed out as a squeal.

"Sofia, I don't know what you're talking about."

Seriously? He was going to play games like that, huh?

"The note where you said you loved me. Why are you doing this? If you don't mean it anymore, then say so." She launched from his lap.

He grabbed her waist and held her down. "What are talking about?"

Tears stung her eyes, but she held them back. Anger, not tears, was what this man deserved. How dare he play with her heart like this? She dug her hand into her pocket, plucked out the little yellow paper and shoved it against his chest. "There. I have it still. You can't deny it."

He picked up the crumpled note with one hand and held her down with the other. After reading the words, his face paled. "Sofia, I didn't write this."

~ * ~

The slap across Gray's face stung.

"Let me go." Sofia struggled against him, tears brimming her eyes.

"No. We need to talk this through. Where did you find this note?"

"Stop it, Gray. I get it, okay? You don't love me. You think I'm nuts." Her breath came up in spurts as she held back her sobs. "Be a man and admit it."

He couldn't release a breath. Air packed his lungs, useless and painful. The note wasn't even in his handwriting, but he had a damn good guess whose it was.

Only problem was how could that be possible?

Sofia squirmed against him again so he drew her into an embrace, shoving aside every other outlandish thought in his head. The woman in his arms was all that mattered now.

"Nothing's over," he said softly against her ear. "I do love you, Sofia. I love you so much it hurts, but I didn't write that note. Now tell me where you found it."

Before she could answer, someone pushed through the cornstalks. A large, husky man with a beard and a black hat stared down at them.

Elijah.

"Everybody okay, here?" he asked.

Gray stood, bringing Sofia with him. He set her down, picked his shirt off the ground, and wiped her tears with it. She let him, staring at him with a stunned expression. Gray wanted to kiss her, but they had an audience.

Thank God. "We're good," Gray said. "We were lost. Sofia got scared."

"Oh?" Elijah looked to Sofia for confirmation and she nodded. "Well, then, you two lovebirds need a ride?"

"That would be great. Thank you."

~ * ~

Sofia sat snug in between the two large men as the buggy sped down the bumpy road with the horses clip-clopping in front. The blanket-covered bench seat bounced them up and down as the wobbly wheels of the carriage dipped in and out of gravelly cracks and grooves.

"Yah, yah," Elijah yelled and cracked the whip. Like they weren't going fast enough. Was the man insane?

Gray's arm tightened around her waist. The poor guy was sitting at the edge and there didn't seem to be much of anything that kept him from falling out with the next big bump.

Sofia got a grip on his jeans belt loop. She wasn't losing him now. Not after hearing that he loved her—for real. She'd nearly lost all sense and reason when he'd told her he hadn't written the note. But, then, who had? A ghost?

Hmm... What about the chilled feeling she'd experienced in the kitchen right before she found the note? No. Spirits couldn't write and leave messages. They didn't have the power to interfere in people's lives. Did they? And, if so, then why? Why would some spirit floating around at Nana's house leave her a love note and sign Gray's name?

Sofia shook the mystery from her head for now. Maybe they'd figure it out later and maybe they wouldn't. She didn't really care. The note didn't need to be real. Just the love.

She met Gray's gaze and he smiled at her. *I love you*, his gorgeous lips said silently.

Yep, that was all she needed. She smiled back, so big that her cheeks hurt.

Quit being a dork, Sofe.

Ah, who cared? Obviously, the man loved dorks.

"Whoa," Elijah said, as they pulled into Tom's Auto Body shop. This was as far as he'd been willing to take them, which didn't bother Sofia one iota. The less time on the horse and buggy, the better.

Gray jumped down and then lifted Sofia to the ground. "We appreciate it, Elijah." He picked his wallet out of his back pocket and began to pull out a twenty.

"Noooo," Elijah grumbled. "Glad to help." He tilted his hat and winked at Sofia. "Take care now. You stop by and visit some time, hear?"

Then he cracked the whip and was off, just like that.

Gray clenched his jaw, probably holding back a growl.

She squeezed his hand. "We made it here alive at least."

His frown thawed into a warm grin, and they turned to see Tom standing at the door to the white building with no windows. Just a garage with an old

Pinto up on the racks.

Tom had on a filthy used-to-be-white tank top that barely covered his beer gut, and suspenders that held up a pair of grubby tan slacks. A toothpick stuck out of his pasty face that displayed a deep scowl. "What you two's want?"

Chapter Sixteen

After Gray had explained their situation, Tom finally let them into his office. Any friend of the Amish was no friend of his, he'd said. Which was odd, considering the location of his shop. But Gray wasn't going to argue. The man had the only phone in a twenty-mile radius.

"I assure you, he was only giving us a lift," Gray had told him. "I can't stand those people myself."

Sofia had nudged him. He'd pay for that later, he was sure. The truth was, he didn't have anything against the Amish, especially after one of them had done him a huge favor by getting him out of a dead-end cornfield in a matter of seconds.

It'd been embarrassing to discover if they'd only walked another ten feet, they would've reached the road, and across it was Elijah's family home. Ten children had scurried outside to see what all the commotion was about, along with a very pregnant wife who didn't smile once.

Gray didn't blame her.

Sofia had cheered up right away, saying hello to each and every one of those kids. Lord, he hoped she didn't want to have that many children. Three was the limit for him. He shrugged. Maybe four.

Gray halted that thought process. Kids? Marriage hadn't even entered his mind. Until now. He watched her charm the suspenders right off Tom with her sweet little smile, and realized he wanted nothing more than to marry and spend the rest of his life with Sofia.

"Gray?" She patted his arm, breaking his thoughts. "Tom says he has a car we can borrow."

"Rent," Tom corrected.

"For a small fee," she added and smiled.

"Sounds great. What is it?"

"It's right out back. Let me show you." Tom gestured for them to follow.

"Wait," Sofia said. "Do you have a restroom I could use?"

"Sure thing. It's right through that door right there. S'cuse the mess. It ain't been cleaned by a lady in a while."

"Oh." The smile disappeared. She looked up at Gray. "I won't be long."

He brought her hand up to kiss. "Meet you out front."

Tom led Gray through the backdoor and into what appeared to be a scrapyard. More than twenty cars were gutted. Others were melded together with mismatched parts. A red hood on a blue car, a primer gray door on a white car, and far in the distance behind a stack of tires, Gray spotted it.

His BMW.

"This here's a fine car." Tom banged the hood of a purple Honda Accord with yellow doors. The car had been lowered to about two inches above the ground. "Have to watch it on the bumps, but it runs like a fox chasing after a jackrabbit."

"That's my car," Gray blurted out, thinking of no other strategy to get his baby back.

"What you talking about?"

"That black BMW over there behind the tires. That's *my* car. Did you find it alongside the road?"

"Maybe. How do I know it belongs to you?"

"Check the registration. My name's on it. Grayson Phillips. And —" He yanked his keys from his pocket and hit the keyless entry button. The lights blinked. "I have the keys."

"Well, now," Tom said with blazing red cheeks. "Why'd you leave a perfectly good car out on the road like that? Someone coulda stole it. Good thing I was there with my tow truck."

"Right." Gray held his tongue. If the car still didn't start, he might need to persuade Tom to take a look at it. To Gray's delight, the engine turned over immediately. And — he did a once-over of the exterior and interior — everything seemed to be in order. No scratches or dents or rips. His baby was perfect, as usual.

He drove the car to the front of the shop and waited for Sofia, proud to be able to show her one of the things he'd accumulated by working his ass off. Over his shoulder, Tom stood at the front door, wringing his filthy car-thieving hands together.

If they hadn't been in a hurry to save people's lives, Gray would've called the cops to send Big Tom to jail for grand theft auto.

"Wow. Tom rented us *this* for a small fee?" Sofia slid into the passenger's seat and ran her fingertips over the beige dashboard and the leather upholstery. "Ooh. Very nice."

Gray wasn't sure why, but he grew hard in his jeans. It was true then that a man's car was an extension of his you-know-what. "Do you like it?"

"I *love* it." She swept a come-hither stare up his body. "It suits you."

"Well, that's good." Gray leaned over and kissed her. "Because it's mine."

"Nuh uh. Are you kidding?"

"I kid you not." Gray revved the engine and left Tom in a cloud of dust.

~ * ~

Penny lay in Sofia's bed, glad to be home from the hospital. It'd been a scare, but everything turned out fine. Herbert had given them a ride home and helped Penny up the stairs. Of course, she didn't need the help. She was finer than fine china. Not an ache in her old body. Nevertheless, it didn't hurt to give the man a reason to stick around the house for a bit.

Just in case she had a relapse.

From the thoughts vibrating from Herbert's mind, he was glad to spend more time with Laura.

With a smile, Herbert said, "Call us if you need anything." Then he closed the door behind him.

Hmm. Daughter down, still working on the granddaughter.

"You feeling better?" Hayes's voice asked from the corner of the room, and then the side of the bed indented.

"Much better. Thank you." Penny wondered why she couldn't read his mind this time. Could it be because he was on his way to crossing over?

"I wanted to thank you, actually, for helping me. Your spell worked out great."

"That's wonderful. So they've said they love each other?"

"Yes, and I think I'll be able to move on now, because Gray seems very happy."

Yes, Hayes was leaving. Penny's heart went out to him. He was such a nice boy. "Wonderful. What of Rachel? Did she find true love?"

"She's well on the way. You might like to know she has a gift like your daughter does. She can see me and touch me. She's even called me, buy I don't think she knows this."

"Interesting. I wonder if I know her mother or grandmother. Gifts run in the family, you know."

~ * ~

Rachel drove up to the Spencer Estate, as her

mother liked to call it. Really, the residence was an immaculate museum, not an appropriate place for a child to grow up. Somehow, Rachel and her sister had managed without breaking too many things.

She felt refreshed since Hayes's last visit. The thought that she, Rachel Spencer, had the potential to do great things had given her a boost of confidence. A small one, but still. It was enough for her to shrug off the idea of dying and concentrate on living, as he'd told her to do. She wanted to make him proud.

Besides, once she'd calmed down she realized taking her life wasn't the answer. The very idea had been ridiculous. Selfish, really, now that she thought it through. Suicide? No, she couldn't do that to her parents and her sister. Hayes was right. She really did have a lot to live for.

Sighing, she shut down the engine and sat there for a moment. Her parents weren't home, she knew. She'd called ahead and asked Therese, the housekeeper, when they'd be back. Therese had said Dad was at work until late, of course, and Mom was out running errands for the wedding.

The wedding had turned into more of a hobby for her mother than anything else. Something she could talk about with her friends at the country club.

Still, Rachel felt obligated to pay back every penny her parents had put into the ceremony. She grabbed the envelope on the seat next to her and made her way across the lush green lawn to the front door.

She rang the doorbell and Therese answered right away. Her silver hair was up in a loose bun and she smelled like Pine Sol, as usual. "Rachel," she said, as though it were a surprise. "What are you doing here? Your parents aren't home." The woman who used to push her on the swings and give her homemade shortbread cookies after school was getting up there in age. It seemed her mind was slipping as well.

"I know, Therese. I just talked to you."

"Oh, that's right. What do you need, my dear?"

"I need a huge favor, actually." Rachel handed Therese the envelope. "That's a letter for my mother, but I was wondering if you could wait to give it to her until after tomorrow."

Rachel wanted to shrink back into her shell for being such a coward. This wasn't exactly how she should be beginning her new life—by not standing up to her mother in person. But sometimes a girl had to start at the bottom to work her way up. That was her excuse, and she was sticking to it.

Therese flipped the envelope back and forth, as if she'd figure out what was inside somehow.

Rachel didn't see any harm in her knowing.

"It's a letter to Mother saying I'll be moving away and a check to pay her back for the wedding. Well, the first installment, anyway."

"You won't be marrying Grayson, then?" Therese gazed at Rachel through silver eyelashes.

"No, I won't."

She smiled mischievously and stuffed the envelope in her apron. "I'll do as you asked, my dear."

"Thank you, Therese." Rachel gave her a partial hug. "You won't forget?"

"No, my dear. I'll be looking forward to it."

Rachel thanked her again and headed back across the lawn.

"My dear?" Therese called out, and Rachel turned around. "Well done."

Well done? The woman always was a little puzzling. Rachel simply waved and hurried to her car before her mom showed up.

~ * ~

Just past two o'clock they arrived at the apartment complex.

Sofia followed Gray through the front door, up the

214

stairs, and down a hallway to where Rachel lived. The building was quaint. The carpets were older. The wallpaper was pretty, but flaking here and there. Not at all swanky, like Sofia had expected.

She'd only seen Rachel once, for a short period of time, but Sofia had gotten the impression of wealth and elegance. She remembered Rachel being stylish and utterly gorgeous. Not the type of girl to burn eggs. More like have them prepared and set in front of her on a silver platter.

However, Sofia's first impressions had been wrong before.

When they reached the door at the very end of the hall, Gray stopped and grabbed Sofia's shoulders. "This is it." He looked as if he might pull out a playbook and show her how to make a touchdown. "She's not like you. She's a little bit shy."

"*I'm* shy." Sofia was offended.

"No, you're not, sugar. You're you, and you're perfect, but you're not even close to being shy."

"Okay." *You learn something new every day.*

"What are you trying to get at?"

"I don't know. I guess I was just prepping you. Shy sometimes comes off as bitchy, especially from someone who looks like her."

Sofia gave him the evil eye, daring him to say anything else about how his ex-fiancée *looked*.

Gray let out a breath. "I love *you*. Okay? I never once said that to her or any other woman, for the matter."

"No?"

"Never."

Sofia smiled. "I love you too."

"Good. Now let's get this over with so I can take you home and finish what we started in that cornfield."

"I can't wait to see your apartment. Is that the place from the dreams?"

"No. I don't where that is."

"Weird."

"I know." Gray knocked on the door and held Sofia's hand.

No answer.

"You don't think the plane was going up today, do you?" he asked.

"It's possible. But I read the dead guy's watch. It said twenty after five."

"And it was a small plane over a mountain range?"

"Yes."

"That could be anywhere. She might've had to take one plane to get to the other."

"I hadn't thought of that. Darn it." Why hadn't she thought of that? She couldn't ask for her Crime Solver Superhero award any time soon.

Times like this Sofia wished someone else had this stupid "gift."

"Don't worry about it." Gray squeezed her hand. "We'll figure it out. Maybe she went to the store or ran some errands. If we get to a phone, I can try her cell."

Sofia nodded, and they turned in time to see Rachel walking up the hall, rifling through her purse as she dug out keys. She was wearing heels, a black pair of slacks and a yellow silk top.

Elegant.

She glanced up, saw them, and stopped dead.

~ * ~

Rachel had thought he was Hayes for a moment. Only briefly, before noticing the woman beside him. The waitress from that night.

But he was Grayson. Not Hayes.

What was he doing here?

Slowly, Rachel walked the distance between them, cautious about where this would lead. She hadn't imagined Grayson would ever want to see her again. Not after she'd told him about the night with Hayes.

Did he want to yell at her? Get some closure?

216

Find out more?

"Hi, Rachel," he said, not looking happy, but not angry either. "This is Sofia, my girlfriend."

Rachel nodded at the woman. Sofia appeared harmless. She had pretty eyes and a smile that was warm and welcoming. Her hair was up in a cute ponytail, and she looked at ease in her jeans and t-shirt. Rachel could easily see why Grayson would like her.

Good for him, she surprised herself by thinking.

"Why are you here?" she asked the both of them.

"We'd like to talk to you for a moment," Sofia said. "It's important and it won't take long at all. I promise."

"I don't know. I'm really busy."

"Packing?" Sofia asked.

"Yes." How did she know?

"Going to the mountains somewhere?"

"Um, where are you getting all this? Grayson, what's going on?"

"Can we come in for a minute?" he asked. "Sofia... She knows things. It's important she get the chance to tell you."

Knows things? If Rachel didn't think Grayson was a decent man, she'd be slamming the door in his face. But he was a good man, and he'd never once hurt her.

She bypassed the couple and unlocked her door. "Just for a moment."

~ * ~

Sofia *loved* Rachel's cute little apartment. The living room was feminine and pink and cozy. The couch looked comfy, as did the matching chair next to it. Now this was a woman who knew how to live.

But she stifled the urge to ask her hostess where she'd found the cute flowered throw pillows, knowing darn well this wasn't the time to ask for decorating tips. She bit her lips shut and took a seat next to Gray on the couch.

"Can I get you a cold beverage, Sofia? Grayson?"

Rachel asked from the kitchenette.

Odd how she kept calling Gray "Grayson." As if she were about to break out a ruler and threaten to smack his hand with it.

"What do you have?" Sofia asked right as Gray said, "No, thank you." And then gave her a look.

Sofia shrugged. "I'm thirsty," she whispered to him.

"Water, diet cola, and orange juice."

"I'd love some water. It feels like we've been out in the sun all day."

"Oh?" Rachel handed her a bottle of water. "That's nice." She handed one to Gray as well, and sat down in the chair with her hands placed neatly in her lap. She let out a small sigh and met Sofia's gaze. "How can I help you?"

Here it goes. This would be the very first time Sofia attempted to prevent tragedy in person. There was nothing anonymous about this interaction. Now, how to begin?

"Sofia dreams of the future," Gray blurted out, and Sofia sucked in a breath.

Sheesh. The man knew how to get straight to the point.

"She what?"

"I'm able to foresee the future." Sofia took over. "For whatever reason, I was given this gift and I've had it since puberty. Strong emotions trigger these visions of fear, love, grief, and so on."

"That's interesting," Rachel said with no facial expression whatsoever. Her hands clasped tighter together.

"Psychic abilities run in my family," Sofia added, wondering if Rachel believed a word she said. "Anyway, I'll get to the point. Lately, I've been having visions of a plane flying through the air, but all of the passengers are, well, they're not breathing. I'm thinking maybe the oxygen depleted from the cabin and the oxygen masks

218

didn't fall down in time to warn them. So they... well, they died."

Rachel wiggled in her seat. "And?"

"And in the dream I had last night, you were on the plane."

"Really? Deceased as well?"

"Yes."

"Is this some kind of a joke?" Rachel rose out of her coma and set a fierce glare toward Gray. "Why did you bring her here? I never took you as the vengeful type. I guess I was wrong."

"No, Rachel. It's not like that. Sofia's telling the truth. I know it's a little hard to believe, but she's the real deal."

"Listen, I'm sorry I slept with Hayes. I was in love with him. I still am in love with him."

"Hayes is dead," Gray said rather gruffly. "This has nothing to do with him."

"He may be dead to you, but not to me."

Oh, boy. Sofia needed to get this back on track. "Sorry to interrupt, but did you recently book that flight? Like yesterday?"

Rachel glanced away from them, ignoring Sofia.

"You took the last seat, did you not?"

"How do you know all this? Do you work for the airline?"

"I told you how I know. One seat was empty— number twenty-two—for the first few dreams I had, and then last night you were sitting there. Look, if you could just tell me the information off the ticket, then we'll leave you alone."

"Why don't you already know that? I thought you were *psychic*?"

Sofia ignored the condescending tone. Obviously, the woman had been through a lot in the past year, and here Sofia was telling her she might die on an airplane that hadn't even left the ground yet.

"What if, hypothetically, I'm right? What if this plane is going to kill everyone on board, including children, and ultimately crash into a mountain that may or may not have people on it? Wouldn't you want to do everything in your power to prevent that tragedy from happening?"

"I don't see what I could do."

"You'd be doing a great thing if you'd only give me some details."

"Great." Rachel hung her head, took a breath and looked up at Sofia. "Fine. What do you need to know?"

Chapter Seventeen

Rachel opened the door for them. She was more than ready to have Grayson out of her sight. He looked so much like Hayes. More than ever, with his hair tousled and his clothes wrinkled and imperfect. These two must've had quite a journey.

But was this for real? Or did Grayson's new girlfriend simply have a vivid imagination and a contact that worked for the airline? Sofia seemed like a sincere and genuine person, though sometimes looks were deceiving. What motive did she have for concocting this story? Rachel already knew why Grayson believed it. He was angry and still a mess from losing his brother.

"Thank you for this, Rachel," Sofia said, waving the paper. "I'm going to do what I can to keep this plane from going up. I hope you'll seriously consider changing your flight."

Rachel nodded. She didn't intend to change anything. If the pair of them could stop this plane from flying, she'd find alternate transportation from Denver to Aspen. Maybe she'd take a different flight or rent an SUV and drive. Or if the plane went up, and Sofia was right...well, then so be it. Fate would lead her to Hayes. Right?

"Take care, Rachel," Grayson said, but he didn't meet her eyes. He wrapped his arm around Sofia and led her down the hall. She whispered something to him, and he leaned down to kiss her.

Hayes had certainly done his job. Grayson was happy. But did that mean Hayes had crossed over? Would she never see him again?

She shut the door and pressed her forehead against it. "Hayes, come to me," she whispered. Calling him had worked before. It had to work again. "Hayes, please come see me. Please."

~ * ~

Sofia read over the information Gray had written down when Rachel finally caved. The day after tomorrow, the flight was scheduled to depart. Saturday. They had forty-eight hours to stop it somehow.

"What can I do?" she muttered, while staring out the car window. "Call and tell them their plane is broken and to fix it?" She snorted. "Yeah, they'll believe some wacko woman from Indianapolis who hasn't even laid eyes on it. What about a bomb threat? That might work."

Gray shook his head and tightened his grip on the steering wheel. "They tend to investigate those. We want to avoid anything that's going to put us in prison."

Sofia liked how he was saying "we" instead of "you." He was in this for the long haul. Her new partner in solving crimes and tragedies.

"Can you read the itinerary back to me again?" He'd gone into detective mode. So serious and analytical.

"DashAir Airlines, flight 221. Leaves at a quarter to five. Saturday from Denver to Aspen, Colorado." She swerved her finger over the way he wrote *Aspen*, and realized this handwriting didn't match the love note at all.

This confirmed he'd been telling the truth. Not that she hadn't believed him. But who had written it then?

"DashAir," he said. "Huh. I think I know somebody who knows somebody who owns that airline."

"Really?"

"A neighbor of mine. He told me his dad owns it."

"You're kidding?"

"I kid you not. We should see if he'll put in a call to daddy."

"That would be fantastic, Gray."

He smiled at her and winked. "Am I still your hero?"

"We'll see later tonight." She slid a hand up his muscular thigh.

How had she gotten this lucky? She only hoped her luck would continue, considering their blooming relationship had so many discrepancies compared to her visions. Different locations, different emotions, everything was altered in some way. She shifted in her seat as an irritating weight of doubt settled heavy in her chest.

Ignore it, Sofe.

This would work. They loved each other. It *had* to work.

~ * ~

Penny ambled downstairs to get a bite to eat. She couldn't stand being cooped up in that bed any longer. Besides, Sofia could be home any minute. It was time for Penny to think about leaving before she was caught in her web of lies.

"Mom?" Laura called from the kitchen table. A garden salad sat in front of her. "You okay to be up and about?"

"I'm fine, dear." Penny poked her head in the refrigerator, but didn't see anything good.

"Where's Herbert?" She turned around to see the blush on Laura's face.

"He had to go into work for a few hours."

"Oh? Will he be back later? He's such a nice gentleman."

Laura finished chewing and swallowed. "You really are the devil in disguise, aren't you, Mother?"

"I prefer the name Cupid, but I won't be picky."

Penny sat down opposite her daughter and eyed the salad. "What do you have there, dear? Trying to stay trim for a reason?"

"Mother, stop it. Herbert's a nice man, I agree. But I want to take it slow and see where it goes."

"I highly recommend the bedroom."

They both broke out in laughter.

Laura put her hand over her heart. "It's been a while, that's for sure."

Penny loved seeing Laura in such good spirits. She couldn't remember the last time they'd laughed together. It had been years. Not since before Michael, her ex-husband and Sofia's father, had up and left. The weasel. He never did understand or appreciate the gifts Laura had been given.

Laura's smile faded as she sipped her tea. "Have you talked to that spirit?"

"You mean Hayes?"

"Mm hmm."

"I talked to him this morning, actually." Penny picked up Laura's fork and scooped a cucumber with extra dressing into her mouth.

"Are you going to leave me hanging, Mother? Or are you going to tell me if my daughter's all right?"

"Of course she's all right. The spell is complete, and they've admitted their love for each other."

Laura clenched her eyes shut and opened them again. "Lovely. Now we wait for the heartbreak?"

"Don't be such a pessimist." Penny poked at a carrot. "The spell worked out for me just fine. Why wouldn't it work for Sofia?"

"Dad told me he was in love with you before you even cast that spell on him." Laura pushed the salad bowl away from her and in front of Penny.

"Could've fooled me."

"Now what? How long until it fades and we find out if he really loves her?"

"Eternal worrywart, that's what you are."

"Answer the question."

"The spell fades after a week or two. The love will last a lifetime." Penny hoped, anyway. You never could be too sure with spells, especially if one didn't practice as much as one should.

"You're going to tell her, Mother. I won't have her heart crushed when she wakes up one morning and sees that he's gone. No note. No nothing."

"Well, he's not Michael, dear."

"You're going to tell her." Laura raised her voice. "And if I find out you've put anymore spells on my daughter, I'll never speak to you again."

Two could play at that game. "Fine, I'll explain everything." Penny raised her voice as well. "But only if you tell her she has more powers than she realizes. She's a witch like you and me and the ancestors before us."

"No way. You know how I feel about that."

"And your reasoning is complete nonsense. You can deny the powers that lie at your fingertips for as long as you like, but Sofia has the right to decide for herself. Don't you think her gift would be a great deal easier to handle if she had a little extra help? A spell to bind a murderer? A protection spell to help the victim? To keep an airplane from flying...or to fall out of love, if need be?"

~ * ~

Gray pulled into his condo's parking garage, questioning how ungentlemanly it would be to take Sofia straight up to his bedroom, lock the door, and throw away the key. The plane wasn't supposed to fly out until tomorrow anyway. They had plenty of time, and her hand on his thigh for the past ten miles had made him quite uncomfortable in his jeans.

He walked her through the lobby. The elevator might be a good place for loving as well. He'd never tried it before, but who better than Sofia to be his first and only?

Her eyes were wide as she took in the high ceilings, extravagant fixtures, and modern furnishings. "This is where you live?"

"My condo is a little more humble." The elevator doors opened, and Gray led her in.

"Hayes and I picked out this condo. He thought the women in his life would give it up easier if he walked them into a place like this. His words, not mine."

"And you?"

"I liked the soundproof walls and windows."

"What is it with you and quiet?" She leaned against the railing and smiled up at him.

Gray moved in front of her, trapping her against the wall. "What is it with me and you?" He brushed his mouth against hers. "I can't seem to get enough. I'm addicted, I think."

She returned the kiss, sliding her tongue along his upper lip. She tasted of sweet tea and red licorice—her afternoon snack she'd picked up while he pumped gas into the BMW.

Gray felt her leg slip up his. It was all he could take. He reached down, cupped her ass, and lifted her against him. He pressed her into his erection to show how much he wanted her.

She rolled her hips forward, rubbing him, making him want her naked and under his sheets, or on top. Whichever was faster.

She moaned against his tongue as he slid it against hers.

The sound of the elevator door opening didn't seem to disturb her, so he continued, getting as much of her as he could until she remembered their self-assigned duty to save thirty-plus lives.

"That is so fucking hot, dude."

Shit. Gray broke the kiss and saw the curly golden-haired neighbor guy staring back and forth from him to Sofia.

"You are my inspiration. I want you to know."

Sofia cleared her throat and wiggled away from Gray. *Damn kid.*

"Sorry to interrupt you guys. You were having a moment there, weren't ya?"

"Oh, don't worry about it," Sofia said, cheerfully. "It's not a big deal."

How did she do that? Gray frowned at her. "Again with the 'no big deal'?"

"Of course you're a big deal, honey." Sofia waved a hand from his toes to his head. "A very big deal. I just didn't want to make your neighbor, here, feel uncomfortable." She held out a hand for the kid to shake. "I'm Sofia."

He shook her hand and eyed her chest. "Andrew Dashmoor. You can call me Andy."

The elevator door began to close, and they all stepped out into the hall.

"Dashmoor?" Sofia's eyes lit up. "As in Dashmoor from DashAir?"

"You got it." He pushed a hand through his hair as if preparing to make a move on Sofia. "My old man owns the whole entire airline."

"That is so neat." Sofia gave her cute smile. "I bet you can get all kinds of deals."

Gray's jaw tightened. Did Sofia not see when men were attracted to her? Maybe she did and was playing it up. Either way, Gray stood behind her and decided to play along. "Do you believe in psychics, Andy?"

"You mean, like, that chick on the Montel reruns?"

"Exactly."

Sofia peered up at Gray with an arched brow.

He would make it up to her later. "Sofia is just like that chick on Montel."

"No way. Are you kidding me?"

Sofia stepped back hard on Gray's big toe. "He kids you not," she said, before he could.

Gray knew damn well her ability was limited to her dreams, but certain circumstances called for certain measures. If they could convince Andy that she was an all-powerful psychic, they could convince him to call his good old daddy to stop that plane from flying. And Gray could have a little fun with Sofia in the process.

"So who or what was I in my past life?" Andy eyed Sofia suspiciously.

"Let's see. I have to touch you to find out. Do you mind?"

"Not at all, dude."

"Close your eyes," Sofia said.

Andy clenched his eyes shut, and Sofia looked up at Gray, sticking her tongue out at him. *You're going to get it*, she mouthed.

Gray was looking forward to it. But did she really have to *touch* Andy?

The elevator door opened again, and Mrs. Farley, Gray's neighbor two doors down, walked out with her cane in one hand and a sparkly pink leash attached to her toy poodle in the other.

"I'm waiting," Andy said with a smile on his face. "Are you going to touch me or not?"

Mrs. Farley gasped, and the poodle barked. The silver-haired woman had been Gray's neighbor since the day he and Hayes had moved in. Lord only knew how long she'd lived here before that. Her hobby was walking around with a notepad and pencil, writing down *occurrences* that happened in the building. She'd gone through a new notebook every week when Hayes was alive. Yep, his brother had kept her very busy.

Gray took Andy by one arm and Sofia by the other. "Why don't we take this somewhere where Sofia can concentrate?"

"Mr. Phillips," Mrs. Farley called out. "Mr. Phillips. Mr. Dashmoor. There is to be no funny business in this building. Do you hear me?"

Gray glanced over his shoulder to see her and the dog scowling up at him. "Of course not, Mrs. Farley." He shoved his key into the lock. Gray had learned a long time ago the less said to the elderly woman, the better. He turned the key in the lock. It worked. The door opened without a problem. His luck was improving.

"Yeah, Mrs. Farley," Andy said. "No worries."

Sofia piped up. "I wasn't going to touch him anywhere inappropriate, I assure you."

"You weren't?" Andy frowned.

"Well," Mrs. Farley huffed. "I'm going to have to write this down on my list of grievances. I would've expected this from your brother, Mr. Phillips, but not you."

Gray blew out a breath. He really wished she hadn't stooped to that level. "Mrs. Farley," he said, after she'd started down the hall. "Your dog pissed against my door again last week. Next time he does that, I'm going to find that notebook of yours and use it as toilet paper to wipe my—"

~ * ~

Sofia hadn't realized she'd had the strength to push a man Gray's size onto his butt. But she did and she had, and now he was sitting on the dark maple hardwood floor in his foyer.

"Super psychic woman, *baby*." Andy put his hand up for a high-five, but Sofia knew better.

She shook her head for him to nix it and looked down at Gray. "I'm so sorry, honey. I had no idea I could do that." She held out a hand for him to grab.

Needless to say, Manly-man didn't accept it. He stood on his own. "Don't worry about it," he grumbled.

"Well, I couldn't let you threaten to—"

"I know, Sofia."

"Don't be mad at me."

"I'm not." He sure the heck sounded like it. He brushed past Sofia and Andy and headed to the kitchen.

"This place is nice, dude." Andy followed him. "Do you have more square footage than I do?"

Sofia glanced around for the first time. The floor plan was open, revealing the living room, dining area and kitchen. The floors were all hardwood. A black leather sofa and loveseat and a glass coffee table sat in front of a flat screen television in the living room. A fireplace posing as a half wall separated the living room from the dining room. The dining table was a dark oak. Four high-back leather dining chairs surrounded it. The kitchen had dark granite countertops and an island bar with stools separating it from the rest of the space.

Everything was very masculine. Of course, Gray and Hayes were the only two people who'd lived here. Bachelors. Sofia was sure Mrs. Farley's comment had hit a nerve with Gray. The twins had grown up together and lived together as adults...and now Gray was alone.

He pulled out two bottles of beer and handed one to Andy. "Sofia, I can open a bottle of wine if you want. Or I have water, but that's about it."

"I'll take a beer." She sat on the bar stool beside Andy.

Gray grinned. "Yeah?"

"Sure. I drink beer sometimes."

"Awesome." Andy leaned toward her. "Super psychic woman who can drink a brewski. I like that. How do you feel about cozying up in a humongous bean bag and watching a football game on a plasma?"

"Um." Sofia wasn't sure how to answer that, but it appeared she didn't have to. Gray walked around, put an opened beer bottle in front of her, and kissed her cheek.

"I love you," he whispered into her ear, and sat down on the stool on the other side of her.

Sofia's skin prickled with delight. She'd never tire of hearing that, and hoped he'd never tire of saying it. The make-out session in the elevator had left her wanting more.

She took a sip of the beer, and from the corner of her eye, caught sight of Gray's upper arm flexing as he leaned against the island. She looked farther up to see him smiling at her.

"Super Psychic Woman," he said teasingly, "are you going to tell Andy his fortune?"

"Wait," Andy said. "Doesn't she have to touch me first?"

"Right." Sofia hopped off the stool and swiveled Andy around to face her. "First, I'll tell you who you were in your previous life." She sized him up like her mother did with all of her clients.

Andy was an average-sized man, but seemed smaller in the presence of Gray. Maybe a couple inches less than six foot. He was lean, but not too skinny. He had some muscle to him. He appeared to be a year or two younger than she was, so maybe he was twenty-one or twenty-two. He wore a shirt with the name of a rock band she'd never heard of and ripped jeans his daddy probably paid a bundle for. He was attractive in a boyish way, with his curly blond hair and puppy dog brown eyes.

"Close your eyes again," she said.

He did, and added the extra step of flinging his head back and bracing his arms against the island. The man was ready to be touched, that was for sure.

Tell him something he wanted to hear. That was always her mother's motto, and it would be Sofia's for this task, since she didn't really know who the guy was in his previous life or even if he had a previous life. Might as well make him happy.

She brought her hand up to his neck and slowly swept it down his chest. Gray cleared his throat and raised his brows at her.

Hello! This was *his* idea. She ignored him and continued with the act, stopping just above Andy's abdomen before starting back up again. She needed more time to think. What would Andy Dashmoor want to hear?

"You were a king," she blurted out. "Of a foreign country. You had several wives that catered to you and fed you grapes from the vine."

Andy smiled, but kept his eyes shut. "What else?"

"The people of your kingdom adored you and bowed at your feet."

"Cool. How did I die?"

"Do you really want to know that?"

"Duh. The Montel chick always 'fesses."

"Okay." Sofia rubbed circles on his chest with the tips of her fingers and thought of how to end the highly fabricated tale. If this didn't please him, she didn't know what would. "Two of your wives were fighting over who was going to sleep with you that night. The argument got out of hand and one of them said if she couldn't have you, no one would, so she stabbed a knife into your heart."

"Dang. That's harsh." Andy opened his eyes and winked at her. "There's plenty of me to go around, as you can see."

"Okay." Gray straightened in his seat. "Can I talk to you in the other room, Sofia? We'll be right back, Andy."

"No prob, dude. You got any chips or anything?"

"Help yourself."

Sofia followed Gray into a hallway. He pushed a door open and gestured for her to enter, all the while not giving her the courtesy of eye contact. *Great.* Was he grumpy again? What happened to the sweet *I love you* in her ear?

His bedroom was large, but taking up most of it was his California King covered by a black and beige striped comforter. The bed frame was a dark mahogany wood that matched his dresser and nightstand. The walls were white, and vinyl blinds covered the window. The man needed some color in his life, for sure.

"Do you want me to paint you something so you can

hang it up in here?" she asked.

The door shut behind her and suddenly she was being picked up and set down on the bed.

Gray's body covered hers as he continued the kiss that had begun in the elevator. His tongue and lips were potent and powerful, like the rest of his body, leaving her senseless and full of desire. She imagined what he could do with that tongue on other parts of her body. She had dreamed that experience before, but as she'd realized, real life was far more satisfying than her visions. Far more emotional, as well.

She eased away from him long enough to tell him she loved him.

"I love you too," he said, "and I want you." He kissed her again. "I know you're having fun out there, but could we move it along so I can be alone with you?"

"Fun?" Sofia looked up into his amused eyes. "You think I was having fun?"

"Well, you were getting into that chest rubbing." He chuckled. "Thought I'd bring you in here and remind you what a real man feels like." He pressed his erection between her legs. "A real king," he said, and chuckled again.

"Oh, ha, ha. *Real* funny. Get off me, now, Grayson Phillips."

"Ah, I'm only playing with you, Sofia. You know I'm teasing. And I'll admit I'm a little bit jealous."

"It serves you right. Why did you bring this whole psychic thing up anyway? I'm in way over my head."

He grinned and whispered his plan into Sofia's ear. "What do you think he'll do if you predict his daddy is going to lose all his money after this plane goes down? *I* predict the families are going to sue, and he'll lose all his business and have to file for bankruptcy, don't you?"

"And then Andy can't depend on Daddy anymore?"

"Exactly."

Chapter Eighteen

Gray had thought a quick telephone call would do the trick. Then he'd have the rest of the evening to spend alone with Sofia. Yet, here he was, driving up the long cobblestone lane of the Dashmoor Estate, preparing himself to meet Andrew Dashmoor Senior, because Andy Junior was a pansy who didn't seem to know how to do anything on his own.

Andy stretched out in Gray's backseat with his hand over his forehead. "This can't be happening. This can't be happening."

"Try to relax, Andy," Sofia said to him from the passenger seat. "We can prevent this, remember?"

"I don't know," Andy whined. "I just can't deal with this in my life right now. I'm under so much stress."

Gray held back a groan. Had he known Andy would've reacted this way, he'd have come up with a different plan. Now, it was too late, and the kid had Sofia feeling sorry for him.

"It'll be a cinch, Andy." Sofia reached back and patted his leg. "You can talk to your father and convince him not to let that particular plane take flight. Then everything will be all right. "

Andy jolted up in between the seats and took Sofia's hand. "You'll go in with me, right? He's never going to listen to me. He hates me. He always has."

"Yes, I'll go." She squeezed his palm. "It'll be okay. Gray will go in too."

Gray shut the engine off when they reached the end of the drive and stared up at the large red brick mansion as dusk descended. Flowering vines crept up the sides of the exterior, and a vast stone staircase led up to the enormous front door.

"It's gorgeous." Sofia's eyes widened. "I can't wait to see the inside."

Only she would find excitement in these circumstances. Gray supposed that was one of the reasons he loved her. He only wished her little "gift" weren't so intrusive. Not when his body ached to have her alone and in his arms. Ah, well. He'd push through this and then take her back to his home.

A leggy, overly tanned blonde stood at the door when they walked up. She wore a cleavage-baring halter-top and a short tennis skirt. Gray didn't think she was much older than Sofia. Apparently, Mr. Dashmoor had his very own trophy wife.

"Hi, Andy!" the woman said, her voice a high-pitched squeal. "We weren't expecting you. Who are your friends?" She ruffled her fingers through Andy's hair.

Andy blushed and did the introductions. Trophy wife's name was Barbie, Andy's newest stepmom. How appropriate.

She took her time shaking Gray's hand, gazing up at him with heavily made-up eyes. "Wow! Aren't you a tall drink of water?"

Sofia's glare bore into Gray. Certain steam was shooting from her ears, he wrapped his arm around her waist and escorted her into the house, holding back a grin the entire time. Didn't she know he only had eyes for her? Guess he'd have plenty of time to show her.

Barbie led them into the enormous living room with vaulted ceilings and an impressive mural of angels flying through clouds painted on two of the walls. Gray sat next to Sofia on one of the dainty vintage-style couches. Definitely not made for a man his size, but he held his tongue and made the most of it.

"Barbie." Andy's face paled again. "We need to talk to Dad. It's really important."

Barbie squealed a little more about who knew what and headed up the grand staircase. Her flip-flops made an annoying clopping sound.

"Your dad's house is beautiful, Andy." Sofia leaned over and patted Andy's hand. "Did you grow up here?"

"Sort of," he mumbled, and stood up from the chair at the sound of Barbie and Mr. Dashmoor striding downstairs.

Gray and Sofia stood as well. Andrew Senior looked like a modern-day Napoleon Bonaparte, and Gray wondered if he had the complex to match. Guess he was about to find out.

"Andy, why are these people in my house?" Napoleon asked, jutting his chubby little chin up at Gray. "I thought we settled that mishap with the bookie."

"Dad, he's not a bookie. He's my friend and neighbor."

Barbie settled onto couch opposite them, pulled out a nail file, and ground it into her fingernail. Could the woman be any more annoying?

"Well, what does he want? I'm a busy man, you know. I don't have time for any of your nonsense today, Andy."

Sofia slowly scooted behind Gray, obviously afraid of Napoleon, who stood eye-to-eye with her.

Enough of this.

236

"I'm Grayson Phillips, sir. This is Sofia Good. We're here because we have reason to believe one of your airplanes is going to kill at least thirty-five innocent human beings and then crash into a mountain. And we want you to stop it."

~ * ~

Twenty minutes later, Sofia could still hear Mr. Dashmoor shouting at poor Andy somewhere on the second story of the gigantic house. The shrieking echoed, bouncing off the walls.

"Maybe we should've been a little more subtle," Sofia said, more to herself than to anyone. She'd had to come out from behind Gray to explain in detail exactly why they believed one of his airplanes was in jeopardy. Mr. Dashmoor obviously hadn't liked the explanation.

"No," Barbie said, suddenly waking from her intense nail filing. She popped the gum in her mouth and straightened her body. "You were right to tell him. Only thing is Andrew doesn't have an open mind like I do. He doesn't believe in psychics and that sort of stuff. Me? I go see my own personal life planner every single week, come rain or shine. She helps me so much, you would not believe."

"That's, uh, great." Sofia felt Gray nudge her leg. He'd appeared aggravated ever since leaving his condo, but Sofia hadn't asked why. She had enough on her mind as it was. Innocent people were depending on her.

Barbie popped her gum again and squinted her eyes at Sofia. "You can really see the future?"

Sofia nodded.

"And if this plane goes up and those people die, Andrew will eventually face bankruptcy?"

Nodding wasn't really lying, was it? The scenario was possible, at least.

"Damn." Barbie stood and started pacing. "As you can see, I didn't marry Andrew for his charisma...or good looks." She turned and pointed the nail file at them.

"Why don't you give me that flight information? I have my ways with Andrew."

"Really?" Sofia said.

Gray perked up beside her.

"Heck, yeah. I've been known to get what I want when I want it. You two get Andy out of here, so I can be alone with my little teddy bear."

Sofia pushed the image from her mind. She'd have to remember that visual next time Nana tried to mind read. "Are you sure you can convince him to stop the flight from going up?"

"Cross my heart. You have Barbie Dashmoor's word."

~ * ~

Gray happily escorted the sobbing Andy down the hall to his condo so Sofia could start a hot bath in Gray's whirlpool bathtub. She'd been excited to hear he had a whirlpool, and he'd been excited to see her excited. Hell, he got excited to see her do anything. Especially if it meant she'd be naked and within his sight.

"He hates me even more now," Andy wailed.

"Shake it off, Andy. Be a man." Gray opened Andy's door for him and shoved him inside.

"But I'm not a man."

"Look. Your dad doesn't have respect for you because you don't have respect for yourself. Get a job, pay your own bills, grow some balls, and you'll be fine. Okay?"

"Okay." More tears.

Gray shut the door and headed back to his place, already growing stiff against his jeans in anticipation. Finally, he had Sofia alone. Finally, he'd be able to woo her exactly how he wanted to.

With a candlelit dinner, soft music, and thorough lovemaking. No questions. Just do it.

After ordering in some salad and pasta, Gray slipped into Hayes's shower. He'd been tempted to join Sofia in the tub. She seemed to be having a good time in there with all the oohing and awing and splashes. But if he started touching her now, he'd never be able to stop.

They had the rest of their lives together, and he desperately wanted to start it out right. Hell, maybe he'd even propose to her tonight.

Shit. Did he really just think that?

Yeah. Yeah, he did.

He shook his head as he toweled himself off and stepped into Hayes's bedroom, suddenly realizing he hadn't set foot in this room since before the funeral. Rachel had come in, made the bed, and picked up whatever mess Hayes had left. She'd cried the entire time.

Gray had listened from the living room, thinking her sympathetic to him. He hadn't had a clue. Rachel had loved Hayes, not Gray.

But then why had she agreed to marry Gray?

Maybe for the same reason he'd asked her—he was lonely. He needed to go on with life and forget the past, or at least find some closure. But that hadn't happened with Rachel.

It was happening with Sofia.

~ * ~

Sofia closed her eyes and let the whirlpool jets beat against her back. She'd been ecstatic to hear Barbie guarantee the plane wouldn't leave the ground, or at least it would be inspected first. Initially, it had all seemed too good to be true. Too easy. But Barbie had assured her she'd call if anything went astray.

Let it go, Sofe.

She'd enjoy the evening with Gray and try to erase the worry from her mind. He needed some peace after all they'd been through, she could see.

And she loved that about him. His desire for quiet, normalcy—and her. She just hoped she could give him what he wanted. Lord knew she needed a little stability for herself as well. Unfortunately, it would never happen as long as she had her gift, and as long as her mother and grandmother had their gifts.

Ugh. When was she going to tell Gray about them and their abilities?

Don't think about it, Sofe. He loves you. He'll understand.

Hopefully.

The bathroom door opened, and Gray stepped in, wearing a terry cloth robe and a pair of silk boxers. His hair was damp, dark, and curly. Had he taken Andy home and showered already? Sofia figured she must've been in the bath for quite some time.

"Hi," she said, as he sat down on the edge of the tub.

His gaze swept over her body, which was fully visible now that the bubbles had disappeared.

Oddly, she wasn't insecure this time. She felt sexy and desired. Loved. How could she not, when he stared at her as if she defined perfection?

"The food is here." He shrugged his arm out of the robe and dipped his fingers into the water. With a tender touch, he ran his hand over the side of her breast and down her belly. She sucked in a breath when he slipped two fingers past her sensitive clit and pressed them inside her.

"Are we hungry?" she asked. She lifted her hips as he reached a delicate area.

"I'm starving." His dark eyes met hers. He kneaded his fingers deeper into *that* spot.

"*There*. Yes," she panted. "Yes." She clamped her knees together as she exploded and jerked against his fingers. Within a matter of seconds. Seconds was all it took for him to make her orgasm.

He slowly withdrew his hand from the water and wiped it dry on a hand towel. Aftershocks rolled through Sofia's body as she tried to gain composure.

He kissed her lips and grinned. "Come eat with me."

240

"Okay."

Then he was gone. *Good Lord.* Could she expect that type of service every time she took a bath? Sofia gathered her wits and wrapped a towel around her body.

No way was she dressing in the clothes she'd worn all day. The light in Gray's walk-in closet was on, so she decided to slip into something more comfortable—one of his dress shirts. His clothes only took up half of the enormous closet. Sofia imagined she could make good use of the other half, except her clothes weren't tailored suits and ties. They were mostly jeans and t-shirts—clothes she wouldn't fret over if she were to get a little paint on them.

She let out a sigh. *Slow it down, Sofe.* Who knew if he wanted her to move in with him? They'd barely revealed they loved each other. *And* it had taken a mysterious note for them to do it.

Someone had wanted them to remain together.

But who?

After toweling off her hair and buttoning up the crisp white dress shirt, she headed out to see the entire open area of Gray's condo was dim except for four candles sitting on the center of the dining table. She didn't bother looking at what he'd ordered for them. Her sights were on the sexy man sitting at the end of the table, gazing her way. No smile, only passion oozed from him. His sultry eyes urging her to go to him without a word being said.

Sex. They screamed sex and a promise of extreme pleasure.

"Why don't we eat, Sofia? You're going to need your energy."

Oh, boy.

Her body trembled as she ambled over and sat beside him, half expecting him to pull her onto his lap and take her right there. She wouldn't object.

She sipped her wine and forked through her salad, wondering if her quivering belly would reject the lettuce. Why was she so nervous? Or was it anticipation? They'd had sex before, but tonight they would make love.

Sofia would know the man who kissed her, penetrated her, and brought her to release, *loved* her. *So much that it hurt*.

"Aren't you hungry?" He ran his hand up her naked thigh.

Dinner was over as far as she was concerned.

"I don't think I am, really." Keeping eye contact, she began unbuttoning her shirt. *His* shirt. "I see that you are, though. Would you like to have me for dessert?"

He dropped his fork onto the floor. "I, uh...Yes, I would."

Sofia remained cool, calm, and sexy for him. He brought the boldness out of her. Made her yearn for it. She finished unbuttoning while he watched attentively.

"Are you done with this, then?" She pointed to his plate.

In response, Gray shoved both their plates toward the center by the candles. The wine glasses tipped over and fell onto the rug below, but he didn't seem to care. He sat back and gestured for her to make herself comfortable.

With as much grace as she could muster, Sofia pulled herself up to sit on the table in front of him. The dress shirt fell open and his jaw clenched. She braced her feet up on each of his armrests, revealing herself to him. He stared intently, licking his lips.

"I really like it when you don't wear panties," he said in a gruff voice.

Sofia leaned onto her elbows and tilted her head back to gaze at the lit candles. "Do you want me to beg, Gray?"

"Yes, I'd like that very much, actually."

The feel of his fingers spreading her apart startled her, briefly. Then he stilled, not giving her any more.

"Please," she whispered.

That simple word was all he needed. His velvety tongue slid across her, warm and firm. He licked her again and then again, faster through each pass, until a surge of marvelous heat rose inside of her, heavy, ready to burst.

Intense pressure built, almost too much to endure. She sat up and thought to push him away, but his rough hands cupped her backside and held her close. He licked and suckled her until finally she screamed from the torturous pleasure.

She gasped out breaths and clasped onto his hair while the aftershocks singed through her.

"Gray. Oh, wow."

His tongue slid inside her, eagerly lapping her up.

At last, he pulled away. A devilish grin spread across his handsome face as he wiped his mouth and licked his fingers. "That was delicious, sugar. Thank you."

Sofia nearly came again.

And once more she wondered how she got so lucky.

After catching her breath, she returned his devilish grin with one of her own. "Can I have my dessert now?" she asked, wanting to return the favor.

"I was hoping you'd ask." He pushed his chair to the wall and slid off his boxers.

Sofia clasped her shirt closed and knelt in front of him. He was fully erect, gorgeous, perfect, but she wasn't quite sure how she'd begin...or end. She'd watched her roommate from art school give her boyfriend a blowjob one night, late, when they'd thought Sofia was sleeping. They both seemed to enjoy it immensely. And of course, she'd done it in one or two of the dreams, but it'd been hazy, like an out-of-body experience. She tried to remember.

He ran his fingers through her hair and lifted her chin up to kiss her. "You don't have to."

"I want to." She craved it. "I just...I've never done it before." Her cheeks warmed and she knew she looked and sounded incredibly naïve. How many women had knelt before him like this? Women who were able to satisfy him as he'd satisfied her?

His mouth twitched to a grin, but he quickly flattened it out. "I'm sorry. I forget that you're new at all of this. You're so amazing, Sofia."

Okay. That made her feel a little better.

"And you've done it in the dreams. Do you remember?"

"I'll try to. This is much more real."

"Are you sure you want to?"

"Yes. Yes, I want to please you."

~ * ~

Gray throbbed, he desperately wanted her mouth on him – her sweet, innocent, untainted mouth. But he would come from the mere sound of her voice if she kept talking like that.

Easy now. Just talk her through it. He could teach her exactly how he liked it.

"Slow," he said. "We can start out slow. Taste me. Run your tongue across to see if you like it."

She nodded, her gaze glossy and wide under her thick lashes.

How did he get so fucking lucky?

He inhaled sharply at the mere sight of her tongue...then she swept it all the way from bottom to head, licking the juice he'd already spent. His mind blurred with lust. "Do you like it?"

"Yes. Very much." She repeated the action, but this time she took his head into her warm mouth.

"That's good, sweetie." He clenched his fists into the armrests so he wouldn't grab her head and force her down on him. "Try to take more in."

She did, and then, as if it were a natural reaction, she began sucking on him. Eagerly, taking more and more of him into her mouth. Her slick tongue pulsed against him, luring him to the edge.

Gray ground his teeth. He was going to explode in her mouth if he didn't gain control.

Maybe that's what she wanted. But what if she were offended? Hell, it was too late. He let go, releasing, quaking his hips up and down again until he was drained.

She swallowed. *Sweet heaven.* Then she drew back and ran a finger across her red, swollen lips. "Did I do okay?"

He nodded, breathing heavily, wanting more. "Like I said – amazing."

She stood to kiss him, her plump breasts crushing into his chest. "I love you, Gray."

The words were simple, but each time she said them, they affected him in a way that astounded him. He'd never thought he needed to hear it from a woman, never thought the sentiment would mean much to him, but now he knew he couldn't live without those three simple words.

How could this have happened in such a short time?

It didn't matter. It felt too good to matter.

He stood and lifted her into his arms. "I love you, too, Sofia. And tomorrow, I want you to pack your things so you can move in with me. If you want to, that is."

She flung her arms around his neck and kissed his cheek. "Gray, I'd love to."

He carried her to the bedroom, somewhat disappointed in himself for not proposing marriage. And somewhat relieved she hadn't expected it. Not yet. His feelings were too deep, too soon. Aching, to be exact. He didn't just *want* Sofia he *needed* her. He thrived on her.

Although it thrilled him to have a woman he was able to care so deeply for, it also scared the hell out of him.

If only he could get this under control.

Chapter Nineteen

The sun started rising, finally. The light poured through the slits in the blinds and took shape across Gray's broad chest, his chiseled jaw, powerful lips, and sleeping eyes. At some point in the early morning, he'd exhausted himself and had fallen asleep.

After massaging, kissing, licking, and suckling every inch of her body. Eating her up like candy, it seemed. He'd savored her, made love to her, talked to her, and repeated the process for hours upon hours. The man had enough stamina to satisfy ten women.

However, Sofia was only one. Although she was completely satiated, she was also completely worn out. Kind of like a sex hangover.

She stretched out her weary arms and legs and yawned. She hadn't been able to fall asleep like Gray, hadn't really wanted to descend into dreamland. Sometimes a girl needed a break from saving people's lives. Sometimes the responsibility was all too overwhelming.

Sometimes it was easier to have this moment in time with this person without knowing what the future held.

She sat up and squelched the urge to run her fingers over his magnificent body. Truth was, if he woke up at that moment and wanted more, she'd give it to him.

She'd do anything for him, to him—whatever he asked, she'd say yes. And she'd be happy to do it.

But he was sleeping soundly, and the whirlpool bath was calling her name. She slipped from the bed, tripped over one of his colossal shoes, redeemed herself, checked to make sure she hadn't disturbed him, and then quietly closed the bathroom door behind her.

Gravity was not her friend at times. However, a hot bath was. She sat at the edge of the cold-tiled tub and started the water. Of course, a man didn't have bottles of bubble bath lying around.

In fact, she was pretty sure she'd been the first person to use this most excellent tub. The shower next to it, on the other hand, had water spots galore on the glass door. Sofia poured a capful of the manly-man scented shampoo into the running water and wondered if Gray had a housekeeper or if he did the cleaning himself.

She had a ton of questions for Gray. Some of them she'd gotten answered the night before, in between being thoroughly explored. His favorite color was brown, of course. He'd spent half of his childhood growing up in the heart of San Francisco, the other half in Indianapolis. Two different worlds, he'd said, and he hoped to one-day move back to San Francisco. Sofia had told him she'd love to see it with him since she'd never been. He'd smiled at that and made love to her again.

Then he'd asked her about her painting and if she wanted to pursue it as a career. Sofia had needed to think about that. Painting as a hobby was one thing, as a career it was something she wasn't sure she had the courage to do. Gray had told her he had every confidence she could do whatever the hell she wanted to do in life, and she'd succeed at it too. In response, Sofia had straddled him, taking the driver's seat for once.

He hadn't been disappointed.

Sofia sank into the hot water and soaked her tender body. The jets and the warmth felt so good that she nearly fell asleep a couple of times. It wasn't until Gray walked in that she fully opened her eyes.

Without a word, he stepped into the other half of the tub and sat down. He plunged his head under the water and then he surfaced, scrubbing his hands over his face and hair.

He gazed at Sofia for a moment before asking, "Last night was too much again, wasn't it?"

"I don't know. Are you usually that...intense?"

"No. Never. Not that many times, not as passionately." He pressed his palms to his bloodshot eyes. "With you, it seems like I can't get enough. Even right now, I'm holding back from touching you because I know I won't want to stop."

Her heart stuttered as his penetrating gaze swept over her again.

"Do you think it's possible to love someone too much?"

Any other time Sofia would've laughed his question away. She would've been flattered and happy to know he loved her so. But his tone wasn't that of adoration – it was of worry. Did he wish to stop loving her altogether?

"No," she said. "Love me as much as you want. I'll love you back tenfold. I promise."

"But, Sofia, I don't want to – "

Before he could say another word, Sofia slid into his lap and pressed her lips to his. She kissed him until he kissed back, wrapping his arms around her waist and gathering her against his hard body. His tongue thrust into her mouth, and she eagerly accepted it, showing him she could handle whatever he delivered.

"Sofia," he whispered.

"Don't talk. Just kiss me."

But he stopped anyway. "Sofia, the doorbell's ringing. I better get it."

~ * ~

Penny slapped at Laura's hand when Laura pushed the doorbell for the third time. "They're probably still sleeping. Whose bright idea was it to drive over here first thing in the morning?"

"I'm worried." Laura pressed the doorbell again. "If they're not at your house and they're not here, then where the hell are they?"

The sound of a deadbolt turning got Penny's undivided attention. This was sure to be exciting, meeting Sofia's love for the first time. If he looked anything like his twin brother, Sofia was one lucky girl.

The door opened halfway, and Penny's question was answered. The twins were identical, although this one had shorter hair, which was nice. His jeans didn't have any holes in them. His t-shirt was black, stretchy, and showing off his muscles. And naturally, this one was alive and thriving.

She read his thoughts while Laura did the introductions.

The image of Sofia in a tub of water vibrated from his mind.

Well, maybe it was best to block the thoughts for a bit. She didn't want to invade anyone's privacy too much.

"It's nice to meet you." He shook both their hands. *Very polite.* "I'm Gray Phillips, but I'm guessing you already know that since you've found where I live."

"That's right, dear." Penny passed by him into the condo. Everything was clean and tidy, except the mess in the dining area. Hmm. What had happened there?

"Is Sofia here?" Laura passed him as well and poked her head around.

"Yes." The young man shut the door. "She's, um, getting dressed. I'll go get her. Make yourself at home."

Penny and Laura both watched him closely as he disappeared down a hallway.

"He's handsome," Penny whispered.

"Yeah, I bet he thinks he can get any woman he wants. I don't trust him for a second." Laura huffed and frowned. "Oh, God. I bet they've slept together."

"Do you think?" Penny rolled her eyes. "It had to happen sometime."

"I know that, Mother. I'm the one who foolishly told her to go do it."

"Oh, *really*? Do you think she wouldn't have if she hadn't had your permission? Don't be naïve, Laura. She's not twelve anymore."

Laura tapped her foot on the hardwood floor. "Can we stop bickering now? They'll be out any second, and I don't want Sofia to worry any more than she's going to already."

"You really need to give her more credit." Penny plopped down on one of the leather sofas and let out a breath. This was not going to go well. She could feel it in the air. Something was amiss. Something was terribly wrong.

~ * ~

Gray shut the bedroom door behind him. Sofia was lying on the bed, wearing nothing but his dress shirt, unbuttoned. She gestured for him to come hither.

His body reacted instantly, but his mind knew better. "Sugar, I'd love to, but you might want to see who's waiting for you in the other room."

She jolted up. "Who?"

"Your mother and your grandmother."

"Oh, my gosh. Shoot. How did they find me?" She quickly began buttoning up.

"I don't know. Have you called them recently?"

"I was going to, but, you know. We were busy saving lives and all that other stuff."

Gray watched her fumble with the last button. He couldn't help but lift her chin up and kiss her just once. "Can we finish what we started in the tub when they leave?"

She smiled halfway. "Yes, I'd love to. I—" She finished buttoning. "I wonder what they want."

"We can go find out," Gray offered. What was she nervous about? Did she think they'd object to him? "Are you going to tell them about moving in with me?"

"Yes. That's a good idea. I—" Her hands trembled as he took them in his.

"What, Sofia? Tell me."

"They have special abilities too."

"So, they have premonitions like you?" Gray wasn't sure what was so horrible about that. He'd already proved he was supportive of Sofia.

"Not exactly. Just don't let my mom touch you, and try to think of Rodney Dangerfield a lot. Okay?"

"Excuse me?"

"I'll explain later. Trust me."

Gray held tight to Sofia's hand as she led him to the living room. Her mother and grandmother stood as soon as they saw Sofia. He searched through his short-term memory for their names. Laura and Penny? Yes, that was what her mother had said. They all had the same eyes. Big and blue. He'd known right away when he opened the door they were related to Sofia in some way.

"Sofia, *what* are you wearing?" Laura asked as she gave Sofia a hug. "No bra?"

"Oh." Sofia blushed and glanced at Gray. "I need to do laundry."

"You look happy, dear," the grandmother said, getting the next hug. "Your face is glowing." She winked.

Gray rolled some of the tension from his shoulders and sat with Sofia on the loveseat. At least her grandmother seemed to like him. The mother, however, couldn't spear swords from her eyes any faster. He took Sofia's hand and squeezed.

Tension was thick in the air.

"So," Sofia started with a hint of uncertainty in her voice. "I'm sorry I left your house unattended, Nana. We had to leave in an emergency. But I left a bowl of food and water for Sam. Is everything okay?"

"It's fine, dear. I went home last night. Sam seemed well taken care of. Thank you for doing that for me."

"Sure. Anytime." She cleared her throat. "You all met Gray, right?"

"Yes, dear."

"He stayed with me at the house for a couple days. We kept having car troubles. It was the strangest thing."

"That's unfortunate," Penny said, but still grinned.

"It was, but, well, we've fallen in love, and now I'm going to move in here with him."

Laura sat up straight at the edge of the couch. "No, you're not."

"Oh, yes, she is," Penny countered. "She's a grown woman, and they're in love. See?"

"Mother." Laura gave her a stern look. "Spill it."

Penny let out a sigh and set her eyes on Gray. "Dear, would you mind if we had a moment with Sofia? We won't be long."

~ * ~

Sofia knew this conversation wasn't going to go well. Not with the way her mother glared at Gray, and the way Nana was being overly cheerful.

"What's going on?" Sofia asked, as soon as the bedroom door clicked shut with Gray behind it. He hadn't appeared altogether happy about having to leave the room in his own home, but still he'd whispered he loved her in her ear and kissed her cheek before stepping away.

"He seems like such a dear." Nana clapped her hands together. "I'm happy for you, Sofia."

"What's going on?" Sofia pointed the question to her mother. "Why wouldn't you approve of me moving in here? I love him, and he loves me."

"Oh, Sofia." Laura sat by her and took her hand. "You don't have a clue, do you?"

"About what?" Sofia panicked. "What is this about? Gray? How did you figure out where he lives, anyway? What are you two up to?"

"Sofia, take a breath," Laura said. "Nana will explain it all to you."

Sofia looked at her grandmother expectantly. "Well?"

"Dear," Nana started slowly, "I noticed you were in the shed to get the toolbox. Did you happen to see my magical goodies?"

"Yes. What was that all about? Have you always had those things?"

Nana waved her hand absently toward Laura. "Your mother will explain more about that later. What's important now is that you know I took the liberty of casting a spell on you and Gray."

"A spell?" Had Nana finally lost it? Sofia straightened her shoulders and tried to stay calm. What the heck was going on here?

"Well, actually, I had to do it twice. You were fighting it, you see. And all the energy I used gave me the worst migraine. Your mother and Herbert had to take me to the hospital. But the ghost helped you through that with the note. He's a really great character. I wish you could've met him."

"Mother," Laura said through pursed lips, "you're rambling. How is she going to understand any of this if you ramble?"

"Wait." Sofia stuck her hand out to stop them. "What is this? Witchcraft? Spells? Ghosts? What are trying to tell me?"

Laura turned to face her. "Your grandmother is attempting to say that the love you and Gray feel for each other may not be real. It's very possible that the strong emotions you're feeling right now will fade when the spell fades."

"Good chance it won't though," Nana added.

"You're kidding?" Sofia pressed her fingers to her forehead to think for a moment. She wasn't surprised Nana had come up with such a crazy idea...but her mother? "You believe this spell business, Mom? You believe it actually works?"

"Yes," Laura said softly. "Unfortunately, it's all true. You know how Nana and I explained that we all carry a gene that allows us our gifts?"

Sofia nodded.

Laura released a breath. "Well, we also have the added benefit of witchcraft to supposedly help us with our gift. Although *some* people get carried away and use it for personal matters, which then gets us into sticky situations like this. That's why I haven't told you before, Sofia. We hold a very powerful tool at our fingertips. It can either prevent or cause tragedies. And in this case, it's likely to bring heartbreak."

Nana huffed. "Don't be so dramatic, Laura. There's no heartbreak here. All I see is love."

"For now, Mother. What about one, two, three weeks from now when that man"—she pointed to the bedroom—"wakes up from the after-effects of the spell and wonders what the hell had gotten into him? He's going to realize he's not really in love with her."

Sofia's mouth dried up, and her heart pounded. "Gray doesn't love me?" It was all very confusing.

"No, Sofia. Not really. The spell lured you together and gave you both very strong feelings for each other, only ending when you both admitted you loved one another. *However*, it takes a while to fade."

"That's not entirely true, Sofia," Nana piped up. "The spell was only a boost to get you started. It could very well be that the love will continue indefinitely. You remember you were dreaming of him. He's in your future. What was the point of waiting?"

"Oh, God. He doesn't really love me." Could it all be true? She'd been stupid to think that a man like Gray could have feelings for her.

"Sofia, dear, the love could be as real as you and I."

"But what if it isn't?" Her eyes stung. "He'll think that I fooled him. He'll hate me."

"I'll never hate you." Gray's voice rumbled from behind her, followed by the click of a door.

Sofia turned quickly to see him.

He frowned, anger in his eyes. "This is the most ridiculous thing I've ever heard." He walked around the loveseat and spoke to her mother. "May I sit by Sofia, please? The woman that I *love*."

~ * ~

Gray had stayed in the room long enough. He'd listened at the door, not being able to help himself. It was obvious when he left that he would be the topic of conversation. He'd been right and what he heard had infuriated him. A spell? *Absolutely absurd.*

Laura glared up at him. "I don't think that's a good idea. Obviously, you've been listening in. You know what's going on. For once, maybe it's time to use your head instead of your dick. Let her leave here with us. You can talk to her later on the phone, if that's what she wants."

Gray stood his ground. "Sofia isn't going anywhere other than to pack her clothes so she can move in here with me. Just as we were planning before you interrupted us."

"You tell her, Gray," the grandmother murmured.

"Gray," Sofia said, tears in her eyes, "maybe we should talk about this."

"No," he said. "This discussion isn't logical enough to give it any more thought. It's comical. It's a fucking joke. I love you because of who you are, not because of some bullshit spell." If they thought his love would simply fade away, they were sorely mistaken.

Sofia stood and took his hand. "But what if it's true? I don't think my mother and grandmother would lie to me about something like this."

"If it's true, Sofe, then you don't really love me. Is that the case?"

"No, of course not."

"Then how can you believe them?"

Laura maneuvered in front of Sofia, forcing their hands apart. "Because the spell hasn't weakened yet. And I'm not going to let my daughter stick around here to wait for you to come to your senses."

Heat rose up his chest, gripped his heart. "Why is it so hard to believe I'll love your daughter now and *forever*? I'm starting to understand why she's never really had a man in her life—you won't let it happen."

Laura poked her finger into his chest. "You're just as idiotic and stubborn as your thickheaded brother."

Gray stepped back, shaken by her words. "How did you know my brother?"

~ * ~

Penny stood, thinking it was probably a good time for her to step in. Laura had muddled this meeting up terribly. What was she thinking, mentioning Hayes?

"Excuse me," Penny said, setting a hand on Gray's forearm. Strong young man, he was.

He looked down at her with narrowed eyes. "How does she know my brother?"

"Hayes visited us in his afterlife, dear." Only partially true, but Gray didn't need to know Laura's part in Hayes's death. Not now. "He's a wonderful young man." Gray's face grew pale, but she continued. "Apparently, he had business to do before he was able to cross over. He needed to see to your happiness and thought Sofia would do the trick. I completely agreed, so we worked collectively to guide you two together. As you can see, it worked. You fell in love. You're happy. Hayes was able to move on. All's well that ends well, right?"

"This isn't funny," he said in a low voice. "This is my brother you're talking about."

"I'm not trying to humor you, dear. Did you and Sofia wonder where that love note came from, Gray? Did you recognize the handwriting?"

Sofia pressed her hand to her heart. "Oh, my. It was his spirit in the kitchen, wasn't it? Right before I found the note, I felt him, the cold breeze on my arm. It was him, wasn't it?"

"Most likely, dear."

Her eyes grew wide. "And the condoms? Did he leave those?"

"No, that was my idea. Definitely my idea. You can't be too safe these days."

Gray broke away from Penny's grasp. "Sofia, why do you believe all of this nonsense?"

"Nonsense?" Laura's face flushed red. "Sofia does not need or want a man in her life who doesn't accept and support her and her family's gifts."

"I support her just fine. But I'll be damned if I'm going to stand here and let you feed her this garbage. None of it makes any sense. Why would Hayes, alive or dead, go to you all to find happiness for me? He didn't even know Sofia." Gray stopped and looked to Sofia. "Did he?"

She shook her head. "I would've recognized him if you two are identical."

Gray clapped his hands together once. "Ladies, your ghost story has a hole in it. Care to explain?"

Penny sighed. Seeing no other choice in the matter, she began to clarify. "Hayes knew Laura."

"What?" Both Gray and Sofia said, and then looked to Laura for an answer.

"Mother, do you think this is necessary?" Laura asked.

"You made your bed, Laura. The young man needs an explanation. You need to give it to him."

Laura rolled her eyes. "I didn't really know him. He came to me for a reading one time, that was all."

Sofia turned to Gray. "My mom is a psychic palm and tarot card reader," she explained. "She works out of our home. And she—" She gasped. "Mom, did you foresee that Hayes was going to die?"

"He wouldn't have believed me, Sofia. You know that. You've seen how people react when I tell them their fate is anything less than perfect."

Penny noticed Gray's hands begin to shake at his sides, but he remained quiet.

"But Mom, you could've warned him." More tears welled in Sofia's eyes. It broke Penny's heart.

"I told him to be careful." Laura's eyes brimmed with redness as well. "It's not my fault," she said to Gray. "He was careless with his life before he even stepped in my door. He wouldn't have listened to me."

Gray cleared his throat, obviously upset. "You saw that my brother was going to die, and you didn't think it mattered enough to tell him? To give him a warning?"

"Like I said, he wouldn't have listened."

"Maybe he would've checked his goddamn parachute then. Maybe he wouldn't have gone up in that airplane. How could you be so heartless?"

"You don't know anything about me," Laura said.

Gray paced the floor until he eventually dropped onto the loveseat, closing his eyes and pinching his nose. "He was my best friend and only family. Do you understand what it felt like to lose him?"

Sofia sat beside him, but didn't seem to have the courage to touch him. "I'm so sorry, Gray."

Laura shook her head. "It wasn't my fault."

"Get out," Gray said, covering his face. "All of you, just get out."

Sofia's face paled. "I'll get my things," she whispered, and hurried into the bedroom.

"Thank God," Laura said.

Penny stepped toward Gray and ran her hand over the top of his head once. "Sofia wasn't a part of this. She loves you."

"Mother, don't tell him that."

"He needs to hear it, Laura. He's not alone in this world."

Gray stood, flushed and trembling. He didn't look at anyone in particular as he disappeared into another room and slammed the door behind him.

Sofia returned, wearing her jeans and holding all of her other items. "Let's go," she said with a sob.

"Go ahead," Penny said. "I'll be right out."

"Nana, just leave him alone, please."

"Don't you worry. It'll only be a minute. I'll meet you at the elevator."

Penny waited until Sofia and Laura left, and then tapped lightly on the door through which Gray had escaped. The poor thing. He'd had so much heartache and now this.

He didn't answer. Penny thought about reading his mind, but wasn't sure she really wanted to know what the young fellow was thinking. Had she done a bad thing here? Putting them together too soon?

"Gray, it's Penny. I don't mean to bother you anymore. I want you to know, if you want to contact Sofia, she'll either be home or maybe at my house. I'll leave her house number and cell phone number. She had these cute little business cards made up. Just for fun, I guess. She actually designed them herself. She's very talented. Anyway, I'll leave that card for you. Here"— Penny pulled one from her wallet—"I'll slip it under the door."

Silence. She bent down and slid the card through.

"If you're worried about the spell, don't be. It'll wear off completely within a week or two. I'm positive Sofia will still be in love with you as you will be with her. And I'd very much like to have you as part of *our* family someday. Whenever you're ready. I know we can't replace your brother, but we'll love you all the same."

Nothing.

Penny couldn't stand it any longer. She opened up her mind and found his thoughts. They were powerful, causing Penny to limit some.

Leave. Leave me. Sofia. Why would she doubt me? Love her so much. Hayes. Her mother could have saved him. God. Hayes could have lived. Why didn't you let him live? Need Sofia. She left. I made her leave. Stupid. She's gone. I shouldn't have sent her away. Need her. Did the grandmother leave? Crazy. All of this is crazy.

Penny took a breath and blocked him out. It was too much, but at least there was potential. He hadn't given up on Sofia. She swiped a tear away, gathered her strength – Lord knew she'd need it for Sofia – and walked out the door.

Chapter Twenty

Sofia ran straight up to her room and fell into bed. Gray was angry with her and with her family, but she loved him and regretted not telling him that before she left.

She should've walked right into that room and kissed him until he kissed her back. Held him until he forgave her. Had she known Hayes had been in her home, had she known he was going to die, Sofia would've done everything in her power to save his life.

No force on Earth could bring Gray's brother back to him now. And nothing would change the fact that Gray's love for her was temporary. How much longer? Today? Tomorrow? Next week? Even if she did gather the courage to go to him, would he push her away? Would she disgust him?

Would he deny he'd ever loved her?

He'd be the same man she'd first met at the restaurant. The one who looked at her as if she were nobody, just some annoyingly clumsy waitress.

Oh, geez. The spell sure had done a number on him, hadn't it? Now, it all made sense.

He'd never really loved her. She doubted he even liked her.

The time they'd spent together had all been too good to be true. She'd known all along Gray could have any woman he wanted. Why would he want her?

Stop it, Sofe. You are just as good as anyone.

"Just as good," she mumbled, as her eyes grew heavy.

Maybe I'll dream of him.

~ * ~

Gray walked through the thick grass, keeping his eyes to the ground as he passed each gravestone. Hayes and his parents were on the far corner of the lot, he remembered. He had a ways to go.

A drop of rain hit his cheek, so he glanced up. Clouds hung low and ominous, threatening to release at any minute. *Perfect.* He couldn't wait to get out of Indiana for a while.

He pulled Sofia's card out of his jeans pocket and read it for the billionth time.

Sofia Good, Painter Extraordinaire. Call me! 555-0122 or…

He stuck the card back in his pocket. He'd memorized the damn thing in a day.

Call her. Tell her you'll always love her.

Would she believe him, though? Or was she stuck on this idea that a spell had made him fall head over heels? The idea was plain ridiculous.

He'd give her time to realize it though. All the time she needed. Besides, Gray needed some space as well. How could he look Sofia in the eyes when he knew her mother could have saved Hayes's life?

They had all these powers, but none of them did any good. None of them could bring his only brother back.

Time to finally say goodbye.

As Gray walked closer to where his family was buried, he noticed a certain strawberry blonde kneeling over Hayes's grave. Rachel. Her shoulders heaved up and down. She was crying.

He kept moving forward. His anger toward Rachel had dissolved. What was the point in being mad at her? What did it matter any more?

They'd both lost Hayes. They both grieved.

"Hey," he said as softly as possible, not wanting to startle her.

She jerked her head up and gasped. "Grayson?"

"Yep, it's me."

She stood and blew her nose. "Sorry, I didn't know you'd be here. I would've given you your time."

"It's no problem."

She nodded, looking down at the grave again.

Gray read the headstone. *Hayes Abraham Phillips.*

"He always hated his middle name," he said. "Abraham. It was Grandpa's but it reminded Hayes of Abraham Lincoln."

"Really?" She met his gaze again. "I didn't know that."

Gray teetered on his feet, recalling another memory, and was happy it was a good one. "Did you know we used to break dance in high school?"

She smiled and sniffed. Her eyes and nose were red and puffy. "No, didn't know that either."

"It's true. We were awesome." He smiled back.

"I have no doubt."

Silence.

"Rache?" Gray kicked at a pinecone lying in the grass. "You remember when you said Hayes was in your apartment? Said he loved me?"

Her gaze darted toward him then back down again. "Yeah."

"Was he really there? You know, his ghost?"

"Yes." She swiped at some stray tears.

"I couldn't see him. I wish I could've."

"I know. I'm sorry."

"Is he gone? You can't see him now, can you?"

She shook her head. "No. He won't come when I call him anymore." More tears.

Gray planted his hand on her thin shoulder. Had she lost weight? "I'm glad that you loved him, Rache. He deserved that."

"Oh, Grayson," Rachel said and wrapped her arms around him.

He hugged her back. "You're a beautiful person. I hope you know that."

She sobbed against him.

"And you know you can call me Gray, right? We're friends now."

The crying transformed to laughing, and she stepped back, wiping her face with a tissue. "I'd love to have you as a friend...*Gray*."

He chuckled. "There you go. That's not bad, huh?"

"No, it's perfect. Thank you."

"For what?"

"For being here. For being you."

He grinned at her. "It's been a while since I've been here and been me, hasn't it?"

"Yes, it has. But I'm glad you're back. So...where's the lady who's responsible?"

"Sofia." His heart ached at the reminder. "I think we're taking a little time apart."

"Oh, I'm sorry, Grayson. I mean, Gray."

He shrugged. "Just for a while. There are some things we have to figure out."

"I hope it works for you. You seemed happy with her." She patted his arm.

"It will. But first, I'm going to check out that loft in San Francisco Hayes chose for us. It's mostly paid for, but I haven't actually seen it yet."

"That sounds exciting. Are you moving out there?"

"Maybe. I might put it on the market and sell it. Hayes and I put a ton of money toward that place. Remember? We had all those plans to buy a boat and sail the coast."

"I remember. It'll be a shame if you don't get to do it."

He shrugged. "Some things are more important. Sounds like you have plans of your own. You were headed to Aspen?"

"I was until I got a visit from my mother. I finally told her the real reason the wedding is off. And I told her I was leaving and never coming back. That I was determined to live my own life and live out my own dreams." She let out a sigh. "But then she made an offer I couldn't refuse. She said she'd forgive whatever debt I owed her for the wedding, and if I continued on with law school, I wouldn't owe her a thing for that either."

"Ah, Rachel. That woman has her claws in you like nothing I've ever seen before."

"I know. I know. She has issues of her own. At least she accepted that there wasn't going to be a wedding between you and me. Now or ever."

"Listen. Let me know how much your parents have put into the wedding and I'll send them a check."

"That's very sweet of you, but it was my fault the wedding was canceled."

"Bull. I think it's fair to say we were equally *not* in love with each other. Don't you think?"

She looked up at him thoughtfully. "What were we thinking?"

"Grief does strange things to a mind."

~ * ~

Sofia ran down the aisle to seat twenty-two. It was empty. *Thank you, God.* At least Rachel wasn't on this doggone plane. She'd believed Sofia. Or she'd thought enough about it to change traveling arrangements. Either way, Sofia had at least saved one person's life.

Evidently, Barbie hadn't gotten her way this time. The plane was still flying in the air. Breathless bodies still filled the seats. And, obviously, Sofia was still dreaming about this tragedy.

She took a quick sweep of the inside of the cabin to see if anything had been altered in any way. Nothing had changed. There was no point in staying in this dream. She had all the information she needed.

Wake up. Wake up, Sofe.

She sat up in bed. Perspiration dampened her entire body, making her hair stick to her cheeks. Rain pelted against the window in large drops. Her room was gloomy, darkened by the storm. How long had she slept?

The alarm clock on the side table read ten after six in the evening. Was it still Friday? Or had she slept all through the day and night?

She threw the covers off her body and ran downstairs. Whispers halted in the kitchen as she stopped at the doorway.

"Sofia?" Nana looked at her from over her teacup. Her mother turned and stared. A bottle of vodka sat between them on the table. "Did you get enough sleep?"

"What day is it?"

"It's still Friday, dear."

Sofia let out a breath. "Thank goodness."

The doorbell rang, and her mother jumped out of her seat. The rims of her eyes were reddened as if she'd been crying. "I'll get it. Sit down with your Nana. Have a drink or two," she said as she jogged past.

Nana appeared to be in good spirits, as usual. She smiled and gestured toward the open seat.

"Sorry, Nana, I don't have time. That airplane is going up tomorrow, and I need to stop it."

"Sit down, Sofia."

"But Nana, I've met the owner of the airline. His wife said she'd take care of it, but for whatever reason she hasn't. I need to run over there and talk to her again. When I get back, I'll sit all you want. You can even read my mind."

"You have plenty of time. Sit. Now."

Sofia pushed a lock of damp hair from her forehead and realized her hands were shaking.

Suddenly light-headed, she slumped down in the chair. "I don't know what do anymore, Nana." She sighed. "It feels like my life is falling to pieces, and I can't pick them up fast enough. People's lives are in my hands, and there's not a danm thing I can do about it. Gray probably hates me, or will any day now. You're a witch and Mom is a palm-reading mercenary."

"Oh, dear." Nana frowned. "Remember? We're *all* witches, have been for generations."

Sofia wrapped her knuckles against the table. "Why is it you've waited this long to tell me? Is that why, when I wished Todd Beltman's pants would rip during a routine at nationals, they actually did?"

"No. Sounds like a good dose of karma to me. That boy was a Neanderthal, calling you fat. No, Sofia, we are good witches. White witches, as they call it. We help people. We don't cause people harm. It's against our nature. Our ancestors believed we were given this ability to practice witchcraft to help us with our gifts."

"What does it all mean? I can cast love spells that fade, and what else? Turn frogs into princes?"

"Frogs into princes? No, dear. But you can protect good people and bind bad people. Do you think that might help you with your visions?" Nana's eyes twinkled as they did so often.

"Maybe." Sofia plucked a tissue out of a box her mother had been using and blew her nose. "Why haven't you told me about this before? Did you think I couldn't handle it?"

"Your mother had her reasons. I think she wanted you to be as normal as was possible, considering."

"I guess I can understand that. But if magic can help me with my dreams, when can I start learning?" There was no time to waste. A little surge of excitement mixed with hope shot through her.

"How about I take a trip with you to meet the owner of this airline? I'll show you how an old witch can work miracles with a ring and the power of persuasion." Nana smiled and winked.

"That sounds wonderful."

~ * ~

By the time Sofia and Nana reached the Dashmoor Estate the rain had stopped. Sofia couldn't help but marvel at the extent of Nana's powers, as if she'd pushed the clouds from the sky, revealing the crescent moon and a mass of stars.

"No, dear. Only God can do that."

"Save the mind reading for the Dashmoors, please, Nana."

"You got it, but we'll have a talk about Gray later, okay?"

"Sure. So, what's the plan? How are we going to do this?"

Nana dug into her purse and pulled out a ring with a large oval onyx stone set in a gold band. She slipped it onto her right hand ring finger. "This lovely piece of jewelry has great power. I've put a spell on it, and whenever I wish to persuade someone to do something, I merely put my hand up and say the words."

"Wow, Nana. That's kind of scary. What if someone bad got a hold of that?"

"I've cast the spell; I'm the only one who can use it. Simple as that. And this is the first I've used it, so let's go give it a test-try. Shall we?"

"Absolutely." Sofia took her grandmother's hand as they walked up the large stone flight of steps.

Barbie opened the door before they were able to press the doorbell. How did the woman know each time? Maybe she had nothing better to do than to wait for someone to pay her some attention.

"Hi, Barbie."

"I know why you're here, and I'm sorry. He won't listen to me. He actually called me crazy. Can you believe that? If he loses all his money, I swear I'm going to divorce his fat ass."

"You will calm down," Nana said, holding an open hand up toward Barbie's face. The black stone drained of its color, giving it a clear, diamond-like appearance.

Barbie visibly relaxed. Her body slumped and one of her spaghetti straps fell off her shoulders.

With her hand still up, Nana said, "You will invite us in to sit while you retrieve your husband."

"Come in. I'll get Andrew," Barbie said and walked away, her flip-flops clomping on the tiled floor.

"It really works. How the heck did you do that?" Sofia whispered to Nana and followed her to the sofa in the living room.

"I'll teach you all you want to know later. Just watch, dear. It'll be fun."

"Goddamnit!" Andrew Dashmoor's voice echoed across the mansion, followed by heavy footsteps down the stairs. "Where is that little bitch? I'll show her what I'm made of."

Barbie tagged behind him meekly, as Mr. Dashmoor, red-faced, charged into the living room. His hairy stomach protruded over his swimming trunks. A white terrycloth robe barely covered the rest of his body.

Nana stood in front of Sofia. "Hello, Andy," she said, smiling.

"Who the hell are you?"

"I'm right. And you are wrong." Nana put up her hand again, but this time reaching it out toward Dashmoor's face.

"What the hell?"

"Calm down." Nana wiggled her fingers and, again, the black drained from the onyx ring. "You will call your airline right now to cancel flight 221, leaving tomorrow at 4:45 PM from Denver to Aspen, Colorado."

He froze, looking bewildered.

Nana's eyes were huge and unblinking. "You will call right now and cancel flight 221."

"Barb, where's my phone?"

Barbie grabbed the cordless off the corner desk and brought it to him. He paused for a moment, a perplexed expression on his face.

"Flight 221 leaving tomorrow from Denver to Aspen, Colorado," Nana repeated. "You will cancel it. You will have your mechanics do a thorough inspection, and you will have it fixed."

Dashmoor dialed a number, asked for a certain person and repeated Nana's orders.

Sofia stifled a smile. This power would *so* come in handy.

When he hung up, both Mr. and Mrs. Dashmoor stared at Nana blankly, as if waiting for more direction.

She obliged them. "Barbie, you will have confidence in yourself, and you will never settle for less than your worth." She turned. "Andrew, you will have your airplanes inspected on a regular basis, and you will not send the airplane for flight 221 up in the air until it is completely safe to fly."

After clapping her hands once, she dropped them to her side. "Sofia, are you ready?"

"Uh, yeah. Is that it?" Sofia whispered.

"Yes, dear. They'll snap out of it when we leave. I'll do a little spell to make them forget we were here."

"You can do that too?"

"Sometimes. *Their* minds are very pliable." She nodded to the couple, who were still standing like zombies. "Easily persuaded. And they live for themselves, so it's easy for them to forget other people."

"Interesting. You can tell that by mind reading?"

"That and instinct. Shall we go?"

Sofia smiled at her grandmother. "Yes. Thank you, Nana."

"You're welcome. Now, let's get me out of all this electricity. My head's starting to throb."

Chapter Twenty-One

Sofia brushed the finishing touches on her latest painting, focusing on how the tiny lines by his eye creased just so when he smiled. She'd tried her damnedest to paint something or someone other than Gray, but he was the muse occupying her mind, day and night.

A week and a half had passed and she hadn't seen or heard from him. She hadn't dreamed of him either. In fact, she hadn't dreamed of anything at all. Which was relieving in one aspect, and heartbreaking in another. It meant thirty-five people's lives had been saved. It also meant Gray wasn't in her future.

The spell had faded, and so had his love for her.

These paintings were a pathetic attempt to keep him close.

Why hadn't her love for him dissolved? If anything, it had grown. She *missed* him.

Everything about him. His smile, his laugh, his touch, his kiss. She even missed the manly-man attitude.

Absence makes the heart grow fonder, right?

"I always hated that saying," she mumbled under her breath.

Her cell phone rang from on top of her bed, and she jumped for it. The caller ID said *Madeleine*. Of course it wasn't Gray. Why would he call?

"Hey, Maddy, what's up?" Madeleine was her best friend and her own personal mechanic. Sofia always returned the favors by painting artwork and murals for her home.

"Are you still sulking? If you are, stop now. I have the greatest news." Madeleine's voice was husky but beautiful. It matched her tomboy slash model-gorgeous appearance.

"What, André agreed to hire me back on?"

Maddy's breath gushed into the phone. "No, I'm sorry. *But* guess what? He bought that empty building by the restaurant. You know, the one where bums used to hide out?"

"Yeah. What is he going to do with it?"

"He's going to turn it into an art gallery for local artists! He said he thought it would be a good way to attract customers. I hope you're not mad, but I told him how talented you are. And he wants to know if you'll show your art for the grand opening. Isn't that great?"

Sofia gulped down the panic rising in her throat. "Uh, I don't know."

"Come on, Sofe. Your paintings are brilliant. I don't know why you're afraid to show them."

Sofia took in a deep breath. The thought of sharing her passion with the public was petrifying. Painting as a hobby was safe, entirely different from setting it up on display for possible rejection and humiliation.

"What could be the worst that could happen?"

"I could have a panic attack, throw up, and be laughed out of the building."

"Sofia, that's silly. Think of it this way— what's the best that could happen?"

"I'll have something to worry about other than Gray?"

"Now there's the Sofia I know and love." Madeleine laughed. "Will you please come? I'll take you out for

274

drinks afterward. We'll have a girl's night out. Maybe you'll meet another guy. How's that sound?"

"Fine," Sofia forced herself to say. "I'll do it."

~ * ~

"Thanks for looking after the place, Mr. Lowell." Gray took the key from the hand of the elderly man who was apparently Gray's new San Francisco neighbor. Now, how to get rid of him? Gray was eager to see the place Hayes had chosen for them to live.

"It was no problem, son. Sorry, again, about your brother. Quite a shame."

"Yep. But he sure the hell knew how to live while he was here." Gray patted Mr. Lowell on the back. Neither Gray nor Hayes needed any pity. Not when Hayes had moved on to a better place, and Gray had so much to live for.

The old man wedged his white disheveled eyebrows together. "I suppose. Glad to see you've passed the grieving stage."

"Absolutely. Hayes wanted me to be happy. I'm going to make him proud."

"Well, then, I'll see you around." Mr. Lowell almost turned to leave, but stopped. "Will you have someone to live with you, by any chance?"

"Honestly, I'm not sure I'll be keeping the place. I may need to sell it. I've got another residence in Indianapolis."

"Better weather here."

"You're right about that." Gray loved this city. Whether it was sunny and bright or chilly and foggy. It was a hell of a lot better than the biting cold winters Indiana produced. Not to mention the scenery here was breathtaking. "I'm going to spend a few days revisiting my old stomping grounds before I make my decision."

"Good. Oh, and Hayes left a note for you inside. I didn't read it, though."

"Thanks again, Mr. Lowell." Gray gave the man another gentle pat. "See you around."

Anticipation sped up Gray's heart as he unlocked the door and stepped inside. Hayes had left him a note, huh? His last words from his brother. He hoped they were good ones.

To Gray's delight and surprise, the place was mostly furnished. When had Hayes had the time or the money to do this?

The downstairs area was laid out much like their condo in Indianapolis. Open, with the living room, dining area and kitchen revealed as you walked in. The furniture wasn't much different either. All leather, dark wood, and heavy glass. Masculine. Instead of it being a single story, to the left was a modern winding staircase that must lead up to the two bedrooms.

The square footage here lacked in comparison to the other place. The price, however, was twice as much as the Indianapolis condo. Even after the supposed good deal they'd gotten for presenting most of the money up front.

Ah, well. It was worth it. At least, it would have been. The loft was only a few minutes from the bay. And the view of the city, Gray noticed, was spectacular.

The piece of paper on the dark granite kitchen counter caught his attention. *Hayes.*

What did his brother have to say? Gray picked it up with trembling hands. He sat on the bar stool, took a deep breath, and read:

Gray,

What do you think? Hope you like the furniture, dude. I figured I couldn't go wrong if I chose most of the same shit we have at our other place. It's pretty cool, right? Call me and let me know what you think of your bedroom, though. It's nothing like your chick-repellent at home. I know you don't like surprises, but I just had to do it. Our lives are about to change like you would not believe.

Love you, man. Can't wait to set sail!

Hayes (the cool twin)

Gray closed his burning eyes and smiled to himself. This was the Hayes he wanted to remember. Giving, loving, and funny as hell. This was the Hayes he'd keep in his heart. His brother—he'd live and thrive in Gray's memory.

Forever.

He set the paper back down and combed a hand through his hair. "I love you, too, Hayes," he whispered, given there might be the slightest chance his brother could hear him. "Now, what did you do to my bedroom?"

Gray wandered up the stairs to the door that had a sticky note that read, *Gray's room*. He slid the partition door open, looked inside, and swallowed down the knot that rose up his throat.

One thing was very clear. He couldn't sell this place.

Chapter Twenty-Two

Sofia tried not to wobble in her heels or worry about the sweat beading on her forehead as people walked by her paintings. They mused, whispered, and moved on to the next. Some smiled, some ignored her.

Some asked for directions to the bathroom.

She was happy to see familiar faces when Nana, her mother, and Herbert strolled up, looking all spiffy and proud.

Herbert held her mom's hand. They'd been on a few dates in the past month. Her mom had told him every secret and every aspect of their family's gifts in excruciating detail. Sofia had wondered if her mother had wanted to scare Herbert off. In any case, he was still around. A few more grey hairs, but still sticking it out.

"It's because he loves her," Nana whispered into Sofia's ear.

Damn the mind reading.

"And your paintings are wonderful, dear," Nana said for everyone to hear.

"They really are," her mother agreed.

Herbert nodded. "Outstanding."

"Thank you." Sofia's cheeks flamed. She'd picked out a few of her best to display, but only one of Gray. It was the painting he'd liked the most, where their bodies were entangled.

Even after two months, it still hurt to think of him. Where was he? What was he doing? Did he ever think of her?

A week ago, she'd gathered the nerve to go to his condo and knock on his door. She'd wanted to invite him to the gallery opening. Just as a friend, if nothing else. A teenage boy had answered the door instead. He'd told her he and his mother had moved in several days prior. He wasn't sure where the old owner had relocated.

Sofia had been devastated. Shoot, she still was. How could he have moved without telling her? He must've really wanted to rid himself of her. Forget she ever existed.

Her mother and Herbert ambled on to view some of the other artwork the local artists had created and displayed along the walls and tables.

But Nana stayed. Her eyes were plastered to *that* painting. "Where do you suppose that dream took place?"

"Nowhere." Sofia didn't want to get into it. That part of her life was over.

"Red sheets. A gold comforter. Deep blue walls in the background. Have you ever seen this bedroom before? Was it his?"

"No, Nana." Sofia tried not to sound too irritated. "I don't want to talk about it, if you don't mind."

"Well, why not?" Nana chuckled. "It's your future."

"It's not, though. I haven't dreamed of him since the spell faded."

"Oh. Do you think maybe the future was altered in some way?"

Sofia stopped an eye-roll midway. They'd been over this too many times to count. Was her grandmother growing senile? "Yes, Nana. I can only assume it's been altered, and that we weren't supposed to meet until later."

"And the love spell screwed it all up?"

Sofia shrugged, not wanting to hurt her Nana's feelings. But, yes, the love spell had done its damage. Gray was gone, out of her life forever.

"We can do a spell to erase your love for him, Sofia. If that would help you."

"No, thank you." She was done with spells that played with emotions. She'd been practicing hard, learning the ones that would help her with her visions. Saving people's lives was how she planned to use them. Any other approach would only get her into trouble, she'd learned the hard way.

"I hate to see you upset."

"I'm fine, Nana. Why don't you catch up with Mom and Herbert? I heard there's some sculptures of naked men just around the corner."

"Hmm... I'll see where the punch is instead. Would you like some? I'll add a little vodka from my flask, if you want?"

Sofia shook her head.

"All right then, dear." Nana leaned forward and whispered, "Good-looking gentleman right behind you. I think he likes the paintings." She winked and left.

Anxious at the thought it might be Gray, Sofia turned too quickly on her heels and fell into the man.

The tall, thin gentleman—who definitely was not Gray—grabbed her elbow and steadied her. "You okay?"

"Yes." Her cheeks warmed. "I'm so sorry. I'm not used to these shoes."

"It's all right." He smiled and turned to her paintings again. "Are these yours?"

"Uh huh." Sofia took in the way his deep green eyes found the different details of the paintings. Like Nana said, he was good-looking. But he was no Gray, and it appeared he was more interested in the stuff on the walls than the stuff under her dress, anyway.

Which was fine with her. She couldn't imagine giving herself to anyone else. Not anytime in the near or far future. She was Gray's. Plain and simple, whether she ever saw him again or not.

"You have quite a talent," the man said.

"Thank you."

"Have you gone to art school?"

"For a year in New York. I had to drop out. Family issues."

"I see." He finally met her eyes. "Do you ever think of going back?"

"I'd love to." Sofia smiled at the thought. "But I don't think I can afford it."

"Yes, it is expensive, isn't it?" He held out his hand for her to shake. "I'm Steven Burns. I'm an admissions counselor for San Francisco Bay Art School."

Sofia shook his hand. "I'm Sofia Good. Nice to meet you. You're a long way from home."

"I'm visiting my mother," he whispered. "She's getting remarried again. Fifth time."

"Ah. Sorry about that."

"No, it's fine. Whatever keeps her happy. But I heard about this gallery opening and thought I'd check it out. I'm glad I came." He pulled out a card and handed it to her. "We have financial aid I'm sure you could qualify for, if you're interested. We're also giving away a few scholarships this year. You might be a candidate for one of them. Why don't you visit us and see what we're about? We need more people like you, Sofia. People with natural talent and obvious passion." He pointed at *that* painting. "There are graduates who don't have your eye for detail. Give us a try, okay?"

Sofia realized her mouth had dropped open, so she shut it and gulped. "Okay. I'll do my best. Thank you."

"See you out there then, Sofia. I'll be looking for you."

~ * ~

Gray sat in the coffee house that housed the first floor of his San Francisco loft. He hauled out his laptop and started his workday. Designing websites. Why he'd never thought of it before he didn't know. People paid him to play around on his computer all day, and he had no one to answer to but his customers. It was perfect. And he was good at it. Business was flourishing.

"What's up, Gray?" his new buddy, Nick, asked as he walked in the door and pulled up a seat at the table next to him. Nick had given him the idea of starting his own business. The surfer/genius spent half his day on the computer and the other half on a surfboard in the ocean.

Gray hoped to one day spend half his day on a sailboat. As soon as he found the right one.

"Not much, Nick. Just got two new accounts I'm going to start working on."

"Awesome." He sipped on his iced coffee and gave Gray a look. "I didn't see you at the party last night. Kari was very upset she didn't get to meet you."

"I was busy." Gray logged onto the Internet and started reading through his emails, hoping to pass right over this conversation.

"Dude," Nick leaned over and said in a low voice, "you know you can tell me if you're gay. I'm totally cool with that."

"I'm not gay," Gray said for the umpteenth time since he'd met Nick. "I like women, trust me. I'm just waiting for the right one."

"You're not going to find her if you're not looking."

"I look every day. Every damn day."

"And? What the hell are you looking for?"

"I'll know her when I see her."

"Huh. You're a weird dude. You know that?" Nick swatted at Gray's arm. "Hey, check out this one. She's kind of cute. A little bit of a mess, but cute."

That description sounded familiar. Gray closed his e-mail and looked up.

And saw Sofia.

She was at the counter, ordering. Her hair was down, pushed back behind her ears. She wore a pair of wrinkled khaki shorts, a blue top, partially tucked in, and brown sandals that had seen better days. She was more beautiful than he'd even remembered.

"Holy hell."

"What?"

"That's her." He grinned, shaking his head.

"Yeah? She the one?" Nick chuckled. "Go get her, dude."

~ * ~

Sofia was running late for her first day of classes, but the coffee shop had practically screamed her name as she passed by the green and white sign. A cold vanilla blended coffee would hit the spot. And— she checked her watch—she did have ten minutes.

"Order's up," the barista called out, and set it on the counter.

"Thanks." Sofia grabbed the cup and turned to head out the door. But ran into a broad, hard chest instead. The lid of her drink popped off and spilled onto the man's white shirt. "Shoot. I'm sorry. I didn't see you—"

"Sofia, it's me."

Gray. Startled by his voice, she dropped the entire cup on the floor. Liquid bounced back and splashed onto his jeans. Slowly, she forced her gaze up to his face. His gorgeous face.

He was smiling at her so large she thought he might start laughing. His hair was a little bit longer, and his face was unshaven, a few days growth at least. He looked happy.

"Hi," she squeaked out. Oh, geez. Here she was seeing him for the first time thousands of miles away from home and she'd gone and spilled a cold drink on him. *Nice going, Sofe.*

"Hi." He picked up the cup and threw it in the trash beside him.

"I'm sorry." She grabbed a napkin and patted at his t-shirt that fit nicely against his chest. "I wasn't expecting to see you here. I guess I freaked out. I didn't mean to—"

"It's okay. They're just clothes."

She continued to pat, partly to get off the whipped cream, mostly to feel him in the flesh. To just feel him. It had been so long.

"Sofia," he said, and took the napkin from her. "It's not a big deal, trust me." He nodded to the brunette barista who was staring up at him. "Can she get another one of these? I'll pay for it."

"Gray, you don't have—"

"So, what are you doing all the way out here?"

Her mind went blank. Why was she here again? Oh yeah. "I'm a student at the art school. It's right across the street." She pointed absently out the coffee shop window.

"That's great, Sofia," he said, but his smile dimmed. "I'm curious. What made you decide to go to this one?" He stood close enough she could smell him. His natural, mesmerizing scent with a splash of whipped topping and caramel.

"Oh, fate, maybe. One of their people saw my paintings in a gallery opening. And...um, what are you doing here?"

Please say you flew out here to find me and sweep me off my feet.

"I live in this building. Do you remember when I told you I owned a place out here?"

"That's right. I do remember. I, uh, went to your condo back home to invite you to the gallery opening, but you'd already moved."

"I'm sorry, Sofia." He skimmed a couple of fingers up her arm.

Her entire body warmed. Did he realize the effect he still had on her?

"I should've called to tell you. But after—" He shook his head. "Listen. None of that matters. Can you come upstairs with me so I can change, and we can continue talking?"

"Yes," she mumbled.

"Yes?"

"I mean, no. I can't right now. I'm running late for my first day." Sofia wondered if she were visibly shaking or if it was all in her head. Her mind was racing with questions. What did he want from her? Was it pity or amusement in his eyes?

"What about later? I'll make you dinner. I've been practicing."

"You have?"

He nodded and handed her the new drink from off the counter. "Will you come over? It's the fifth floor. Number 501. Around seven? Will that work?"

"I think so." *I think so? Come on, Sofe. Get it together.* "Er. That'll be fine. Number 501 at seven o'clock?"

"Yeah." He brushed a kiss across her cheek. "Good luck on your first day. I'll see you later."

Her feet started moving before her mind did, and she was out the door before she let out a breath. *Shoot.* She hadn't even said goodbye. But she couldn't go back. She was late and she'd look like a dork rushing back in there. She'd just have to wait.

She headed across the busy street as a thought dawned on her, settling in her belly like a cement brick. Did he want her to come to dinner so he could be with her, or officially break it off?

What other reason could he have for disappearing and not calling?

Just get through the day, Sofe.

~ * ~

The day couldn't have gone better, Sofia thought as she pushed the number five button on the elevator wall. She'd made new friends. The classes were interesting and thought provoking. Steven Burns had offered her a job in the admissions office, so she didn't have to take that barmaid position.

It was everything she could've hoped for and more. Her life was finally on the right path. But as she walked through the elevator doors and ascended floor after floor after floor, the nerves in her body launched an all-out attack on her stomach, making her wonder if she just might die. Or throw up.

Ding. The doors opened, and right in front of her was the number 501 tacked onto a black paneled door. His door. He was right behind it, probably making her dinner.

Because he'd practiced.

Why? Did he want to be even more perfect before he dumped her? Before he told her, "It was fun while it lasted but…" Before her heart leaped up into her head and made an escape route out through her ears, because what heart would want to spend any more time in her pathetic, loveless, sexless body?

Get a grip, Sofe. Maybe he got sick of eating burned eggs.

She stepped out into the hardwood hallway. A black and white checkered rug ran from one end to the other. All she needed was some red and black checkers and she'd have a very good reason not to ring that doorbell.

Her finger thought otherwise. It pushed the little gold button, sending a buzzing noise into the other side. She heard a man's laugh and then the doorknob turned. A man, a stranger, held a beer bottle as he stood at the threshold.

Maybe this was her lucky day?

Sofia checked the apartment number again. "I'm sorry. I guess I have the wrong – "

"Are you Sofia?"

"Yes," she said, her voice making it sound more like a question than an answer.

"Don't worry. This is Gray's place. I was just making sure he doesn't burn down the building, especially since I live one floor below him."

"Oh. Okay." *Darn.*

"Come in, Sofia," Gray called. "I'm in the kitchen."

The man gestured for her to enter, and she slipped by him. The layout of the loft looked like a mini version of his condo, except for the stairs that led up to a second story.

Gray stood at the island, opening a bottle of wine. He was clean-shaven but his hair still sat shaggy against his ears and forehead. Sofia liked the new carefree look, maybe a little too much.

Her gaze wandered down to the blue, thin knit sweater that emphasized his every muscle. Behind him, steam rose from a pot. A lemony aroma filled the air.

He set the corkscrew down and walked around to greet her, planting a kiss on her cheek.

High cheek, far away from the lips.

"I'm glad you came," he said. "This is my friend, Nick. He was just leaving."

Nick held out a hand for her to shake. "Yep, I'm leaving. Actually, Gray wanted me to leave an hour ago, but I wanted to meet the famous Sofia."

Sofia shook his hand lightly, afraid her palm was clammy. She couldn't recall when she'd ever been this nervous. Was there a spell that got rid of the urge to vomit?

No. No more spells for personal use. Look at the mess it had gotten her into already.

"Famous?" she asked, the word finally registering.

"Yeah." Nick winked. "Gray was telling me about your adventures together."

Gray patted his friend's back, giving him a slight shove. "See you tomorrow, Nick."

"Okay. Okay. I'll take the not-so-subtle hint. You two have fun catching up."

Nick left, leaving Sofia alone with Gray.

"I didn't tell him the private details." He cleared his throat. "Why don't you sit while I check on our dinner?"

~ * ~

Gray poured her a glass of wine as she settled onto one of the barstools. She was damn sexy in her little flowered dress that curved at all the right places. When he'd kissed her cheek, he'd inhaled her scent, remembering the vanilla. Remembering everything. How could he forget?

He turned to dump the pasta into the colander.

Please, God, do not let me screw up the dinner. Any part of it.

He poured the sauce in with the chicken, but her stare bore into him, penetrated through to his marrow. She was being too quiet, but what did he expect? He'd moved across the country without telling her. She probably thought he was an asshole. *Again.*

Hopefully, she'd believe his reasoning.

"So," he began, without looking back, "how was your first day of school?"

"Good. It went well." Her voice was unsteady.

He glanced her way and noticed her hands trembled against the wine glass. "I'm glad. This is all quite a coincidence, don't you think? You and I meeting here?"

She nodded.

Gray took in a breath and got back to work, pouring the chicken, sauce, and pasta all into one bowl. The recipe said he should pair it with asparagus, but he hated asparagus. Broccoli would have to do. He scooped everything onto two separate plates. Nice plates he'd bought for this occasion.

"Do you like broccoli?" He turned to ask, and saw that her wine glass was empty.

"Yes. Everything smells great." A forced grin spread across her glossed lips.

He poured her another glass. She was as nervous as he was, maybe even more with the way her face was flushed.

"Are you okay?" he asked.

She nodded again, pursing her mouth. What she must think of him. He could only imagine.

"I, uh…" *Tell her you love her. Tell her you never once stopped loving her.*

Not yet. The timing wasn't right. She needed to see the bedroom first.

"I'll take your plate to the table if you want to carry your wine."

She agreed, and he followed her, setting a plate down in front of her and placing one at his place. He'd already set the table, so he poured himself a glass of wine and sat.

Everything was in place. Nothing had burned, and he hadn't said anything too idiotic. Yet.

"Where are you staying?" Nice, safe topic.

She looked up from forking a noodle around. "I'm staying in a hotel room right now. I have a scholarship, but it doesn't pay for housing, so I'm looking for a roommate who doesn't charge too much."

Gray had an extra room. But he didn't want her sleeping in there. He wanted her sleeping with him. Just as they'd planned before any of this love spell crap happened.

"You can stay with me," he offered.

"Here? But—"

Mozart starting ringing from her purse sitting at her feet.

"Sorry. It's probably my mom."

"Sure, no problem."

She pulled out a glittery pink phone and answered. "Hello?"

The volume on her phone must have been turned to the max or her mother had an extremely loud voice, because he could hear every word. Gray figured it was the latter.

"Hi, Mom." She held the phone away from her ear some. "I'm safe and everything is going well. Can I call you back?"

"You can spare a moment, can't you? Your Nana's here. We called to see how you did on your first day of school."

"It was... Hold on." She fiddled around with some buttons, but gave up. "It was good. It went really well."

"Nana wants to know if—wait. I'll put her on the phone. She's driving me crazy with all these questions."

"Sofia?" Her grandmother was even louder. Did they ever use the telephone?

"Hi, Nana."

"Sofia, did that Steven guy ask you out on a date yet?"

"What?" Sofia's cheeks flared red, and Gray's heart stopped beating. "No, Nana. That's not going to happen."

Thank God. The last thing Gray needed was competition.

"Nana, can I call you guys back later? I'm kind of busy right now."

"Well, what's so important? Are you on the toilet? Having sex? What?"

"No, I'm having dinner with Gray. I ran into him this morning. He lives out here."

Silence.

"Nana?"

"Yes, dear. Call me back as soon as possible. I want to hear all about this."

"Sorry," Sofia said as she closed the phone. "I guess distance doesn't stop me from having a nosy family."

Mozart blared again. She checked the caller ID and simply powered it off.

"No problem. Who's Steven?" He couldn't help but ask.

"You heard all that, didn't you? Dang it. Steven is the man who discovered my paintings and then helped me get into the school for next to nothing."

"Sounds like a great guy." Jealousy started in again.

"He is, but he's not interested in me the way Nana thinks he is. I don't have the heart to tell her he has a boyfriend."

"He has a *boyfriend?*"

"Yes. I've had dinner at their house. They're both very nice. And they have the most amazing art collection." Her eyes softened, and she seemed to relax for the first time.

Gray smiled, hoping he'd get one back.

He did, but lost it when her gaze dropped down to her plate again.

She forked at a piece of broccoli. "Gray?"

"Yeah?" His pulse quickened as he waited for her next words.

"I'm sorry for everything that happened. My mom's reading. The love spell. I want you to know I wasn't behind any of it. And my mom has agreed to start being more honest with her clients. She was very upset by what had happened to Hayes. And Nana, well, she hasn't agreed to anything, but she—"

Gray put up his hand to stop her, surprised she was apologizing to *him*. "It's all in the past, Sofia. I'd rather look to the future."

"Okay," she said, and pushed a lock of her hair behind her ear.

"I've missed you." He couldn't hold back any longer.

Her eyes widened. "You have?"

"God, yes."

She still looked surprised. Maybe too surprised. Another rush of panic rounded over him. Had he waited too long?

"I…" he began again, feeling desperate to make her understand just how much he had missed her. "I always think about you."

"You do?"

"Yeah. I think of everything. The sweetness of your smile. The genuineness of your laugh. The soft sound of your voice. Your kindness. Your smell. The warmth of your body when you're lying up against me. Touching you. Being inside you. Everything."

The words spilled from his mouth, releasing and exploding into the air between them like a heartrending bomb. They must have hit her the wrong way because she didn't look too thrilled. Confused was a better word.

"I have to use the restroom," she said, and rose from the table.

"The restroom?"

"Yes. Where is it?"

He set his napkin on top of his untouched food and stood. For the first time since they'd separated, he let himself question if maybe Nana's love spell hadn't been so ridiculous.

What if, just what if, Sofia's love for him had faded?

He hadn't wanted to believe any of her grandmother's nonsense, and he'd purposely and patiently waited for destiny to catch up—for Sofia to make her way to San Francisco. He knew she'd eventually come. It was their fate. The dreams had made that clear.

And once she saw the bedroom, she'd forget about the spell, and she'd realize his love was real.

The only question was did she still love him?

He had to find out.

But first he'd tell her where the bathroom was. "It's right over there." He pointed to the door next to the kitchen.

She headed that way, almost passing him, but stopped abruptly and stared up at him. "I don't really have to go," she said.

"I didn't think you did."

"I was going to go in there, splash cold water on my face and try to come up with a reasonable explanation as to why you left me. I probably would have blamed it on the spell or my mother. I might've thought you needed some time to cool off. Most likely, I would've started to doubt myself and my gift. I would've wondered if you left because you couldn't accept me and all the crazy stuff that comes with me. Or maybe you found another woman, had an affair—"

"Why don't you ask me?"

She planted her feet stubbornly in front of him and met his eyes. "Why did you leave me, Gray? I loved you and I needed you and you weren't there for me. I thought I'd never see you again. I thought you hated me. And I just…" She shook her head. "I don't know if I can be here with—"

"Wait. Just wait." Damn, he was going to lose her.

Don't ask. Just do it.

Confused as to what else to do, Gray grabbed her by the waist and lifted her over his shoulder. "I'm taking you to the bedroom."

"What?" She kicked and swatted at him. "No, you aren't, Grayson Phillips. I need an explanation."

He took the stairs as fast as he could, making sure he didn't bump her head into the railing. One hand gripped firmly on her thigh, the other around her waist. Lord, did he miss touching her, even if she loathed every minute of it.

"I'm not having sex with you, Gray. You can't walk back into my life and expect me to simply spread my legs for you. I'm not that type of woman, and if you think I am, then you don't know me at all."

"Oh, I know you better than you realize." He used his foot to push open the partition door, stepped inside and dropped her on the bed.

She glared up at him. "Who do you think you are?"

"I'm the man from your dreams." He knelt down on the bed and drew her to him. "Look around, Sofia. Look around at this bedroom."

"What are you talking about?" she asked, but did as he said.

Her mouth gaped open as she took in every detail. The deep blue walls around her, the red sheets, and gold comforter beneath her, the large wooden posts that stood prominently at each corner of the bed.

"This is it," she whispered. "From my dreams."

"And my dreams too. This is why I didn't come back. This is why I couldn't sell this place. Hayes decorated this room. When I saw it, I knew it was in our destiny. I knew you would come to me eventually, but I didn't want it to be unnatural. I didn't want to screw with our destiny. And I thought you'd need time to realize your feelings for me didn't have anything to do with a spell." He gathered her closer, reveling in the way her soft breasts pressed against his chest. "I'm so glad you finally showed up, sugar. I was going nuts without you."

Her body slackened in his arms, and her eyes brimmed with tears. "You weren't trying to get rid of me?"

"No, Sofia. Never. I love you. I'll always love you."

She took in a tiny gasp of air, the sound sweet to his ears. "I love you, too, Gray."

"Good." Gray breathed out a sigh of relief, then brought his hands up to cradle the face of the woman who'd changed his life forever. "Now, why don't we make our dreams come true?"

~ * ~

Sofia grabbed Gray by his shirt and hauled him down onto the bed with her. He gave a hearty laugh, one that echoed throughout the loft and into her soul.

This was the place. This was their destiny.

As Gray lay on top of her, his hand slipped under the bottom of her dress, massaging her thigh on the way up.

A thought occurred to her. "But I haven't dreamed of you since the last time we were together."

"You didn't need to." He pulled her bottom lip in with his teeth, and slowly released it.

She inhaled the scent of his musky aftershave. Masculine and sexy. "I didn't?"

"No." He kissed softly, seductively. Her mouth, cheek, chin, licking at the space right below her ear. "The future was already well on its way. I found this place, and I waited for you. Simple as that."

"But what if I hadn't come?" Her hands searched over his broad shoulders and back. Hard and powerful.

"Oh, you're gonna come," he whispered into her ear. "I'll see to that." His fingers slid into the sides of her panties and peeled them down.

Sofia lifted her bottom to help. "That's not what I meant, Gray."

"I know." He sat up, yanked off her sandals and panties in the same sweep, and tossed them to the floor. "Let's get you undressed. I want to see you. It's been too long."

At his words, Sofia unzipped and tugged her dress over her head. Nothing had changed— she'd still give him whatever he wanted.

Nevertheless, she had questions. "What would you have done if we hadn't reunited?"

His dark gaze slowly swept over her naked body. "I'd have flown to Indiana and kidnapped you," he said. "Just last night I was considering buying a plane ticket to Indianapolis. More than once I've fantasized about getting in my car and driving until I found you, waking you in the middle of the night, tying you up and bringing you here. Just so I could see you again. Feel you. Taste you."

"Really?" The idea sort of excited Sofia. She settled back against the pillow and rested her hands under her head.

"Really." He yanked his shirt off and worked on his belt and jeans buttons.

Sofia licked her lips as she appreciated his well-built muscles, especially the one that was hardening and emerging while he pushed his jeans and underwear down and off. Thick, solid, tempting.

He skimmed his hand over the length and back down again. "Do you want me inside of you?" he asked, his voice husky, wanting.

Speechless, she nodded her head and spread her knees apart.

He grinned, slid two fingers over her, and into her heat. "Because I've been dying to be here."

"Take me, Gray," Sofia managed to say with a shallow breath. "Please."

He maneuvered over her, bracing one hand by her head, the other hand guiding himself inside of her. Her body jolted from the instant pleasure. He filled her, stretched her, and found *that* spot.

She bit her lip. "Have you been practicing this as well?"

He chuckled. "Didn't I say I knew you better than you think?"

"I suppose you did."

He eased out and slid back in. Again and then again.

She grasped onto his biceps as an orgasm manifested. Her thighs trembled and her belly surged with heat. She thrived on the aftershocks until he released and filled her with his warmth.

They lay together for what felt like hours. Lazy and in love. Exploring each other's bodies with languid fingers. Whispering adoration and contentment. Finally together.

Until another thought occurred to Sofia. "How do I know you'll always love me? Never grow sick of me and my gift?"

A slow smile curved his full lips. "I thought you'd never ask." He reached over her to his bedside nightstand and pulled out a small, velvety black box.

Sofia stopped breathing.

"Come here." He tugged at her hand until she sat on the side of the bed. With the sheet wrapped around him, he knelt before her. "Sofia Good, I couldn't be more certain of my love for you. I want you with or without your dreams. I'll accept and love your family as my own. And I promise to help you through it all. Crazy or normal. Thrilling or average. It doesn't matter to me. I want you to be my wife." He opened the box and removed the diamond ring. "Please say yes."

"Okay," she said without delay, taking in the size of the rock. *Okay? Come on, Sofe. Give him a better answer than that.* "I mean, absolutely. I'd be honored and so, *so* lucky to be your wife." She made a grab for the ring.

Gray kept it out of her reach. "Not lucky, Sofia."

"No? What then?"

"Destined."

"Hmm. I guess that'll work too."

"Can I have your hand now so I can put this ring on your finger? I've been waiting forever, you know."

Sofia held out her hand. "It's yours."

"Just the way I like it."

~ * ~

Once Sofia knew Gray was sleeping, she sneaked back down the stairs. She searched through her purse, pulled out her cell phone, and dialed her mother's house.

Nana answered on the second ring. "What happened?"

"Oh, good. You're still there. Were you sleeping?"

"No. What happened?"

"Nana, I have one question for you, and you better tell the truth."

"Then you're going to tell me what happened?"

"Yes."

"Go for it."

"Did you cast another spell on Gray and me?"

"Of course not."

She sat down and released a relieved sigh. "Just checking."

"Well?"

"He asked me to marry him."

Nana shrieked into the phone. "I knew it! I knew he still loved you. You said yes?"

"I did." Sofia looked down at her hands that were still shaking. The ring on her finger sparkled up at her. "It's hard to believe it's all real."

"Well, there's one way you can find out."

"Really? This doesn't have to do with a spell, does it?"

"Maybe."

Sofia thought it over. "Okay. Tell me."

Before she could get an answer, she felt Gray's hand on her shoulder. He took the phone from her and put it to his ear. "Hi, Nana. I'm taking Sofia back to bed now. No spell needed for what I'm going to do with her."

"Oh, my," Sofia heard Nana say loud and clear.

"She'll call you in the morning to tell you if it worked." He shut the phone and dropped it in Sofia's purse. Then he grabbed and gathered her to his naked body. "No more spells on me," he said, not looking very happy.

"I wasn't really going to—"

His powerful lips shut her up, kissing her with the passion only a man in love could generate. Then he pulled away.

She gulped.

He smiled. "If you ever want to know how real my love is for you, just ask. I'll tell you."

"Okay," she squeaked out.

"And if you want to know how much I want you – " He walked away, up to the top of the stairs, his body hard *every*where. "Come back to bed," he said, and disappeared through the bedroom door.

Holy cow. This scenario was much better than anything a spell could produce.

With wobbly legs, she hiked upstairs.

He was sprawled over the red sheets, uncovered and waiting. "Good choice."

"I thought so too."

~ * ~

The next morning, Sofia woke and smiled to herself. She'd dreamed once again.

There had been a wedding out in a field by a familiar lake. People were happy and laughing. Gray was handsome and seemed relaxed in his tuxedo. Panic rose in Sofia as she searched around for the bride.

But couldn't find her until she glanced down at herself...in a wedding gown.

ABOUT THE AUTHOR

Viola Estrella loves a story with flawed characters, paranormal elements, humor and romance. She tries to include these aspects in all that she writes and loves every minute of it. When she's not writing, reading, and designing cover art, she's spending time with her husband and four sons in their Colorado home.

Viola is a 2010 RITA® finalist. Also in 2010, she was honored by her local RWA® chapter, Colorado Romance Writers, with the Writer of the Year award.

Find out more about Viola Estrella's writing at www.ViolaEstrella.com.